THE
MERCHANTS'
WAR

THE
MERCHANTS'
WAR
by Frederik Pohl

· · ◆ · ·

A Sequel to

THE SPACE MERCHANTS

by Frederik Pohl & C. M. Kornbluth

ST. MARTIN'S PRESS
NEW YORK

Design by Janet Tingey

Library of Congress Cataloging in Publication Data

Pohl, Frederik.
    Merchants' war.

    Sequel to: The space merchants.
    I. Title.
PS3566.036M47   1984   813'.54   84-18394
ISBN 0-312-53010-2

First Edition

10 9 8 7 6 5 4 3 2

For
John and David
and for
Ann, Karen, Fred the Fourth and Kathy
with abiding love

Why do I write satire?
Ask, instead, how can I help it?
—Juvenal

THE
MERCHANTS'
WAR

Tennison Tarb

··◆··

I

The woman was a wimp. Pathetically she had tried to make herself pretty for the interview. It was a waste of time. She was a sallow, sickly-looking little creature, and she licked her lips as she stared around my office. It is not an accident that the walls of the interview office are covered with full-D, full-movement advertising posters for brand-name goods. "Gee," she sighed, "I'd do just about anything for a slug of good old Coffiest!"

I gave her my most dishonest look of honest bewilderment. I touched her dossier display. "That's funny. It says here that you warned Venusians that Coffiest was addictive and health threatening."

"Mr. Tarb, I can explain!"

"And then there's what it says on your visa application." I shook my head. "Can this be right? 'The planet Earth is rotten to the core, raped by vicious advertising campaigns, the citizens mere animals and the property of the rapacious advertising Agencies'?"

She gasped, "How did you get that? They said the visa documents were secret!" I shrugged noncommittally. "But I had to say that. They make you abjure advertising or they won't let you in," she wailed.

I maintained my bland expression—seventy-five per cent "I'd

1

like to help you," twenty-five per cent "But you really are *disgusting.*" The whole performance was old stuff by now. I'd been seeing this wimp's kind at least once a week for the four years of my tour on Venus, and habit didn't make them any more attractive. "I know I made a bad mistake, Mr. Tarb," she whimpered, voice full of sincerity, eyes big and staring out of an emaciated face. Well, the sincerity was fake, although well enough done. But the eyes were terrified. The terror was real, because she surely didn't want to stay on Venus any more. You could always tell the desperate cases. The emaciation was the tip-off. The medics call it "anorexia ignatua." It's what happens when a decent, well-brought-up Terrestrial consumer finds himself in a Veenie store, day after day, and can't ever figure out what to buy for dinner because he hasn't had the wise and useful counseling of brand-name advertising to guide him. "So please, I beg you—can't I have a return visa?" she finished, with what I suppose she thought was a prettily pleading smile.

I winked up at the hologram of Fowler Schocken on the wall. Normally I would have left the creature to stew in the room with the commercials for ten minutes or so while I went off on some pretended errand. But my instincts told me she didn't need any more softening up—and besides, a little tingle in my glands reminded me that I was not talking only to the wimp.

I let down the hammer; nice-guy time was over. "Elsa Dyckman Hoeniger," I barked, reading her name off the visa application, "you are a traitor!" The bony jaw dropped in shock. The big eyes started to fill with tears. "According to your dossier you came of good consumer stock. Member of the Junior Copysmiths as a child. A fine education at G. Washington Hill University in New Haven. A responsible job in Customer Relations with one of the largest credit jewelry chains—and, I see, with a lifetime refund ratio of less than one tenth of one per cent, a record that got you a 'Superior' rating in your personnel file! And yet you turned your back on all of it. You denounced the system that gave you birth and defected to this sales-forsaken wasteland!"

"I was misled," she whimpered, the tears spilling down.

2

"Of course you were misled," I snarled, "but you should have had enough common decency to keep that from happening!"

"Oh, please! I'll—I'll do anything! Just let me come back home!"

It was the moment of truth. I pursed my lips in silence for a moment. Then, "Anything," I repeated, as though I had never heard such a word from a chickened-out turncoat before. I let her sob herself dry, peering into my face with fear and despair. When the first touch of hope began to show through, I made my pitch.

"There *might* be a way," I said. And stopped there.

"Yes, yes! Please!"

I made a production of studying her dossier all over again. "Not right away," I cautioned at last.

"That's all right," she cried eagerly. "I'll wait—weeks, if I have to!"

I laughed scornfully. "Weeks, eh?" I shook my head. "Elsa," I said, "I don't think you're serious. What you did can't be paid for in a couple of lousy weeks—or months, either. You've got the wrong attitude. Forget what I said. Application denied." And I stamped her form and handed it back to her with a big red legend that glittered *Refused*.

I leaned back and waited for the rest of the performance. It came just the way it always did. First there was shock. Then a searing glare of rage. Then, slowly, she got up and blindly pushed her way out of my office. The scenario never changed, and I was really good at my part.

As soon as the door was closed, I grinned up at Fowler Schocken's picture and said, "How'd it go?" The picture disappeared. Mitzi Ku grinned back at me.

"First-rate, Tenny," she called. "Come on down and celebrate." It was the right answer, and I paused only long enough to stop by the commissary and pick up something to celebrate with.

When they built the Earth Embassy in Courtenay Center—it would be more accurate to say when they dug it—they had to use

3

native labor. It was a treaty rule. On the other hand, the crumbly, fried Venusian rock is easy to dig. So when the first lot of dips moved in, their Marine guard was given double duty for a year. Four hours in smart uniform, standing outside the Embassy lock; another four hours down in the depths of the Embassy, quarrying out extra space and lining it for our War Room. The Veenies never guessed we had it, in spite of the fact that half the Embassy was swarming with Veenie workers during business hours—they weren't allowed into the dips' lavatories, and through the end cubicle in each toilet was the secret entrance to what was, primarily, the place where Cultural Attaché Mitsui Ku kept her noncultural records.

When I got there, breathless and balancing the bottle of genuine Earthside drinking whiskey and ice on a tray, Mitzi was patterning data on the wimp into her file. She raised a hand to keep me from interrupting and pointed to a chair, so I mixed a couple of drinks and waited, feeling good.

Mitzi Ku is a brassy lady—starting with her skin color, which is that creamy Oriental tone; and she talks brassy and acts brassy. Just the type I like. She has that startlingly black Oriental hair, but her eyes are blue. She's as tall as I am, though a lot better built. Take her all in all—as I was always anxious to do—and she was about the best-looking agent-runner we'd ever had in the Embassy. "I wish I weren't going home," I offered, as she came to what seemed to be a pause.

"Yeah, Tenny," she said absently, reaching out for her drink. "Real damn shame."

"You could rotate, too," I suggested—not for the first time —and she didn't even answer. I hadn't expected her to. She wasn't going to do that, and I knew why. Mitzi had only eighteen months on Venus, and you don't get Brownie points from your Agency for anything less than three years hard duty. Quick-trick people don't really pay their travel expense. I tried a different tack: "Think you can turn her?"

"Her? The wimp? God, yes," said Mitzi contemptuously. "I watched her leave the Embassy on the closed-circuit. She was

4

breathing flame and fury. She'll be telling all her friends that Earth's even rottener than she thought when she defected. Then it'll begin to hit her. I'll give her another couple days, then call her in for—let's see—yeah, to straighten out some credit charge from back on Earth. Then I'll give her the pitch. She'll turn."

I leaned back and enjoyed my drink. "You could say a little more," I encouraged.

Those blue eyes narrowed alarmingly, but obediently she said, "You did a good job on her, Tenny."

"More than that even, maybe," I persisted. "Like, 'You did a good job on the wimp, Tenny dear, and why don't we get back together again?'"

The narrowed eyes became a genuine frown—a serious one. "Hell, Tenny! It was great, you and me, but it's over. I'm reupping and you're going back, and that's the end of it."

I didn't have the sense to give up. "I'm here for another week," I pointed out, and she really flared.

"Cut it out, damn it!"

So I cut it out. And I damned it. Especially I damned Hay Lopez—Jesus Maria Lopez on the books—who was not as handsome as I, or (I hoped) as good in bed as I, but had one big advantage over me. Hay Lopez was staying and I was going home, and so Mitzi was taking thought for the morrow.

"You can be a real pain, Tenny," she complained. The frown was solid. When Mitzi frowned you knew she was frowning. Even before she frowned, while the tempest was still gathering on the horizon, you could see the clouds, two narrow vertical lines above her nose, between her pencil-thin brows. They meant, *Beware! Storm coming!* And then the blue eyes would freeze, and the lightning would flash—

Or not. This time it was not. "Tenny," she said, relaxing a bit, "I've got an idea about the wimp. Do you suppose we could work her into the Veenie spy system?"

"Why bother?" I grunted. The Veenies just didn't have the brains to be good spies. They were dregs. Half the crazy Conservationists that emigrated to Venus were going to wish they'd never

5

come within the first six months, and half of those were going to beg to be let back on Earth. I was the one in charge of telling them they didn't have a prayer—my main title at the Embassy was Deputy Chief of Consular Services. Mitzi was the one who picked them up a little later and turned them into her agents. Her title was Associate Manager of Cultural Relationships, but the main Cultural Relationship she had with the Veenies was a bomb in an airport locker or a fire in a warehouse. Sooner or later the Veenies would wake up to the fact that they couldn't beat a planet of forty billion people, even if it was a long way off in space. Then they'd be down on their knees begging to be let back into the fellowship of prosperous, civilized humanity. Meanwhile, it was Mitzi's job to keep them from getting comfortable out in the cold. Or, more accurately—considering what sort of a hellhole their planet was—out in the hot. Spies? We didn't have to worry about Veenie spies! "—What?" I said, suddenly aware she was still talking.

"They're up to something, Tenny," she said. "Last time I went to Port Kathy my hotel room was searched."

"Forget it," I said positively. "Listen. What shall we do with the time I've got left?"

The twin creases above her nose flickered for a moment, then waned again. "Well," she said, "what've you got in mind?"

"A little trip," I offered. "The shuttle's at the PPC now, so I'll have to go up there for the prisoner bargaining—I thought you might want to come along—"

"Aw, Tenny," she said earnestly, "you have the *worst* ideas! Why would I want to go there?" It was true that the Polar Penal Colony wasn't high on Venus's list of tourist attractions—not that there was anything else on the list to speak of, either, Venus being what it is. "Anyway the shuttle's coming here next, and I'll be up to my ears. Thanks. But no." She hesitated. "Still, it's a pity you didn't see the real Venus."

"The real Venus?" It was my turn to scoff. The heat of real Venus would melt the fillings in your teeth if you ever exposed yourself to it—even around the cities, where there's been substantial climate modification, the temperature is still awful and the air is poison gas outside the enclosures. You want to know what the "real" Venus was like? Look in an old-fashioned coal furnace after the fire's gone out but it's still too hot to touch.

"I don't mean the badlands," she said quickly. "What about Russian Hills, though? You've never been to see the Venera spacecraft, and it's only an hour away—I mean, if we wanted to spend a day together."

"Fine!" I could think of better things to do on a day together, but was willing to settle for any offer. "Today?"

"Hell, no, Tenny, where's your mind? It's their Day of Planetary Mourning. All recreational things will be shut down."

"When, then?" I pressed, but she only shrugged. I didn't want the frown lines to set in again, so I changed the subject. "What are you going to offer her?"

She looked startled. "Who? Oh, you mean the renegade. The usual thing, I guess. I'll get five years as an agent out of her, then we'll repatriate her—though only if she's done a good job."

I said, "Maybe you don't have to go that high. I was watching her closely, and she's prime. How about if you just give her PX privileges once a month? Once she gets in the store and gets some of those good old Earth brand names she'll do anything you want."

Mitzi finished her drink and put the glass back on the tray, looking at me in a peculiar way. "Tenny," she said, half-laughing, half-shaking her head, "I'm going to miss you when you rotate. You know what I think sometimes, like when I can't get to sleep right away? I think maybe, looked at in a certain way, it's not such a morally good thing I do, turning ordinary citizens into spies and saboteurs—"

"Now, wait a minute!" I snapped. There are some things you don't say even as a joke. But she held up her hand.

"And then I look at you," she said, "and I see that, viewed in a certain way, compared to you I'm practically a saint. Now get out of here and let me get back to work, will you?"

So I got, wondering whether I'd gained or lost by that little

7

discussion. But at least we had a sort of date, and I had an idea for improving on it.

The Day of Planetary Mourning was one of the nastiest of the Venusian holidays. It was the anniversary of the death of that old bastard Mitchell Courtenay. So naturally the Veenie clerical help and porters took the day off, and I had to get my own coffee-sub to take to the second-floor lounge. From there I had a good look at the "celebrations" outside the Embassy.

Your basic Veenie is a troglodyte, which is to say a cave dweller, which is to say that, Hilsch tubes or none, they're a long way from blowing off all the nasty gases that stink up their air. I admit they've made progress. You can go outdoors in a thermal suit and air-pack if you want to, at least in the suburbs around the cities—personally, I seldom wanted to. But even there the air is still poison. So the Veenies picked out the steepest, deepest valleys on the planet's cracked and craggy surface and roofed them over. Long and narrow and winding, your typical Veenie city is what Mitzi calls an "eel's lair". But your typical Veenie city isn't anywhere near being a real city, of course. The biggest of them is maybe a pitiful hundred thousand people, and that's only when pumped full of tourists on one of their disgusting national holidays. Imagine celebrating the traitor Mitch Courtenay! Of course, the Veenies don't know the inside story of Mitch Courtenay the way I do. My grandmom's dad was Hamilton Harns, a senior vice-president at Fowler Schocken Associates, the very Agency that Courtenay had betrayed and disgraced. When I was little, Grandmom used to tell how her father had spotted Courtenay for a troublemaker at once—Courtenay had even fired him, and a bunch of other loyal, sales-fearing executives in the San Diego branch, to cover up his wickedness. Of course, the Veenies are so crazy they'd call that a victory for right and justice.

The Embassy is located on the city's main drag, O'Shea Boulevard, and of course on a day like this the Veenies were busy at their favorite sport—demonstrations. There were signs saying *No advertising!* and signs saying *Earthmen go home!* The usual stuff.

8

I was amused to see the morning's wimp appear, wrench a banner from a tall man with red hair and green eyes and go marching and shouting slogans back and forth in front of the Embassy. Right on schedule. The fever in the wimp was rising, and when it fell she would be weak and unresisting.

The lounge began to fill with senior staff for the eleven o'clock briefing session, and one of the first to arrive was my roommate and rival, Hay Lopez. I jumped up and got his coffee-sub for him, and he looked at me with suspicion. Hay and I were not friends. We shared a duplex suite: I had the top berth. There were real good reasons for us not to like each other. I could imagine how he had felt, all those months, listening to Mitzi and me in the bunk above. I didn't have to imagine, really, since I had come to know what it was like to hear sounds from below.

But there was a way of dealing with Hay Lopez, because he had a black mark on his record. He had fouled up somehow when he was a Junior Media Director at his Agency. So naturally they furloughed him to the military for nearly a year, on reservation duty, trying to bring the Port Barrow Eskimos up to civilized standards. I didn't know exactly what he'd done. But Hay didn't know I didn't know, and so a couple of judicious hints had kept him worried. He ran scared anyway, trying to erase that old blot, working harder than anybody else in the Embassy. What he didn't want was another tour of duty north of the Arctic Circle; after the sea-ice and the tundra, he was the only one among us who never complained about the Venusian climate. So, "Hay," I said, "I'm going to miss the old place when I get back to the Agency."

That doubled the suspicion in his eyes, because he knew that was a lie. What he didn't know was why I was telling it. "We'll miss you, too, Tenny," he lied back. "Got any idea what you'll be assigned to?"

That was the opening I wanted. "I'm thinking of putting in for Personnel," I lied. "I think it's a natural, don't you? Because the first thing they'll want is updates on performance here—say," I said, as though suddenly remembering, "we're from the same

9

Agency! You and me and Mitzi. Well, I'll have a lot to say about you two! Real star-class performers, both of you." Of course, if Lopez thought it over he'd realize the last thing I'd put in for— or get—would be Personnel, because my whole training was Copy and Production. But I only said Hay was hard-working, I never said he was smart; and before he knew what was happening I'd got his promise to take over my Polar Penal Colony trip for me —"to break in in case he got the assignment when I left." I left him puzzling it out and went over to join a conversation about the kinds of cars we'd owned back on Earth.

The Embassy had a hundred and eight on the duty roster—the Veenies were always after us to cut the number in half, but the Ambassador fought them off. He knew what those extra sixty people were there for—of course, so did the Veenies. I was maybe tenth or eleventh in the hierarchy, both because of my consular duties and my side assignment as Morale Officer. This meant that I was the one who selected commercials for the in-house TV circuits and—well—kept an eye on the other hundred and seven for Conservationist leanings. That didn't take much of my time, though. We were a hand-picked crew. More than half of us were former Agency personnel, and even the consumers were a respectable bunch, for consumers. If anything, some of the young ones were *too* loyal. There'd been incidents. A couple of the Marine guards, just weeks before, had got a little too much popskull into them and flashed eye-resonating commercials at three of the natives with their hand weapons. The Veenies were not amused, and we'd had to put the Marines under house arrest for deportation. They weren't present now, of course; the eleven o'clock briefing was only for us twenty-five or so seniors. I made sure there was a place next to me when Mitzi came in, late as usual; she glanced at Hay Lopez, sulking by the window, then shrugged and sat down to join the conversation.

"Morning, Mitzi," grunted the Protocol Chief, just in front of us, and went right on: "I used to have a Puff Adder, too, but pumping with your hands that way you can't get the acceleration—"

10

"You can if you put the muscle in it, Roger," I told him. "And, see, half the time you're stuck in traffic anyway, right? So one hand's plenty for propulsion. You've got the other free for, well, signaling or something."

"Signaling," he said, staring at me. "How long have you been driving, Tenny?" And the Chief Code Clerk leaned past Mitzi to put in:

"You ought to try a Viper, with that lightweight direct drive. No pedals, just put your foot down on the roadway and push. Talk about get-up-and-go!"

Roger looked at her scornfully. "Yeah, and what about braking? You can fracture your leg in an emergency stop. No, I say the foot pedal and chain drive is the only way to go—" His expression changed. "Here they come," he grunted, and turned around to face front as the heavyweights came in.

The Ambassador is a really imposing man, Media back on Earth, with that pepper-and-salt curly hair and that solid, humorous, dark-complected face. He wasn't from our Agency, as it happened—the big ones took turns naming the top people, and it hadn't been our turn—but I could respect him as a craftsman. And he knew how to run a meeting. First order of business was the Political Officer, fluttering anxiously over one more of the crises that plagued his days. "We've had another note from the Veenies," he said, wringing his hands. "It's about Hyperion. They claim we're violating basic human rights by not allowing the gas miners freedom to choose their own communications media— you know what that means."

We did, and there were instant mutters of "What nerve!" "Typical Veenie arrogance!" The helium-3 miners on the moon Hyperion only amounted to about five thousand people, and as a market they'd never be missed. But it was a matter of principle to keep them well supplied with advertising—one Venus in the Solar System was enough.

The Ambassador was having none of it. "Reject the note," he rapped frostily. "It's none of their damned business, and you shouldn't have let them hand it to you in the first place, Howard."

"But how could I know until I read it?" wailed the Political

Officer, and the Ambassador gave him the I'll-see-you-later look before relaxing into a smile.

"As you all know," he said, "the Earth ship has been orbiting for ten days now, should be sending the shuttle down here any time. I've been in touch with the captain, and there's good news and bad. The good news is they've got some fine stuff for us— a troop of ethnic dancers, disco and Black Bottom, as cultural exchange, Mitzi, you'll be in charge of them, of course. They've also got ten metric tons of supplies—Coffiest, ReelMeet, tapes of the latest commercials, all the goodies you've all been waiting for!" General expressions of joy and satisfaction. I took the opportunity to reach out for Mitzi's hand, and she didn't withdraw it. The Ambassador went on: "That's the good news. The bad news is, as you all know, when the shuttle takes off she'll be taking with her one of our favorite members of our happy family here. We'll say good-by to him in a better way the night before he leaves— but meanwhile, Tennison Tarb, would you like to stand up so we can show you how much we're going to miss you?"

Well, I hadn't expected it. It was one of the great moments of my life. There is no applause like the plaudits of your peers, and they gave it unstintingly—even Hay Lopez, though he was frowning as he clapped.

I don't know what I said, but when it was over and I was back in my chair I was surprised to find I didn't have to reach out for Mitzi's hand again. She had taken mine.

In the afterglow I leaned over to whisper in her ear, meaning to tell her that I'd fobbed the Polar Penal Colony trip off on Hay, and so we could have the whole suite to ourselves that night. It didn't get said. She shook her head, smiling, because the Ambassador had sneaked the new commercial tapes down early in the diplomatic pouch, and of course we all wanted to be quiet while we watched them.

It never did get said. I sat there, dumb and happy, with my arm over Mitzi's shoulder, and it didn't even strike me as worrisome when I noticed Hay's eye on us, glum and resentful—not until he edged his way over to the Ambassador and began whisper-

12

ing in his ear as soon as the films were over. And then it was too late. The son of a gun had thought it through. As soon as the lights went up he came grinning and nodding toward us, all cheer and good-fellowship, and I knew what he was going to say: "Hell, Tenny boy! The damnedest thing! I can't take that PPC sortie for you. Big huddle with the Ambassador tomorrow—know you'll understand how it is—hell of a thing to make you do in your last days here—"

I didn't listen to the rest of it. He was right. It was a hell of a thing to make me do, and I did understand. I understood real well that night, fretfully trying to pillow my head on the uncomfortable seat-back of the supersonic flight to the Polar Penal Colony. It would have been a lot easier to get my head comfortable if I hadn't been so dismally sure that I knew exactly where Hay Lopez was pillowing his.

II

At eight o'clock the next morning I was sitting in the conference room of the prison, across from the Veenie Immigration and Passport Control bureaucrat. "Nice to see you again, Tarb," he said, unsmiling.

"Always a pleasure to meet with you, Harriman," I answered. Neither of us meant it. We'd sat opposite each other every few months, every time a prison ship came in from Earth, for four years, and we knew there was nothing nice or pleasurable to be expected.

The Polar Penal Colony wasn't really "polar" exactly, because it was up in the Akna Montes, about where the Arctic Circle would have been if Venus had had one. Naturally it wasn't arctic. It wasn't even appreciably less hot than the rest of the planet, but I guess the first Agency survey ships thought it would be. Otherwise why would they claim some of the least desirable real estate on Venus? It was Earth property, precariously established before the Veenie colonists were strong enough to do anything about it,

13

and retained out of habit, like the foreign compounds in Shanghai before the Boxer Rebellion. At the moment we were on Veenie territory, in one of the few aboveground buildings at the perimeter of the PPC itself. The Veenies had rigid roofs over valleys. The prisoners—*greks,* we called them—had caves. The whole Polar Prison Colony was right outside our window, but you couldn't see it. Here, too, since the kiln-dried Venusian rock was easy to dig, the prison had been dug.

"I ought to tell you, Tarb," he said smiling, but the tone was ominous, "that I've had some criticisms aimed at me since our last meeting. They say I've been too flexible. I don't think I can be as accommodating this time."

I responded to the ploy instantly: "Funny you should say that, Harriman, because I've had the same thing. The Ambassador was furious over my letting you take those two credit delinquents." Actually the Ambassador hadn't said a word, but then neither had Harriman's bosses. He nodded, acknowledging the end of the first round with no decision either way and began to roll the dossiers.

Harriman was a hardball bargainer, and sneaky. So was I. We both knew the other fellow was out to gain victories, straight mano-a-mano, the only difference being that the best victories were when the other fellow never found out what he had lost. Earth had emptied its jails and dumped the worst of the scum here. Murderers, rapists, credit-card frauds, arsonists were the least of them. Or the worst, depending on your point of view. We didn't want the occasional mugger, for instance—didn't want the expense of feeding him, didn't want the task of keeping him in line. Neither did the Veenies. What the Veenies wanted out of each prisoner contingent was the vilest of the traitors. Conservationists. Contract Breach felons. Antiadvertising zealots, the kinds that deface billboards and short-circuit holograms. They wanted to make them full Venusian citizens. We didn't want to give them up. They were the kind we used to brainburn, sometimes still do, and if they were lucky enough to get away with five or ten PPC years from some soft-hearted judge we felt they should serve them out in full. Those people *earned* their sentences!

14

Letting them go free into the Venusian population was no punishment at all. In practice, it came down to a horse trade. Both of us gave a little, took a little; the art of the bargaining was to reluctantly "give" what you were really anxious to have the other guy take.

I plinked the display key and cursored the top six names. "Moskowicz, McCastry, Bliven, the Farnell family—I suppose you want those, but you can't have them until they've served at least six months hard."

"Three months," he bargained. They were all down as CCs —criminal Conservationists—just the kind of misfits the Veenies welcomed into their population.

I said positively, *"Six* months, and I ought to hold out for a year. On Earth they're the worst kind of criminals, and they need to be taught a lesson."

He shrugged, disliking me. "What about this next prisoner, Hamid?"

"Worst of the lot," I declared. "You can't have him. He's convicted of credit-card larceny, and he's a Consie to boot."

He tensed at the epithet but inspected the printout. "Hamid wasn't convicted of, ah, Conservationism," he pointed out.

"Well, no. We couldn't get a confession." I smiled confidentially, one law-enforcement officer to another. "We didn't have any firsthand witnesses, either, because, as I understand it, his whole cell was picked up and liquidated some time ago, and he was never able to make contact again. Oh, and there's some evidence 'Hamid' isn't his real name—the technicians think his Social Security tattoo's been altered."

"You didn't prosecute him for that," said Harriman thoughtfully.

"Didn't need to. Didn't need to press the Conservationist count, either—we had him fair and square on credit-card. Now," I said, rushing him on, "what about these three? They're all Medicare malingerers, not a very serious offense—I could commute them right away if you want to take them in—"

If there's one thing Veenies hate, it's being put in a position

15

where their "ideals" tell them one thing and their common sense something else. He flushed and stammered. Theoretically the Medicare frauds were perfect candidates for Venusian citizenship. They were also *old*, and therefore liabilities in what is still, after all, a pretty rugged frontier society. It took his mind right off Hamid, as I had wanted it to do.

Four hours later we were at the bottom of the list. I'd given him fourteen greks, six right away, the others over a matter of months. He'd refused two, and I'd held onto another twenty or so. We still hadn't settled Hamid. He glanced at his notes. "I am instructed," he said, "to inform you that my government is not satisfied with your compliance with the Protocol of '53. Under it we have the right to inspect this prison at yearly intervals."

"Reciprocally," I corrected him. I knew the Protocol by heart; each power had agreed, fulsomely and generously, to let the other inspect all penal, corrective or rehabilitative institutions to assure compliance with humanitarian standards. Fat chance! Their Xeng Wangbo "retraining center" was in the middle of the Equatorial Anti-Oasis, and no dip had ever been allowed near it. Of course, what we did inside the PPC was none of their business, either. Veenie law insisted that every grek get his own bunk with a minimum of twenty-four cubic feet of space. That was no punishment at all! There were plenty of sales-revering consumers back home that never saw that much space. There was no use arguing about it, though. The Veenie building inspectors had insisted we build in that much space, but as soon as the prison was finished the warden just closed off a couple of bays and doubled everybody up.

"It's a matter of basic human standards," he snapped. I didn't bother to answer, only laughed at him silently—I didn't have to mention Xeng Wangbo. "All right," he grumped, "then what about commercials? Several parolees have testified that you're in violation there!"

I sighed. Same old argument, every time. I said, "According to section 6-C of the Protocol a commercial is defined as 'a persuasive offering of goods or services.' There's no offer, is there?

16

I mean, the things can't be *offered* when they're not available, and the greks can't ever have such things. It's part of their punishment." The rest of their punishment, to be sure, was that they were continually bombarded with advertising for the things they couldn't have. But that, too, was none of his business.

The quick gleam in Harriman's eye warned me I had fallen into a trap. "Of course," I backtracked swiftly, "there are exceptions to the general rule, so trivial in nature that one need not even mention them—"

"Exceptions," he said gleefully. "Yes, Tarb, there are exceptions, all right. We have affidavits from no fewer than eight parolees stating that prisoners have been driven by the commercials to write their families and friends back on Earth for some of the advertised goods! In particular, we have evidence that Coffiest, Mokie-Koke and Starrzelius brand Nick-O-Teen Chewies have been included in prisoners' Red Cross packages for that reason. . . ."

We were off. I abandoned all hope of catching the return flight that night, because I knew we would be haggling now well past midnight.

So we were, with much consultation of "clarificatory notes" and "position statements" and "emendations without prejudice." I knew he wasn't serious. He was just trying to establish a bargaining position for what he really wanted. But he argued tenaciously, until I offered to cancel all Red Cross packages completely for the greks if that would make him happy. Well, obviously he didn't want that, so he offered a deal. He dropped the question of commercials in return for early commutation for some of his pet greks.

So I gave him slap-on-the-wrist, token ten-day sentences for Moskowicz, McCastry, Bliven, the Farnell family . . . and Hamid. As I had planned to all along.

Harriman was all smiles and hospitality once I'd given him what he wanted—or thought he wanted. He insisted I spend the night in his pied-à-terre in the Polar town. I slept badly, having refused

17

his offer of a nightcap or several—I didn't intend to take chances on spilling information I didn't want him to have. Also, all night long I kept waking up with that panicky agoraphobic feeling you get when you're in a place that's *too large*. Crazy Veenies! They have to fight for every cubic foot of living space, and yet Harriman had *three whole rooms!* And in an apartment he didn't use more than ten nights a year! So I got up early the next morning and by six A.M. I was standing in line at the airport check-in counter. Ahead of me was a teenage Veenie with one of those "patriotic" tee shirts that say *Hucks Go Home* on the front and *No *DV*RT*S*NG* on the back—as though "advertising" were a dirty word! I wouldn't give him the satisfaction of looking at him, so I turned away. Behind me was a short, slim black woman who looked vaguely familiar. "Hello, Mr. Tarb," she said, amiably enough, and it turned out she was familiar enough—a local fire inspector or something back at the port. She'd toured the Embassy a few times, checking for violations.

She turned out to be my seatmate on the flight, as well. I had automatically assumed she was a Veenie spy—all the natives who got into the Embassy for any reason at all, we knew, were likely to file reports on what they'd seen. But she was surprisingly open and friendly. Not your typical Veenie crackpot at all. She didn't talk politics. What she talked about was a lot more interesting to me: Mitzi. She'd seen the two of us together in the Embassy and guessed we were lovers—true enough then!—and she said all the right things about Mitzi. Beautiful. Intelligent. Energetic.

What I had intended to do on the return flight was sleep, but the conversation was so congenial that I spent the whole time chatting. By the time we touched down I was babbling about all my hopes and dreams. How I had to return to Earth myself. How I wished Mitzi would rotate with me, but how determined she was to stay on. How I dreamed of a longtime relationship—maybe even marriage. A home in Greater New York, maybe out toward the Forest Preserve Acre at Milford . . . maybe a kid or two. . . . It was funny. The more I said, the sadder and more thoughtful it seemed to make her.

But I was sad enough myself, because I couldn't believe that any of that was going to happen.

III

But things began to brighten astonishingly when I got back to the Embassy. First I encountered Hay Lopez, coming out of the men's room—coming out of Mitzi's hideaway, I was pretty sure. But he didn't say anything, just growled as we passed. The expression on his face, glum and irritated, was exactly what I might have hoped to see.

And when I flushed my way through the private door into the War Room, the look on Mitzi's face was just as good. She was grimly punching data into her files, flustered and annoyed. Whatever had gone on those two nights I had been away, it was no idyll. "I got Hamid in," I reported proudly, and leaned over to kiss her. No problem! No enthusiasm, either, but she did kiss me back, tepidly.

"I was sure you would, Tenny," she sighed, and the frown lines began to dwindle; they hadn't been aimed at me. "When can he report for duty?"

"Well, I didn't actually talk to him, of course. But he's got a ten-day parole. I'd say two weeks at the outside."

She looked really pleased. She made a note to herself, then pushed back her chair and gazed into space. "Two weeks," she said thoughtfully. "Wish we'd had him here for the Day of Planetary Mourning—he could have heard all kinds of things in that crowd. Still, there's other stuff coming up—they're going to have one of their elections next month, so there'll be all sorts of political meetings—"

I put my finger on her mouth. "What's coming up," I said, "and that tomorrow night, is my farewell party. Would you be my date for the party?"

She gave me an actual smile. "On your big night? Of course I will."

19

"And maybe take the day off tomorrow so we can do something together?"

Faint shadow of the frown lines coming back. "Well, I'm really awfully busy right now, Tenn—"

I took a chance. "But not with Hay Lopez, right?"

Frown lines deep and blazing. "No chance!" she hissed dangerously. *"Nobody* can treat me the way he wants to—thinks he owns me!"

I kept my face bland and sympathetic, but inside I was grinning the top of my head off. "So about tomorrow?"

"Well, why not? Maybe we'll—I don't know—go out to Russian Hills maybe. Something, anyway." She leaned forward and pecked my cheek. "If I'm going to take tomorrow off I've got a heavy day today, Tenny—so clear out, will you?" But she said it fondly.

To my surprise, she was serious about making us visit the old Russian Venera rocket. I humored her. I suppose, in a way, it would have been missing something for me to leave Venus without taking a look at one of its most famous artifacts. We ducked out of the Embassy early and took an electrohack to the tram station before the streets were really crowded.

Around the major cities the Veenies have managed to grow some grass and weeds and even a few spindly things they call trees —of course, they're specially engineered genetically, somehow or other, but they do show some green now and then. Russian Hills, though, hasn't been changed at all. On purpose.

Do you want to know what kind of crackpots the Venusians are? All right, let me tell you one simple anecdote. You see, they've got that huge planet—five times as much land area as the whole planet Earth, you know, because there aren't any oceans yet. In order to make it into something decent, they've been busting their backs for forty years and more trying to make green things grow. But that's hellishly difficult, because of the kind of planet Venus is. Plants have a tough time. One, there's not really enough light; two, there's damn near no water at all; three, it's

20

way too hot. So to make anything grow at all takes all kinds of technological wizardry and enormous effort. First they had to nuke some tectonic faults to set off volcanos—that's to bring whatever water vapor there is up out of the core (that's the way the Earth got its water billions of years ago, they say). Second, they had to cap the volcanos to catch the water vapor. Third, they had to provide something cold enough to condense the vapor to a liquid; that's the cold end of the Hilsch tubes—you see them on mountaintops all over Venus, big things like one-hole piccolos, with the hot end blasting gases out through the atmosphere to get lost in space and the cold end providing cooling for the cities— and generating a little electricity while they do it. Fourth, they have to pipe that trickle of water to where things are planted, and they have to do it underground so it won't boil away in the first ten feet. Fifth, they have to have special, genetically tailored plants that can whisk that water up through their stems and leaves before letting it boil away—it's a miracle they got any of this done, especially considering they don't have much work force to spare for big projects. There are only about eight hundred thousand Veenies all in all.

And yet—here's the funny thing—if you take the tram out to Russian Hills, the first thing you see in the park itself is a six-man crew working all around the clock, climbing those ugly sharp rocks with hundred-pound backpacks of plant killer, zapping every green thing they see!

Crazy? Of course it's crazy. It's the insanity of Conservationism carried to its lunatic conclusion: the Conservationists want to keep the Venera setting just the way it was when the probe landed. But the lunacy isn't really surprising. "If Veenies weren't crazy they would have stayed on the Earth in the first place," I told Mitzi as we rattled along the tramline. "Look at the dumps they live in!" We were passing through roofed-over suburbs. They were supposed to be high-class residential areas, and yet they were filled with scraggly weeds and pressed-plastic tenements; they didn't even have Astro-Turf!

It occurred to me that I might be talking a little too loudly.

The other passengers, all Veenies, were turning around to look at me. That was no big treat. Veenies are almost all grossly tall—even taller than Mitzi, usually—and they seem to take pride in their fishbelly-white skins. Of course, they never get any sun. But they could use UV lamps like we do—all of us—even Mitzi, who doesn't need tanning to have that nice velvet-brass skin.

"Watch your mouth," Mitzi whispered nervously. The Veenie family just in front of us—Daddy, Mommy and four (yes, I said *four!*) kids—were half-turning their heads to get a look at us, and their expressions weren't friendly. Veenies don't like us much. They think we're city slickers trying to gobble them up. That's a laugh, because what have they got worth gobbling? And if we're taking an interest in their affairs, obviously it's for their own good—they're just not intelligent enough to realize it.

Fortunately we had entered the tunnel that goes through the ring of peaks around Russian Hills. Everybody began getting ready to get out. As I started to rise, Mitzi nudged me, and I saw a grossly tall he-Veenie, green eyes and red hair with that ugly dead-white skin, giving me a bad look. I took Mitzi's hint. I gave the Veenie my sweetest forgive-me-for-my-blunders smile and slipped past him out the door. While I stopped to buy a souvenir booklet, Mitzi was standing behind me, gazing after the man with the traffic-light head. "Look at this," I said, opening the guide book, but Mitzi wasn't listening.

"Do you know," she said, "I think I've seen him before. Day before yesterday. When they were demonstrating."

"Come on, Mitz! There were five hundred Veenies out there!" And so there had been—maybe more—at the time, I could have sworn half of Venus was silently parading around our Embassy with their stupid signs—"No Advertising!" and "Take Your Filth Back Where It Belongs!" I didn't mind the picketing so much—but, oh, the pathetic amateurishness of their slogan writers! "They're crazy," I said—a complicated shorthand that didn't mean "crazy" for thinking we would use advertising techniques on them, but "crazy" because they were getting upset about it—as though there were any possibility that, given a chance, we wouldn't.

22

I also meant crazy in the specific context of incompetent copysmithing, and that was what I wanted to show Mitzi. I glanced around the noisy car barn—another was just rattling up toward the switching point for the return trip to Port Kathy. No Veenies were within earshot. "Look here," I said, opening to the page marked *Facilities—Food and Drink.* It said:

If for any reason you do not want to bring your own refreshments while visiting Russian Hills, some items like hamburgers, hot dogs and soy sandwiches are available in the Venera Lounge. They're inspected by the Planetary Health Service, but the quality is mediocre. Beer and other drinks can also be purchased, at about twice the cost of the same things in town.

"Pathetic?" I groaned.
She said absently, "Well, they're honest."
I raised my eyebrows. What did honesty have to do with moving product? And this place was a copysmith's dream! They had a captive clientele, one. They had a theme to hang the copy on, two. And they had customers who were in a holiday mood, ready to buy anything that was for sale, three, and most important of all! All they had to do was call their hot dogs "Genuine Odessa Wurst" and the hamburgers "Komsomol Burgers" to give the consumers an excuse to buy—but instead they talked them right out of it! Consumers didn't expect to *get* what advertising promised. They just wanted that one tiny moment of hope before the "Sleep-Tite Super-Soft" mattress stuck a spring into their bottoms and the "Nature-Fresh Golden-Tropical-Fruit Elixir" turned out to taste of tar. "Well," I said, "we've come this far. Let's go look at their damn space probe."

Venus was a garbage planet to start out. The air was poison, and too much of it, so the pressure was appalling. The heat boiled everything boilable away. There was nothing growing that was worth talking about when the first Earth ship landed, and fifty years of human colonization hadn't made it good: just microscopically less awful. The Veenies' attempts to turn the atmosphere into something a human being could stand weren't finished, but they'd gone far enough that in some places you could get around without a pressure suit nowadays . . . though you needed to carry a breathing tank on your back, because there was precious little oxygen.

This part they called the "Venera–Russian Hills Planetary Park"—so the sign at the tram stop said—wasn't really much worse than the rest of it, no matter how much the Veenie Conservationists patted themselves on the back for retaining its "unspoiled wilderness quality." I gazed at it through the window, and felt no impulse to get closer.

"Let's go, Tenn," Mitzi urged.

"Are you sure you want to do this?" It was nasty enough in the tram station, with the noise of the cars and the Veenies with their giggling brats. Going out of doors meant a whole higher order of nastiness. We'd have to put on the air tanks and sip air from tubes in our mouths, and it would mean even more heat than the interior ovens the Veenies seemed to thrive on. "Maybe we should eat first," I offered, eyeing the refreshment stand. Under the painted legend "Chef's Recommendation for Today" someone had chalked, "Stay away from the scrambled eggs."

"Oh, come on, Tenn! You're always telling me how much you hate Veenie food. I'll go get us a couple of breathers."

When you don't have any choice, go along—that's the motto of the Tarbs. It has served our family well, for we've been members of the advertising profession since the old days of Madison Avenue and the Pepsi-Cola jingle. So I strapped the damn tank on my back and put the damn tube in my mouth and, whispering around the mouthpiece, said, "Into the valley of death, march on!"

Mitzi didn't laugh. She was in a sort of down mood that whole day, I know—I assumed because I was leaving. So I clapped her on the back and we stumbled down the path to the Venera.

The Venera space probe is a hunk of dead metal, about the size of a pedicab, with spiky rods and dishes sticking out of it. It is not in good shape. Time was when it perched on top of a rocket in snowy Tyuratam and blasted its way across a hundred million miles of space to come blazing down through Venus's blistering air. It must have made quite a sight, but of course there wasn't anybody there to see it. After all that trouble and expense it had a working life of a couple of hours. It was long enough for it to radio back some pressure and temperature readings, and transmit a few out-of-focus distorted pictures of the rocks it was sitting on. That was its whole career. Then the poison gases seeped in, and all the circuits and gadgets and gizmos died. I suppose, really, that you'd have to say that the Venera was quite an accomplishment for those old pretechnological days. Those foggy gray camera eyes produced the first look at the surface of Venus that any human being ever had, and when the Veenies stumbled across it, in their first months of colonizing the planet, you would have expected them to want to celebrate it as a triumph, right? Oh, hell, no. The reason the Veenies made such a fuss about this hunk of junk was just more of their weirdness. See, back in those days the Russians were what they called Soviets. I'm not real sure what Soviets were —I always get them mixed up with the Scientologists and the Ghibellines—but I do know that they didn't believe in—wait for it!—in *profit!* That's right. Profit. They didn't believe in people making money out of things. And as for profit's major handmaiden, advertising, well, they just didn't have any! I know that sounds strange, and when we were taking History I back in college I couldn't believe it, so I checked it out. It's true enough. Bar some piddly little things like electric signs boasting about steel production and TV commercials begging the factory hands not to get drunk in working hours, advertising just didn't exist. But it was almost the same now, with the Veenies, and that's why they made a shrine out of two tons of scrap metal. The big difference between the Veenies and the Russians is that after a while the Russians smartened up and joined the free confraternity of profit-loving people, while the Veenies tried their best to go the other way.

After half an hour of climbing around the Venera I'd had

about enough. The place was full of Veenie tourists, and I can get real tired of drinking my air out of a soda straw. So while Mitzi was bent over, her lips moving as she tried to make out the Cyrillic script on the nameplate, I reached behind me to the relief valve on my oxygen tank and gave it a little twist. It made a shrill squeal as the gas poured out, but I took a fit of coughing at that moment, and, anyway, the scream of the Hilsch tubes on the hills all around us drowned out most minor sounds. Then I nudged her.

"Oh, damn it all to hell, look at this!" I cried, and showed her my oxygen gauge. It was way down into the yellow, almost touching the red danger zone—I'd cut it a little finer than I intended. "Damn Veenies sold me a half-empty tank! Well," I said, tone reeking with resignation, "I'm sorry about this, but I'm going to have to get back inside the station. Then maybe we should think about heading home."

Mitzi gave me a funny look. She didn't say anything, just turned and started back up the slope. I had no doubt that she had checked the tank gauge when she paid for it, but it wasn't likely she would be *sure* she had. To take the sting out of it, while we were trudging back I caught up with her, took the tube out of my mouth and suggested, "How about a drink in the lounge before we catch the tram?" It's true that I can't stand Veenie food— it's the CO_2 in the air, it makes things grow real fast, and besides the Veenies eat everything fresh, so you never get that good flash-frozen tang. But liquor is liquor, anywhere in the solar system! And besides, eighteen months of dating Mitzi had taught me that she was always a lot more fun with a couple of drinks in her. She brightened right away, and as soon as we'd ditched the tanks—I persuaded her not to make a fuss about the light load in mine—we headed for the stairs to the lounge.

The tram station was typical Veenie construction—it wouldn't have passed muster for a Consumer-level comfort station back home. No vending machines, no games, no educational displays of new products and services. It was hollowed out of the solid rock, and about all they'd done to beautify it was to slap some paint on the walls and plant some flowers and things. The tramline came in through a tunnel at one end. They'd blasted and dug a space for the tram platforms and a waiting room and things like that. They hadn't wanted to spoil the capital-N-Natural capital-B-Beauty of the park, see, so they hid the station inside the hill.

The worst thing about it, I thought at first, was the noise. When a tram barreled into that hard-surfaced echo chamber it was like demolition day in a scrap-iron plant. I almost changed my mind about the drink, but I didn't want to disappoint Mitzi. Then, when we got settled in at a table in the upper-deck lounge, I found out what was even worse. "Look at this," I said in disgust, turning the menu card so we could both read it. It was more of that sickening Veenie "candor," of course:

All cocktails are canned premixes, and they taste like it.

The red wine is corky and not a good year. The white is a little better.

If you want anything to eat you'd do better to go downstairs and bring it up for yourself—otherwise there's a $2 service charge.

Mitzi shrugged. "It's their planet," she said, determined to have a good time, and craned her neck to peer out the window. And that was another thing. So as not to spoil the looks from outside they had artfully hidden the windows in clefts in the rock. From outside it was maybe a good idea; but from inside you couldn't see out without straining, and what's the use of an observation window you can't see out of?

Grin and bear it! I was on my way out of this hellhole anyway. We ordered the white wine, obediently, and Mitzi commented, "Look, there's an ambulance chopper by the path. I wonder if somebody got hurt."

"They probably keep it there for the people they swindle on the oxygen," I joked, bending to look out. The chopper had been there a while, because the rotors were still. Two men were having

27

some kind of an argument beside it. I was mildly surprised to see that one of them was the man with the traffic-light head from the tram. That wasn't so surprising, because there are just so many Veenies and you can't help running into the same ones over and over. But I was beginning to get a little tired of this particular one. "Drink up," I said, dismissing him and paying the waiter at the same time. "A toast! To our good times together—past, present and future!"

"Ah, Tenn," said Mitzi, raising her glass, "I wish. But I'm still going to reup."

The wine was good and cold—well, no; it wasn't all that good, but at least it was cold. Thinking about Mitzi wasting herself for another year and a half, at least, on this smelly cinder of a planet spoiled it for me. "They say if you spend too much time with the Veenies you'll turn into one." I was half-joking—half at the most. And immediately she got her defensive look.

"My Agency has no reason for dissatisfaction with my work," she said stiffly. "The Veenies aren't so bad! A little misguided."

"A little." I gazed around the lounge. The tables were bare plastic. There was no Muzak, no friendly advertising posters decorating the walls.

"It's just a different life-style," she insisted. "Of course, compared to what we have on Earth it's *pathetic*. But all they want from us, really, is just to be left alone."

The conversation was not going at all the way I wanted it to. Sometimes, when I was talking to Mitzi when she was off-duty and off-guard, I wondered if the old saying wasn't true for her. She had been on Venus for eighteen months. She had covered the whole planet, just about, and she had dealt with its seamiest citizens, the turncoats. If there was anybody in the Embassy who should have been sick and disgusted with this primitive place it was Mitzi Ku. But she wasn't. She was going to sign up for another hitch in the oven. She even, sometimes, acted as though she *liked* it here! There were even stories that sometimes she went shopping in the Veenie stores instead of the PX. I didn't believe them, of course. But sometimes I wondered. . . . And yet what

28

she said was true. Her Agency, which was the same as my own, could certainly find nothing wrong with her record on Venus. Her official designation at the Embassy was "visa clerk," but her real work was running a network of spies and saboteurs that stretched from Port Kathy to the Polar Penal Colony. She did it superbly. The computer analyses said the Veenie Gross Planetary Product was off a good 3 per cent just because of Mitzi's work.

And yet she said such strange things! Like, "Oh, Tenn, give them credit. They took a planet that an Arizona rattlesnake couldn't stay alive on, and in less than thirty years they've made it livable—"

"Livable!" I sneered, gazing meaningfully out the window.

"Sure it's livable! At least where they've covered it over. Naturally it's not a South Seas paradise, but they've done a pretty good job, considering what they had to work with." She glanced irritably across the room, where a Veenie family was trying to quiet a screaming child. Then she shrugged. "Oh, they're annoying," she admitted. "But they're not such bad people. Consider what they started from—half of them came here because they were misfits on the Earth and the other half got exiled as criminals."

"Misfits and criminals, right! The dregs of society! And they haven't got much better here!"

But there was no sense spending our last day together arguing politics. I swallowed and changed direction. "Some of them aren't so bad," I conceded. "Especially the kids." That was safe enough, everybody's in favor of kids, and the poor little tyke hadn't stopped screaming. "I wish I could cheer him up," I offered tentatively, "but I think I'd scare him out of his mind—some big huck coming at him that way—"

"Let him yell," said Mitzi, gazing out the window.

I sighed—but silently. There were times when I wondered whether it was worthwhile trying to keep up with Mitzi's moods and peculiarities. But it was. The important thing about Mitzi Ku was that she was a gorgeous woman. She had that perfect silky-brassy honey-almond skin and, for a person of Oriental ancestry, quite a womanly figure. Her eyes weren't that Oriental shoe-

29

button black, either; they were light blue—some fooling around among the progenitors, no doubt. And she had perfect teeth and knew just when to, very delicately, use them. Take her all in all, she was well worth the taking.

So I tried again. I reached out for her hand and said sentimentally, "There's something about that little boy, honey. I look at him and I wish you and I could some day have—"

She flared, "Knock it off, Tarb!"

"I only meant—"

"I know what you meant! Let me tell you the facts. One, I don't like kids. Two, I don't have to like kids, because I don't have to have any—there are plenty of consumers to keep the population up. Three, you're not interested in a kid anyway, you're only interested in what you do to get one started, and the answer is *no.*"

I let it drop. It wasn't true, though. Not much more than half-true, anyway.

But then things began to get a little better. I had a powerful ally in the Veenie wine; however it tasted, it had a handsome kick. And the other ally I had was Mitzi herself because the logic of the situation convinced her the way it had convinced me: there was no sense getting into a spat when we had so little time left.

By the time we finished the capsule I had moved over next to her. When I slid my hand around her waist it was just like old times, and, like old times, she leaned into my arm. With my free hand I lifted my glass, with the last quarter-inch of wine in it, and offered a toast: "Here's to us, Mits, and to our last time together." Funny, I thought, peering past her—that bus-person clearing off the tables at the far end of the room: she looked a lot like the woman I'd sat next to on the flight from the Pole.

But I thought no more of it, because Mitzi raised her own glass, smiling at me over the brim, and gave back the toast: "To our last day together, Tenn, and our last night."

That was as clear an exit line as I'd ever heard. We got up and headed for the stairs to the tram station, arms around each other.

We were definitely fuzzy from the wine, but even so I nudged Mitzi as we passed the table by the door. Half the Veenies I had ever met seemed to be in this place today; this one was old red-hair green-eyes again. Evidently he'd settled his argument out at the ambulance chopper because he was sitting alone, pretending to be reading the menu—as if that could take more than ten seconds! He glanced up just as we passed. What the hell. I wouldn't have to be seeing any of their bleached dumb faces any more after the shuttle took off, so I gave him a smile. He didn't smile back.

I didn't expect him to, after all. So I just led Mitzi out the door and down the stairs, and forgot the whole incident—for a while.

Hand in hand we strolled to the nearest platform where a tram was waiting. I had thought I had seen people boarding it, but as we were about to get on a Veenie guard hurried up. "Sorry, folks," he panted, out of breath, "but this one's out of service. It's got, uh, a mechanical defect. The next one out—" he pointed—"will be right over there on Platform Three."

There was no tram at Platform Three, but I could see that there was one at the junction point, its nose just poking out from the tunnel, waiting for the signal lights to clear so it could enter the platform.

For some reason I was feeling a little dizzy and generally vague. The wine, I assumed. It kept me from wanting to argue. We turned to start back down the platform but the guard waved us across the tracks. "Save time if you just cut through here," he said helpfully.

Mitzi seemed a little blurry, too, but she asked, "Isn't that dangerous?" And the guard gave us an indulgent let's-not-hit-the-booze-so-hard-next-time chuckle and guided us to the track. No, he didn't guide us. He *shoved* us . . . just as there was a clatter from the end of the platform.

Out of the corner of one eye I saw the tram galumphing down on us. We were right bull's-eye in its path.

"Jump!" I yelled, and, "Jump, Tenny!" yelled Mitzi at the

same moment, and jump we both did. I grabbed for Mitzi, and she grabbed for me, and it would have worked out really well if we had jumped in the same direction. But we didn't. We bumped each other. If Mitzi had been smaller, instead of taller, than me, I might have tossed her or tugged her clear; as it was she went one way and I went another, but not quite in time. The tram slammed me out onto the platform, with yells and cursing and screeching of brakes. Flames of pain ran up my legs as I slid across rough concrete on my knees. Somewhere along the line I hit my head a good one—or the tram did.

The next thing I knew my knee and my head were competing to see which one could hurt me the most, and I was hearing yelling voices—

"—couple of hucks tried to cross the track—"

"—one dead and one pretty bad—"

"Get that medic in here!"

And somebody out of the tram was leaning over me, ruddy whiskered face pop-eyed with surprise, and to my astonishment it was Marty MacLeod, the Deputy Station Chief.

I don't remember much of the next little while. There are only flashes: Marty demanding I be taken at once to the Embassy, the medic obstinate that ambulance patients went to the hospital and nowhere else, someone peering over Marty's shoulder and blurting, "Jeez! It's the male huck, and he's alive!" The someone was the traffic-light Veenie.

Then I remember the cement-mixer bumps and jolts of the ambulance chopper as it leaped the hills around the park, and I went quietly to sleep. Thinking about Mitzi. Thinking about how I felt. Thinking that it wouldn't be right to say that I loved her, exactly, and certainly nothing she ever said to me, in bed or out, sounded like she felt anything like that . . . but thinking mostly that it was really sad that she was dead.

But she wasn't.

They kept me an hour in the emergency room—a couple of Band-Aids and an X-ray series—and when they released me into Marty's custody they told me Mitzi had nine fractures counted and at least six internal ruptures that showed on the tomography. She was in intensive care, and they'd keep us posted.

Good news! But it didn't make my heart sing. Because by then I was getting my head straight, and the straighter it got the more certain it became in my mind that the accident had been no accident.

I will say for Marty that when we got inside the bug-proof Embassy compound she listened seriously while I told her what I thought. "We'll check," she promised grimly. "Can't do anything till we see what Mitzi has to say, though—and for now, you're going to sleep." It wasn't a suggestion. It wasn't even an order. It was a fact, because they'd slipped me a shot when I wasn't looking, and it was bye-bye time.

When I woke up I had barely time to dress and get down to the farewell party in my honor.

Now, really, that's kind of a joke. The Veenies don't have many public holidays, but the ones they have they celebrate with a lot of enthusiasm. That's embarrassing for us dips. We need to be part of the festivities, because that's what diplomacy is all about, but we certainly can't admit to celebrating most of their holidays—they have names like "Freedom from Advertising Day" and "Anti-Christmas." Still, we have to do something, so for every holiday we cook up an excuse to hold a party—for a totally different reason, of course—at that time. There's always some excuse. Sometimes the excuses are arranged before the dip gets assigned here. There's old Jim Holder, for instance, from Codes & Ciphers; they say he was sent here because he happened to be born on the same date as the renegade Mitchell Courtenay.

So tonight's party was—nominally—a send-off for me. All the people I ran into congratulated me on shaking this place loose at last—and, a couple of steps down on the priority list, oh, yes, your lucky escape from the tram, too, Tenny. That is, the Earth people did that; the Veenies were as always a whole other thing.

Let's be fair to the Veenies. They don't like these ceremonial parties any more than we do, I guess. If they're high enough on

33

the totem pole they get invited. If they get invited they come. Nobody says they have to enjoy themselves. They're polite about it—reasonably polite—if they're female they dance two dances with two separate male Earth dips. I think they like that part, at least, because they're almost always taller than their partners. The conversation is almost always about the same—

"Hot today."

"Was it? I didn't notice."

"The new Hilsch plant's coming along nicely."

"Thank you."

—then the second obligatory dance with a different partner and then, if you happen to look around for them—though why you would do that I can't guess—they're gone. The male Veenies do about the same, except that it's two drinks at the bar instead of two dances, and the conversation isn't about the weather, it's about Port Kathy's chances against North Star in the rolley-hockey league. It's just as bad when we have to go to one of their formal parties. We don't linger, either. Mitzi says that her spies tell her the Veenies' parties usually get to be real hell-roaring balls after we leave, but none of us are ever urged to stay. Dips' parties are meant to be diplomatic: nothing heavy discussed, and certainly not much fun.

But sometimes it doesn't go like that. My first duty dance was with a slim young thing from the Veenie Department of Extra-planetary Affairs—fishbelly skin, of course, but it went well enough with her almost platinum hair. If I hadn't been so sore about Mitzi I might have enjoyed dancing with her, but she would have spoiled it anyway. "Mr. Tarb," she said right off, "do you think it's fair to make the Hyperion miners listen to your advertising slop?"

Well, she was *very* junior. Her bosses wouldn't have said anything like that. The trouble was, it was my bosses who were nearby, and the conversation got worse: Why were armed Earth spacecraft orbiting Venus every now and then without explaining their errands? And why had we refused permission for the Veenies to send a "scientific" mission to Mars? And—and everything else was pretty much the same. I made all the right defensive replies, but she'd been speaking pretty loudly and people were looking at us. Hay Lopez was one of them; he was standing with the Chief of Station, and they exchanged glances in a way I didn't much like. When the dance was at last over I was glad to head for the bar. The only open space was next to Pavel Borkmann, head of some section of the Veenie Department of Heavy Industry. I'd met him before and intended ten minutes of nonthreatening chat about how their new Hilsch barrage in the Anti-Oasis was going, or whether they were satisfied with the new rocket plant. That didn't work out either, because he too had heard snatches of my little dialogue with the Extraplanetary Affair. "You ought not to get into fights where you're overmatched," he grinned, referring both to my late dance partner and to the obvious scars I had collected from the tram. If I'd had any sense I would have chosen the meaning that was least chancy and told him all about the tram accident. My feelings were ruffled; I took the other course, "She was way out of line," I complained, signaling for a drink I certainly didn't need.

But Borkmann had had a drink more than he needed too, it seemed, because he too took the path with the beartraps in it. "Oh, I don't know," he said. "You have to understand that we Free Venusians have moral objections to forcing people to buy things—especially at the point of a gun."

"There aren't any guns pointed at Hyperion, Borkmann! You know that."

"Not yet," he admitted, "but haven't there been such cases right on your home planet?"

I laughed, pitying him. "You're talking about the abos, I suppose."

"I'm talking about the pitiful few corners of the Earth that haven't yet been corrupted by advertising, yes."

Well, by then I was getting irritated. "Borkmann," I said, "you know better than that. We do maintain a peacekeeping body, of course. I suppose some few of them have guns, but they're only for protection. I did my own reserve training in

35

college; I know what I'm talking about. They are *never* used offensively, only to preserve order. You must realize that even among the worst of the aboriginals there are plenty of people who want to have the benefits of the market society. Naturally, the old fuddy-duddies resist. But when the better elements ask for help, why, of course we give it."

"You send in the troops," he nodded.

"We send in advertising teams," I corrected him. "There is no *compulsion*. There is no *force.*"

"And," he mimicked, "there is no *escape*—they found that out in New Guinea."

"It's true that things got out of hand in New Guinea," I admitted. "But really—"

"Really," he said, slamming down his glass, "I have to be going now, Tarb. Nice talking to you." And he left me fuming. Why, there was really nothing wrong in New Guinea! There had been less than a thousand deaths all told. And now the island was firmly a part of the modern world—we even had a branch of the Agency in Papua! I swallowed my drink in one gulp and turned away . . . and almost bumped into Hay Lopez, grinning at me. Walking away, glancing back at me over her shoulder, was the Chief of Station. I saw her join the Ambassador and whisper in his ear, still looking at me, and realized this was turning out to be a pretty bad day. Since I was on my way home anyway there was little the Embassy people could do to me, but still I resolved to behave like a proper dip for the rest of the evening.

That didn't work out, either. Through the luck of the draw, the second partner I drew was Dirty Berthie, the Turncoat Earthie. I should've been faster on my feet; I guess I was still a little groggy. I turned around, and there she was, boozy breath, sloppy-fat face and hair piled up on her head to make her look taller. "My dance, I believe, Tenny?" she giggled.

So gallantly I lied, "I've been looking forward to it!" What you can say for Dirty Berthie is that even in those spike heels and haystack hairdo, she doesn't tower over you the way the natives do. That's about all you can say for her. Converts are always the worst, and Bertha, who is now Deputy Curator for the entire planet-wide Venus library system, was once a Senior Research Vice-President for the Taunton, Gatchweiler and Schocken Agency! She gave all that up to migrate to Venus, and now she has to prove with every word she says that she's more Veenie than the Venusians. "Well, Mr. Tennison Tarb," she said, leaning back against my arm to study my shiner, "looks like somebody's husband came back when he wasn't supposed to."

Just a harmless jocularity, right? Wrong. Dirty Berthie's little jokes are always nasty. It's "How's organized lying today?" for a hello, and, "Well, I mustn't keep you from peddling some more poison baby food," when she says good-by. *We* aren't allowed to do that kind of thing. To be fair, most of the native Veenies don't, either, but Bertha is the worst of both worlds. Our official policy on Bertha is smile and say nothing. That's what I had done for all those long years, but enough was enough. I said—

Well, I can't defend what I said. To understand it you have to know that Bertha's husband, the one she gave up her star class job on Earth for, was a pilot on the Kathy-to-Discovery airline, who lost part of his right leg and an unspecified selection of adjacent parts in a crash the year after they were married. It's the one thing she's sensitive about. So I gave her a sweet, sweet smile and said, "I was just trying to do Carlos's work as a favor to him, but I got the wrong house."

My joke wasn't very funny. Bertha didn't even try for one in response. She gasped. She pushed free of my arms, stood stock-still in the middle of the dance floor and cried, loud and clear, "You bastard!" There were actual tears in her eyes—rage, I guess.

I did not have a chance to study her reaction. A beartrap grip closed on my shoulder and the Chief of Station herself said politely, "If I can borrow Tenny a moment, Bertha, there are some last-minute things we have to settle. . . ." Out in the corridor she squared off, head to head. "You *ass*," she hissed. Sprinkles of saliva like snake venom ate pits in my cheeks.

I tried to defend myself. "She started it! She said—"

"I heard what she said, and the whole damned room heard

what *you* said! Jesus, Tarb!" She had let go of my shoulder, and now she looked as though she wanted to take me by the throat instead.

I backed away. "Pam, I know I was out of line, but I'm a little shook up. Don't forget somebody nearly murdered me today!"

"It was an *accident.* The Embassy has officially listed it as an *accident.* Try to remember that. It doesn't make sense any other way. Why would anybody bother to murder you when you're on your way home?"

"Not me. Mitzi. Maybe there's a double agent among the spies she's recruited, and they know what she's doing."

"Tarb." There was no snake venom this time and no hiss, not even anger. This was just an icy warning. She looked quickly around to make sure no one was nearby. Well, of course I shouldn't have said anything like that while there were Veenies in the building—that was Rule Number One. I started to say something, and she raised her hand. "Mitsui Ku is not dead," she said. "They've operated on her. I saw her myself in the hospital, an hour and a half ago. She hadn't regained consciousness, but the prognosis is good. If they wanted her dead, they could have done it in the operating room and we never would have known it. They didn't."

"All the same—"

"Go back to bed, Tarb. Your injuries are more severe than we realized." She didn't let me interrupt, but pointed toward the private rooms. *"Now.* And I've got to get back to my guests—after I stop in my office to add some remarks to an efficiency report. Yours." She stood there and watched me out of sight.

And that was the last I saw of the Chief of Station, and almost the last I saw of anything at all for quite a while—two years and a bit—because the next morning I was hustled out of bed by two Embassy guards, bundled into a station car, hurried to the port, packed into a shuttle. In three hours I was in orbit. In three hours and a half I was lying in a freezer cocoon, waiting for the sleepy drug to put me out and the chill-down to start. The space liner was not due to start its main engines for another nine orbits—

more than half a day—but the Ambassador had given orders to get me put away. And get me put away they did.

The next thing I knew I was being eaten alive by fire ants, that unbearable arm's-asleep feeling you get when you're first thawed. I was still in the cocoon but I was wearing an electrically warmed skinsuit with only my eyes exposed, and bending over me was somebody I knew. "Hello there, Tenn," said Mitzi Ku. "Surprised to see me?"

I was. I said I was, but I doubt that I managed to express just how surprised I was, because the last thought I remembered, just before the whirly-down sleepiness took over, was rueful regret that I hadn't had that last farewell appearance in Mitzi's bed, and was not likely ever to get a chance to make it up.

I was startled at her appearance. Half her face was bandaged, only the mouth and chin exposed, with two little slits in the dressing for eyes. Of course, that was natural enough. Healing doesn't take place when you're frozen. Effectively Mitzi was only a few days out of surgery. "Are you all right?" I asked.

She said sharply, "Sure I am. I'm fine! I mean," she qualified, "I probably won't be *all* fine for weeks yet, but I'm ambulatory. As you see," she grinned. I *think* she was grinning. "When the doctors said I could leave the hospital I made up my mind that Venus had seen the last of me. So I tore up my reenlistment papers and they got me on the last shuttle. I stayed unfrozen for a while, until they could get the stitches out—and here I am!"

The itching had dwindled to the almost bearable range. The world suddenly looked brighter, and I started to peel off the hotsuit. Mitzi nodded. "That's the spirit, Tenn! We touch down on the Moon in ninety minutes—better get your pants on!"

Tarb's Homecoming

·· ◆ ··

I

To my surprise, the two deported Marines were on the same ship. That was a good thing. Without them helping me limp off I doubt I would have made it. Mitzi, all bandaged and broken, was fine. I was not. I was sick, and by that I mean, man, *sick*. I've always been susceptible to motion sickness, but it had never occurred to me that it was just as bad to be on the Moon.

Venus is terrible, sure, but at least on Venus you weigh what you expect to weigh. The Moon isn't that friendly. They say after the first six weeks you stop throwing your coffee across the room when you only want to put it to your lips but I'll never know that for myself—I don't like the place. If we'd come on a regular Earth rocket we'd have shuttled down to the surface right away, but it was a Veenie vessel and had to stop at quarantine.

And that, really, was a farce! I'm not saying anything against the Agencies. They run the Earth very well. But the whole idea of quarantine is to keep Veenie diseases out, right? That includes the worst Veenie disease, the political pestilence of Conservationism. So you'd expect that on the Moon they'd give the Veenies a hard time in Customs and Immigration. In fact Immigration waved them past with no more than a cursory look at their passports. I don't mean just the crew, who weren't going anywhere but the nearest flopjoint anyway. Even the handful of

40

Veenie business people and dips, transshipping to the Earth, got greased through in no time.

But us Terrestrials—wow! They sat Mitzi and me down and magnetic-checked our papers and pried through our bags, and then the questions began. It was report all contact with Venusian nationals in line of duty for past eighteen months; give purpose of contact and nature of information communicated. Report all such contacts *not* in line of duty—purpose and information included. We were three hours in that sealed cubicle, filling out forms and answering questions, and then the interrogator got serious. "It has been ascertained," he said—grammatically speaking the voice was passive, but the actual voice rang with loathing and contempt, "that certain Earth nationals, to secure easy admission to Venus, have performed ritual acts of desecration."

Well, that was true enough. It was just another typical lousy Veenie trick, like the Japanese making Europeans trample on Bibles centuries ago. When you got to the Veenie Immigration checkpoints you had a choice. You could go through four or five hours of close questioning, with all your belongings opened and most likely a body search. Or you could take an oath renouncing "advertising, publicity, media persuasion or any other form of manipulation of public opinion"; toss off a few slanders of your Agency; and then, depending on how good an actor you were, breeze right through. It was a big joke, of course. I chuckled and started to explain it to him, but Mitzi cut in ahead of me. "Oh, yes," she said, nodding earnestly, her expression as disapproving as his own, "we've heard that, too." She gave me a warning look. "Do you happen to know if it's true?"

The Immigration man put down his stylus to study her face. "You mean you don't know whether that happens or not?"

She said carelessly, "One hears stories, sure. But when you try to put your finger on it, you just can't find a single concrete bit of evidence. It's always, no, it didn't happen to me, but I heard from this person that he had a friend who— Anyway, I can't really believe a decent Terrestrial would do such a thing. *I* certainly wouldn't, and neither would Tennison. Apart from the plain immorality of it, we know we'd have to face the consequences when we came back!"

So grudgingly the man passed us, and as soon as we were outside I whispered to Mitzi, "You saved my tail—thanks!"

"They just started doing that a couple years ago," she said. "If we'd admitted taking a false oath it would go on our records—then we'd be in the stuff."

"Funny you heard that that was happening and I didn't."

"I'm glad you can see the humor of it," she said bitingly, and for some reason, I perceived, she was furious. Then she said, "Sorry. I'm in a bad mood. I think I'll try to get a few more of these bandages off—then it'll be time for the shuttle!"

Earth! The birthplace of homo sapiens. The homeland of true humanity. The flowering of civilization. When we came to the shuttle in its lock and I caught a glimpse of its graffiti I knew I was home. "Everett Loves Alice." "Tiny Miljiewicz has herpes in his ears." "Rams all the way!" There's nothing on Venus like our native Terrestrial folk art!

So we came down from the sky, jolting and slamming; I worried about Mitzi's healing scars, but she only mumbled and turned over to sleep. Out over the wide ocean, greeny gray with slime—clear across the wide, welcoming North American continent, with its patchwork carpet of cities glowing welcomingly up through the smog—then the sun we had left behind rising again before us as we skidded out over the Atlantic, made our U-turn to spill out the last of our altitude and speed, and touched down finally on the broad runways of New York Shuttleport. Little old New York! The hub the universe spins on! I felt my heart throbbing with pride, and with joy at homecoming . . . and Mitzi, strapped in beside me, had slept through the whole thing.

She sat up drowsily while we were waiting for the tractor to hook on and tow us to the terminal. She made a face. "Isn't it great to be back?" I demanded, grinning at her.

She leaned over me to stare out the window. "Sure is," she said, but her tone was a long way from enthusiastic. "I wish—"

42

But I never found out what she wished, because she broke out in a fit of furious coughing. "My God!" she gasped. "What's that stuff?"

"That's good old New York City air you're breathing!" I told her. "You've been away too long—you've forgotten what it's like!"

"At least they could filter it," she complained. Well, of course it *was* filtered, but I didn't bother to correct her. I was too busy getting our stuff out of the overhead racks and lining up to disembark.

It was seven A.M., local time. There weren't too many people in the terminal yet, which was a plus, but the minus that balanced that in the equation was the lack of baggage handlers. Mitzi trailed sulkily after me to the baggage claim, and there I got a surprise. The surprise's name was Valentine Dambois, Senior Vice-President and Associate General Manager, pink cheeks, twinkly blue eyes, plump figure jiggling as he hurried across to greet us.

I told myself that I shouldn't have been surprised—I'd done a good job on Venus, and I'd never doubted that the Agency would treat me kindly when I got back. But not *this* kindly! You didn't get a star-class executive to welcome you home at that hour of the morning unless you were really *special.* So, full of cheer and great hopes, I stuck out my hand to him. "Great to see you, Val," I began—

And he went right past me. Right to Mitzi.

Val Dambois was a tubby little man, and the fattest thing about him was his face; when he smiled he looked like a Halloween pumpkin. The smile he gave Mitzi was like a pumpkin on the verge of splitting in two. "Mitzi-wits!" he yelled, though he was only two feet away from her and closing fast. "Missed you, sweety-bumps!" He flung his arms around her and stood on tiptoe to give her a big kiss.

She didn't kiss back. She pulled her head back so the kiss only got as far as her chin. "Hello," she said—"Val."

His face fell. For a minute I thought Mitzi had blown every

43

chance of promotion she ever had, but Dambois did a great reconstruction job on his smile. By the time he put it back on his face it was as good as new, and he patted her rump affectionately —but hastily. He stepped back, chuckling. "You sure made yourself a killing," he said warmly. "I take my hat off to you, Mits!"

I didn't know what he was talking about, of course. For a minute I didn't think Mitzi did, either, because a swift shadow clouded her eyes and her jaw tensed, but Dambois was already looking at me. "Missed the boat, I guess," he said good-naturedly —rueful good nature, that was, with just a slight shading of contempt.

Now, I wasn't too surprised by the way Dambois greeted Mitzi. There were little bits of gossip here and there about Mitzi and one or two star-level agency executives, Val Dambois included. It meant nothing to me. Hell, it's a rough course you have to run if you want to get ahead in the advertising business. If you can help yourself along by giving a little joy to the right parties, why not? But she hadn't said anything to me about a killing. "What are you talking about, Val?" I demanded.

"She didn't tell you?" He pursed his plump little lips, grinning. "Her damage suit against the tram company. They settled out of court—six megabucks and change—it's all waiting for her right now in the Agency bank!"

I had to try twice to say it. "Six—Six mill—"

"Six million dollars tax-free and spendable, right on!" he gloated. The man was as pleased as though the money had been his own—maybe he had some idea of making it so. I cleared my throat.

"About this damage suit—" I began, but Mitzi leaned past me to point.

"There, that one's mine," she said as the bags began to come off the conveyor. Val leaped forward and, puffing, swung it off and set it beside her.

"What I mean—" I began. Nobody was listening.

Dambois said jovially, slipping a pudgy arm around Mitzi's

waist—as far around as it would go: "Well, that's the first bag. Probably not more than another twenty or so, eh?"

"No, that's the only one. I like to travel light," she said, and moved away from his arm.

Dambois looked up at her reproachfully. "You've changed a lot," he complained. "I think you even got taller."

"Comes from being on a lighter planet." That was a joke, of course. Venus is only minutely smaller than the Earth. But I didn't laugh, because I was puzzling over why it was that Mitzi had got herself a whopping chunk of change and I hadn't—then that was driven out of my mind as I saw what was coming down the conveyor.

"Aw, *shit*," I cried. It was the bag I had marked Delicate Handling—the steamer trunk, with sturdy sides and a double lock. They hadn't been enough to save it. The trunk looked as if somebody had run one of the spacecraft tractors over a corner of it. One side was squashed like a fallen soufflé, and it was leaking an aromatic slop of liquor, colognes, toothpaste and god-knows-what. Naturally I had put all the breakables in it.

"What a mess," Dambois complained. He tsked impatiently a couple of times and glanced at his watch. "I was going to offer you a lift," he said, "but really—that stuff in my car would smell it up for weeks—and I suppose you've got other bags—"

I knew my lines. "Go ahead," I said glumly. "I'll take a taxi." I watched them go, wondering a lot about why I hadn't been allowed to get in on the damage suit, but actually wondering even more just then whether I should hightail it for the baggage claim office or wait for the rest of my stuff.

I made the wrong decision. I decided to wait. After the last visible bag had long since been removed and the conveyor had stopped running I realized I had a problem.

When I reported the problem the superintendent in charge of denying all responsibility for anything, ever, told me that he'd check out the missing pieces, if I wanted him to, while I filled out the claim forms, if I thought that was worthwhile—although it

45

looked a lot to him, he said, as though the damage to my case was old stuff.

He had plenty of time to check, because there was plenty to fill out. When I turned in the claims he kept me waiting only another half-hour or so. I called the Agency to say I'd be delayed. It didn't seem to worry them. They gave me the address of the housing they'd lined up for me, told me to settle in and said I wasn't expected until tomorrow morning anyway. It is nice to be missed. Then the claims superintendent reported that the rest of my bags seemed to have gone either to Paris or Rio de Janeiro, and in neither case was I likely to see them for a while.

So, bagless, I joined the glum queue waiting for the next city subline.

Half an hour later, finally at the head of the line, I realized I hadn't changed any Veenie currency and so I didn't have enough cash for the fare—found a cash machine, punched in my I.D., got a bodiless voice cooing, "I am deeply sorry, sir or madam, but this Kwik-Check One-Stop Anytime cash dispenser terminal is temporarily out of service. Please consult map for nearest alternate location." But when I looked around the booth there wasn't any map. Welcome home, Tenn!

II

New York, New York. What a wonderful town! All my fretful annoyances were submerged, even the one about why Mitzi cut me out of the gravy train. Ten years didn't seem to have changed the tall buildings that disappeared into the gray, flaky air. The *cold*, gray, flaky air. It had gone winter again; there were patches of dirty snow in corners, and an occasional consumer furtively scooping them up to take home to avoid the freshwater tax. After Venus, it was heaven! I gawked like a Wichita tourist at the Big Apple. I walked liked one, too, bumping into scurrying pedestrians, and things worse than pedestrians. My traffic skills were gone. After the years on Venus I just wasn't used to civilized ways.

46

There was a twelve-pusher pedibus here, three cabs competing for one gap in the flow there, pedestrians leaping desperately between the vehicles all over—the streets were jammed, the sidewalks were packed, every building pumped a few hundred more people in and out as I passed—oh, it was marvelous! For me, I mean. For the people I was bumping into or tripped or made dodge around me, it might not have been so delightful, I suppose. I didn't care! They yelled after me, and I don't doubt what they yelled were insults, but I was floating in sooty, choky, chilly bliss. Advertising slogans flickered in liquid-crystal display on every wall, the newest ones bright as sunrise, the older ones muddied and finally buried by graffiti. Samplers stood along the curbs to pass out free hits of Glee-Smoke and Coffiest, and discount coupons for a thousand products. There were hologram images in the smoggy air of miraculous kitchen appliances and fantastically exotic three-day tours, and sales jingles ringing from everywhere—I was *home.* I loved it! But it was, admittedly, a little difficult to make my way through the streets, and when I saw a miraculously clear stretch of sidewalk I took it.

I wondered at the time why the elderly man I pushed aside getting to the sidewalk gave me such a strange look. "Watch it, buster!" he called. He was waving at a signpost, but of course it was graffiti-covered. I wasn't in a mood to worry about some minor civil ordinance. I walked past—

And WOWP a blast of sound shook my skull and FLOOP a great supernova flare of light burned my eyes, and I went staggering and reeling as tiny, tiny elf voices shouted like needles in my ears *Mokie-Koke, Mokie-Koke, MokieMokieMokie-Koke!* And went on doing it, with variations, for what seemed like a hundred years or more. Stenches smote my nose. Subsonic shivers shook my body. And—a couple of centuries later—while my ears were still ringing and my eyes still stinging with that awful blast of sound and light, I picked myself up from where I lay sprawled on the ground.

"I warned ya," yelled the little old man from a safe distance.

It hadn't been centuries at all. He was still standing there, still

47

with the same peculiar expression—half-eagerness, half-pity. "I warned ya! Ya wooden listen, but I warned ya!"

He was still waving at the signpost, so I staggered closer and blearily managed to decipher the legend under the graffiti:

Warning!
COMMERCIAL ZONE
Enter at Own Risk

Evidently there had been some changes while I was away, after all. The man reached cautiously past the sign and tugged me away. He wasn't all that old, I realized; mostly he was *used*. "What's a 'Mokie-Koke'?" I asked.

He said promptly, "Mokie-Koke is a refreshing, taste-tingling blend of the finest chocolate-type flavoring, synthetic coffee extract and selected cocaine analogues. You want some?" I did. "You got money on you?" I had—a little, anyway—the change left over from the cash dispenser I'd finally located. "Would you tip me one if I showed you where to score some?" he wheedled.

Well, who needed him for that? But I couldn't help feeling sorry for the woebegone little guy, so I let him lead me around the corner. There was a vending machine, just like all the other Mokie-Koke machines I'd been seeing all along, on the Moon, in the spaceport, along the city streets. "Don't fool with the singles," he advised anxiously. "Go for the six-pack, okay?" And when I gave him the first bottle out of the batch he pulled the tab and raised it to his lips and swigged it down where he stood. Then he exhaled loudly. "Name's Ernie, mister," he said. "Welcome to the club!"

I had been drinking my own Mokie-Koke curiously. It seemed pleasant enough, but nothing special, so that I wondered what the fuss was all about. "What club are you talking about?" I asked, opening another bottle out of curiosity.

"You been campbelled. You shoulda listened," he said virtuously, "but, say, long as you didn't, you mind if I walk along with you wherever you're going?"

Poor old guy! I felt so sorry for him that I split the six-pack

48

as we headed for the address the Agency had given me. Three shots apiece. He thanked me with tears in his eyes but, all the same, out of the second six-pack I only gave him one.

The Agency had done well by me. When we got to my new home I shook Ernie off and hurried in. It was a new sea-condo just towed in from the Persian Gulf—former oil tanker—nearly a hundred square feet of floor space with kitchen privileges just for me, and it was about as convenient to the Agency building as you could hope, moored right off Kip's Bay, only three ships out into the river.

Of course, the bad side was what it cost. All the savings I'd accumulated on Venus went to the down payment, and I had to sign a mortgage for three years' pay. But that wasn't so bad. I'd served the Agency well on Venus. There was little doubt in my mind that I was due for a raise—not only a raise, but a promotion —not only a promotion, but maybe a corner office! Altogether I was well satisfied with the world (not counting a couple little questions that nagged at my mind, like that damned lawsuit I hadn't been invited to join) as I relished a Mokie-Koke and gazed around my new domain.

But to work! There was so much to do! Until they located my bags, if that ever happened, I needed clothes and food and all the other necessities of life. So I spent the rest of the day shopping and lugging packages back to the sea-condo, and by dinner time I was just about settled in. Picture of G. Washington Hill over the foldaway bed. Picture of Fowler Schocken on the hideaway bureau. Clothes in one place, toilet stuff in my personal locked cabinet in the bath—it took all day, and it was tiring, too, because the heat was on full blast in my room and there didn't seem to be any way to turn it off. I had a Moke and sat down to think it over, enjoying the spaciousness and the quiet luxury. There was a special condo-only band on the vid, and I watched it reel off the many attractions available to us lucky tenants. The condo had its own pool, with seating for six at a time, and a driving range. I made a note to sign up for that as soon as I got my own cue. The future looked bright. I dialed back to the pool—gallons and gallons of sparkling pure water, nearly armpit deep—and sentimental thoughts began to steal into my mind: me and Mitzi side by side in the pool . . . me and Mitzi sharing the big foldout bed . . . me and Mitzi— But even if Mitzi decided after all to share my life, with six megabucks of her own to throw around she'd probably want to share it in some fancier place than even the sea-condo. . . .

Well, rework that daydream. Leave Mitzi out for a minute: the future was still bright. Even though I'd signed up for heavy money to get the condo, I should still have spare purchasing power. A new car? Why not? And which kind of car—a direct-drive model where you kneel one leg on the seat and push with the other, or some fancy geared-up make-out wagon?

It was getting very hot. I tried again to turn off the heat, and failed again.

I found myself drinking Mokes one after another. And, actually, for a moment I thought seriously about pulling out the bed and getting a good night's sleep.

Tired or not, I couldn't spend my first night home that way! It called for a celebration.

A celebration called for somebody to celebrate with. Mitzi? But when I called Agency personnel they didn't have a home number for her yet, and she had already left the office. And all the other dates I could think of were either years stale, or millions of miles away. I didn't even know which were the in places to celebrate in any more!

That part, anyway, could be handled. I had a neat Omni-V console that came along with the apartment, two hundred and forty channels. I ran through the selector—housewares commercials, florists' commercials, outerwear commercials (male), outerwear commercials (female), news, restaurant commercials—yes, that was the channel I wanted. I picked a nice place only two blocks from the sea-condo, and it was all that I'd wanted. Because I had made a reservation I was only kept an hour or so in the bar, drinking gin-and-Mokes and chatting up my neighbors; the dinner was the best of brand-name soya cutlets and reconstituted mashed veggies; there was brandy with the coffee, and two waiters dancing attendance to unwrap my portions and pull the tabs on my drinks. There was one little funny thing. When the check came I looked at it quickly, then more slowly, then called the waiter over again. "What's this?" I said, pointing at the column of printouts that said,

Mokie-Koke, $2.75
Mokie-Koke, $2.75
Mokie-Koke, $2.75
Mokie-Koke, $2.75

"They're Mokie-Kokes, sir," he explained, "a refreshing, taste-tingling blend of the finest chocolate-type—"

"I know what a Mokie-Koke is," I interrupted. "I just don't remember ordering any."

"I'm sorry, sir," he said, all deference. "Actually you did. I'll play back the voice tape if you like."

"Never mind the voice tape," I said. "I don't want them now. I'll just go."

He looked shocked. "But, sir—you've already drunk them!"

Nine A.M. Bright and early. I paid off my pedicab, pulled the soot-extractor plugs out of my nostrils and strutted into the main lobby of the huge Taunton, Gatchweiler and Schocken Agency Tower.

We get older and we get cynical, but after the years of absence there was almost an epiphany of feeling that shook me as I entered. Imagine two thousand years ago entering the court of Augustus Caesar, and knowing that here, in this place, the affairs of the entire world had their control center and inspiration. With the Agency, the same. True, there were other agencies—but it was a bigger world, too! Here was where Power was. The whole vast building was dedicated to one sublime mission: the betterment of mankind through the inspiration to buy. More than eighteen thousand people worked in that building. Copysmiths

51

and apprentice word-jugglers; media specialists who could sound a commercial out of the ambient air or print a message on your eyeball; product researchers dreaming up, every day, new and more sellable drinks, foods, gadgets, vices, possessions of all sorts; artists; musicians; actors; directors; space buyers and time buyers —the list went on indefinitely—and above them all, on the fortieth floor and higher, there was Executive Country where the geniuses who directed it all brooded and conceived their godlike plans. Oh, sure. I joked about the civilizing mission of us who dedicated our lives to advertising—but under the joking was the same real reverence and commitment that I'd felt as a cub scout in the Junior Copywriters, going after my first merit badges and just then beginning to perceive where my life could lead. . . .

Well. Anyway. There I was, in the heart of the universe. There was one funny thing. I had remembered it as vast and vaulted. Vaulted it was—but vast? Actually it seemed tinier, and more crowded, than the Russian Hills tram station; so those years on Venus had corrupted my sensibilities. The people even looked shabbier, and the guard at the weapons detector gave me a surly and suspicious look as I approached.

No problem there. I simply put my wrist into the scanner, and the data store recognized my Social Security number at once, even though it had been ten years since its last use. "Oh," said the guard, studying my stats as the recognition light flashed green, "you're Mr. Tarb. Nice to see you back!" There was a false implication there, of course. From the look of her she'd still been in high school last time I entered the Agency building, but her heart was in the right place. I gave her bottom a friendly pat and swaggered toward the lift. And the first person I saw on forty-five as I let go of the handbar was Mitzi Ku.

I'd had twenty-four hours to get over resentment at that lawsuit deal. It hadn't been enough, really, but at least the sharp edges of jealousy had blunted a bit, and she really looked good. Not perfect. Although she was out of her bandages, that funny blurring around the eyes and mouth told you she was wearing plastiflesh where healing had not quite finished. But she was

52

smiling at me tentatively as she said hello. "Mitzi," I said, the words popping out of my mouth unexpectedly—I had not known I had been thinking them—"shouldn't I sue the tram people, too?"

She looked embarrassed. What she would have said I don't know, because from behind her Val Dambois popped out. "Too late, Tarb," he said. I didn't mind the words. I minded the contemptuous tone, and the grin. "Statute of limitations, you know? Like I told you, you missed the boat. Come on, Mitzi, we can't keep the Old Man waiting—"

The morning was one shock after another; the Old Man was who I was going to see. Mitzi allowed Dambois to take her arm, but she hung back to peer at me. "Are you all right, Tenny?" she asked.

"I'm fine—" Well, I was, mostly, not counting a slightly frayed ego. "I'm a little thirsty, maybe, because it's so hot in here. Do you happen to know if there's a Mokie-Koke vending machine on this floor?"

Dambois gave me a poisonous look. "Some jokes," he gritted, "are in lousy taste."

I watched him flounce off, dragging Mitzi after him into the Old Man's sanctum. I sat down to wait, trying to look as though I had simply decided to rest my feet there for a moment.

The moment turned out to be well past an hour.

Of course, nobody thought anything of that. Over in her own corner of the cell the Old Man's sec[3] kept busy with her communicator and her data screen, glancing up to smile at me now and then the way she was paid to do. People who wait only an hour to see the Old Man generally gave thanks for their blessings, since most people never got to see him at all. Old Man Gatchweiler was a legend in his own time, poor boy, consumer stock, who rose out of obscure origins to pull off so grand a scam that it was still whispered about in the Executive Country bars. Two of the grandest old-line Agencies had wrecked themselves in flaming scandals, old B. J. Taunton nailed for Contract Breach, Fowler Schocken dead and his Agency in ruins. Their Agencies carried on a spectral existence as shells, written off forever by the wiseacres. Then Horatio Gatchweiler appeared out of nowhere to swallow the wreckage and turn it into T., G. & S. No one wrote Taunton, Gatchweiler and Schocken off! We were tops in Sales and Service. Our clients led the charts in Sales, and as to Service, well, no thousand-dollar-a-hit stallion ever serviced his mares as thoroughly as we serviced the consumers. A name to conjure with, Horatio Gatchweiler! It was almost literally a name to conjure with, for it was like the unspeakable name of God. No one ever spoke it. Behind his back he was the "Old Man," to his face nothing but "sir."

So sitting in his tiny sec³'s anteroom while I pretended to study the *Advertising Age* hourlies in the tabletop screen was nothing new for me. It was even an honor. At least, it would have been except for the sulky, nagging annoyance at the fact that he had given Mitzi and Val Dambois precedence.

When at last the Old Man's sec³ turned me over to the sec², who led me to the secretary, who admitted me to his own private office, he did try to make me welcome. He didn't stand up or anything, but, "Come right in, Farb!" he boomed jovially from his chair. "Good to see you back, boy!"

I had almost forgotten how magnificent his place was—two windows! Of course, both had the shades drawn; you can't take chances on somebody bouncing a pencil-beam off the glass to pick up the vibrations of secret talks inside. "That's Tarb, sir," I offered.

"Of course it is! And you're back from a tour on Venus—good work. Of course," he added, peering up at me slyly, "it wasn't *all* good, was it? There's a little note on your personnel file that you probably didn't bribe anybody to put there—"

"I can explain about that Agency party, sir—"

"Of course you can! And it won't stand in your way. You young people who volunteer for a tour on Venus deserve well of us—nobody expects you to stand that kind of life without a little, uh, strain." He leaned back dreamily. "I don't know if you know this, Farb," he said to the ceiling, "but I was on Venus myself once, long ago. Didn't stay there. I won their lottery, you know."

I was startled. "Lottery? I had no idea the Veenies ever ran a lottery. It seems so out of character for them."

"Never did again," he guffawed, "since a huck won the first one! They gave up the idea right after that—besides declaring me persona non grata, so I got hustled right back here!" He chuckled for several seconds at the fecklessness of the Veenies. "Of course," he said, sobering, "I kept my skills up while I was on Venus." From the way he peered at me I knew it was a question.

I had the right answer, too. "So did I, sir," I said eagerly. "Every chance I got! All the time! For instance—well, I don't know if you've ever seen the inside of what the Veenies call a grocery store—"

"Seen a hundred of them, boy," he boomed jovially.

"Well, then you know how incompetent they are. Signs like, 'These tomatoes are all right if you're going to eat them today, otherwise they'll spoil,' and 'Prepared mixes cost twice what making the dish from basic ingredients would'—things like that."

He laughed out loud, and wiped his eyes. "Haven't changed a bit, I guess," he said.

"No, sir. Well, I'd go through the store and then come back to the Embassy and write *real* copy for them. You know? Like for the tomatoes, 'Luscious ripe flavor-full at the peak of perfection' or 'Save! Save! Save precious time with these chef-prepared ready-to-cook masterpieces!' That sort of thing. And then I'd review all the latest Earth commercials for the staff—at least two hour-long pep meetings every week—and we'd have contests to see who could come up with better original variations on the basic sales themes—"

He looked at me with real affection. "You know, Tarb," he said, with kindness verging on sentimentality, "you remind me of myself when I was your age. A little. Well, listen, let's get ourselves comfortable while we decide what you'd like to do for us now that you're back. What'll you have to drink?"

"Oh, I think a Mokie-Koke, sir," I said absently.

The climate in the room took a swift change for the worse. The Old Man's finger stopped over the call button that would have summoned his sec², in charge of bringing in coffee and refreshments. "What did you say, Farb?" he gritted.

I opened my mouth, but it was too late. He didn't let me speak. "A *Moke?* Here in my office?" The expression went clear across the scale, from benevolence through shock to wrath. Livid, he stabbed down on a completely different button. "Emergency services!" he roared. "Get a medic in here right away—I've got a Moke-head in my office!"

They got me out of the Old Man's office fast as any leper ousted from the sight of Louis XIV. Treated me that way, too. While I was waiting for the results of my tests I sat in the common-clinic waiting room in Subbasement Three, but, although it was crowded, there were empty seats on both sides of me.

At last, "Mr. Tennison Tarb," crackled the voice from the overhead speaker. I got up and stumbled through the underbrush of hastily moved legs and pulled-aside ankles to the consultation room. It was like walking the Last Mile in those old prison movies, except that there were no mumbled words of encouragement from my fellow cons. There was the same expression on every face, and it said, *Thank God it's you, not me!*

I expected that past the sliding door would be the doctor who would prescribe my fate. Surprisingly there were two people there; one the doctor—you could tell by her ritual stethoscope around the neck—and the other, of all people, little Dan Dixmeister, grown all lank and gloomy. "Hey, there, Danny!" I greeted him, sticking out my hand for old time's sake.

And for the same sake, I guess—his version of it—he studied my hand for a moment before reluctantly putting out his own. It wasn't a shake. It was more like his offering his hand for me to kiss—no grip, just a limp touch and withdrawal.

Now, Danny Dixmeister had been my copy cub trainee half a dozen years earlier. I went to Venus. He stayed behind. Clearly he hadn't wasted his time. He wore Deputy Department Head epaulettes and, on his sleeve, fifty-thousand-a-year stripes, and he looked at me as though I were the new apprentice and he the exec. "You really screwed up, Tarb," he rasped joylessly. "Dr. Mosskristal will review your medical problem for you." And the tone said *bad news.*

Bad news it was. "What you've got," said the doctor, "is a Campbellian addiction." Her tone was neither kind nor unkind. It was the tone in which a doctor announces a white-blood-corpuscle count in a laboratory animal, and the look she turned on me was exactly the same look as Mitzi used to give a would-be returnee who might be recruited for her spy chains. "I suppose you could be reprogrammed," she said, studying the results on the display before her. "Hardly worth the effort, I'd say. A very uninteresting chart."

I swallowed. It was hard for me to take in that it was my *life* they were talking about. "Tell me what I'm up against," I begged. "Maybe if I understood what was wrong I could fix it."

"Fix it? *Fix* it? You mean overcome the programming by yourself? Oh-ho-ho-ho," she laughed, glancing at Dixmeister and shaking her head humorously. "What strange notions you laymen have."

"But you said there was a cure—"

"You mean reprogramming and detoxing," she corrected. "I don't think you want to go through *that.* Maybe ten years from now it might be worth a try, although there's about a forty per cent mortality rate. But in the early stages, right after exposure —uh-uh." She leaned back, pressing her fingertips together, and I got ready for the lecture. "What you have," she explained, "is a Campbellian reflex. Named after Dr. H. J. Campbell. Famous pioneering psychologist in the old days, inventor of limbic-pleasure therapy."

"I never heard of limbic-pleasure therapy," I said.

"No," she admitted, "the secret was lost for many years." She leaned forward, depressed an intercom button and called, "Maggie, bring in the Campbell. According to Dr. Campbell," she resumed to me, *"pleasure* is the name we give to the feeling we experience when the limbic areas of our brain are electrically active. He was first led to this research, I believe, when he discovered that many of his students were deriving great pleasure from what was called rock music. Saturating the senses in this way stimulated the limbic area—thus pleasure—thus, he discovered a cheap and easy way of conditioning subjects in desirable ways. Ah, here we are." The sec^2 had brought in a transparent plastic box containing—of all things!—a *book*. Faded, tattered, hidden inside its plastic case, it was still about the best example I had ever seen of that quaint old art form. Instinctively I reached out for it, and Dr. Mosskristal snatched it away. "Don't be silly," she rapped.

But I could read the title: *The Pleasure Areas,* by H. J. Campbell. "If I could just borrow it," I pleaded. "I'll bring it back within the week—"

"You will, *hell.* You'll read it here, if you read it at all, with my sec^3 watching you and making sure you pump the nitrogen back in when you put it back in the box. But I'm not sure it's a good idea. Laymen shouldn't try to understand medical problems, they're simply not equipped. Let's just say that you've had your limbic areas stimulated; under the influence of that great upwelling of pleasure you've become conditioned to associate Mokie-Koke with joy, and there's nothing to be done about it." She glanced at her watch and stood up. "Now I've got a patient to visit," she announced. "Dixmeister, you can use this room for your interview with the patient if you like—just so you're out of here in twenty minutes." And she flounced away, clutching her book.

And leaving me with Danny Dixmeister. "Pity," he said, shaking his head at the screen, which still displayed my test results. "You probably had a reasonably good future ahead of you at one time, Tarb, if you hadn't got yourself hooked."

"But it's not fair, Danny! I didn't know—"

He looked honestly perplexed. "Fair? True, campbelling is something new—I don't suppose you were watchful enough. But the areas for limbic commercials are clearly marked."

"Clearly!" I sneered. "It's a dirty, vicious trick and you know it! Certainly our own Agency would never do such a thing to move goods!"

58

Dixmeister pursed his lips. "The question," he said, "hasn't come up, since the competition owns the patents. Now. Let's talk about you. You realize, Tarb, that any kind of high-level position is out of the question for you now."

"Now hold on, Danny! I don't see that at all. I just put in a lot of lousy years on Venus for this Agency!

"It's a simple matter of security," he explained. "You're a Moke-head. You'd do anything for a Mokie-Koke, including betraying your grandmother—or even the Agency. So we just can't take the chance of letting you work on any high-security area—not to mention," he added bitchily, "that you've shown a certain lack of moral fiber in letting yourself get hooked in the first place."

"But I have seniority! Tenure! A record of—"

He shook his head impatiently. "Oh, we'll find something for you, of course. But not creative. How are your typing skills, Tarb? No? That's a pity—well, that's a problem for Personnel, after all."

I leveled a look at him for a moment. "Danny," I said, "I must have given you a harder time than I realized when you were my stooge."

He didn't answer. He only gave me a look that was both cryptic and long. I was out of that room, up the elevator to *Personnel—General Service* on the fifth floor, waiting my turn with the fresh, young college kids and the middle-aged semi-employables before I quite deciphered that look. It wasn't dislike, or even triumph. It was pity.

What Dr. Mosskristal didn't tell me about was one of the side effects of campbellization. Depression. She didn't warn me, and when it happened I didn't recognize it for what it was. I guess that's what depression is. When you're having it, it just seems like the way the world is. You never think of it as a problem, only a state of being.

I had a lot to be depressed about. They found work for me, all right. Delivering art, carrying flowers to the stars of our commercials, dashing out into the street to flag and hold a pedicab for somebody from Executive Country, fetching soyaburgers and Coffiest for the secretaries—oh, I had a million things to do! I

59

worked harder as a General Services dogsbody than I ever had as a star-class copysmith, but of course for that kind of work they don't pay star-class money. I had to give up the sea-condo. I didn't mind. What did I need such luxury for except to entertain, and who was there to entertain? Mitzi had moved herself up to a loftier sphere. All my old girl friends were transferred or married or promoted, and the new crop didn't seem to want to get involved with somebody in the deep freeze.

Speaking of deep freeze, the thing I had mostly forgotten about home was what it was like to be cold. I mean capital-K-*cold*. Cold to where the pedicab-pullers' breath steamed out around their faces, and they'd slip and stumble on the icy streets. Cold to where I could almost wish to change places with them for the exercise instead of sitting in the hard, bare seat with my teeth hurting from the wintry New York air—well, I said "almost." Even being a messenger boy was better than pulling a cab.

Especially now that it was getting cold. Those six years on Venus had thinned my blood. Even if I could have afforded to go out very often, the desire wasn't there. So I spent my days in the messenger pool, and my evenings at home, watching commercials on the Omni-V, talking with my new roommates when they were around—sitting. Mostly just sitting. And it was quite a surprise when the buzzer sounded, and I had a visitor, and the visitor was Mitzi.

If she had come to be nice to me, she had a funny idea about how to do it. She looked around with her nose wrinkled and her lips clamped shut, as though the place smelled of decay. She seemed to wear the twin frown lines between her brows all the time now. "Tenn," she said sternly, "you've got to pull yourself out of this! Look at you! Look at this dump! Look at what a shambles you've made of your life!"

I looked around the room, trying to see what she meant. Of course, when I couldn't afford the sea-condo payments any more I had to make other arrangements. It wasn't easy. Getting out of the contract cost me most of my saved-up pay, and this shared-time condo was about all I could afford. It was true that my roommates were pretty sloppy. One was into junk food, the other had gotten himself into one of those interminable collections of Nearly Silver Miniature Presidential Busts from the San Jacinto Mint. But still! "It's not so bad," I said defensively.

"It's *filthy*. Don't you ever throw out those old Moke bottles? Tenn, I know it's hard, but there are people who successfully take the cold turkey cure every year—"

I laughed. I was actually sorry for her, because she simply didn't understand how it was, having never been hooked. "Mitzi," I said, "is that why you came here, to tell me what a shambles I'm making of my life?"

She looked at me silently for a moment. "Well, I suppose the cure's pretty dangerous," she admitted, looking around for a place to sit. I cleared some of Nelson Rockwell's Hittite Emperors and a few of Charlie Bergholm's taco wrappers off the second chair. "I'm not really sure just why I did come here," she said, inspecting the seat carefully before sitting down.

I said bitterly, "If it was for a roll in the hay, forget it." I pointed to the closed bed box, where Rockwell, my two-to-ten roomie, was taking his share of sack time.

She—I was about to say flushed, but I guess darkened is a better word. "I guess in some way I feel a little responsible," she said.

"For not telling me about the damage suit? For letting me go broke while you collect millions? For some little things like that?"

She shrugged. "Something of the sort, maybe. Tenny? All right, I accept that you can't rise very high in the Agency again while you're a Moke-head, but there are plenty of other things you can do! Why not go back to school? Learn a new skill, start over in some other profession, I don't know, doctor, lawyer—"

I looked at her in amazement. "And give up *advertising?*"

"Oh, God! What's so holy about advertising?"

Well, that one took me back. All I could find to say was, "You've sure changed a lot, Mitzi." And I meant it as a reproof.

She said morosely, "Maybe I made a mistake coming here." Then her face brightened. "I know! What would you say to

Intangibles? I think I could get you in there—not right away, of course, but when there's a vacancy—"

"Intangibles!" I sneered. "Mitzi, I'm a *product* person. I sell *goods*. Intangibles is for the has-beens and the never-wases—and, anyway, what makes you think you could do it?"

She hesitated, then said, "Oh, I just think I could. I mean—well, you might as well know, although it's a company secret for a while. I've taken my damage money and they've let me buy into the Agency."

"Buy in! You mean a stockholder?"

"Sure, a stockholder." She seemed apologetic about it—as though there were any reason for that! To be a stockholder in the Agency was about the next thing to being God. It had simply never occurred to me that anybody I knew would ever have the capital to do something like that.

But I shook my head. "I'm Product," I said proudly.

"Really," she flashed, "do you have any better offers?"

And of course I hadn't.

I surrendered. "Have a Mokie-Koke," I said, "and let's talk it over.

So I went to bed that night, even if alone, nevertheless with something I hadn't had before: hope. As I drifted off to sleep I was thinking impossible dreams: back to school, get that Master of Advertising Philosophy degree I'd planned for when I was a kid, learn some additional skills, do some research into Intangibles . . . kick the Moke habit.

They all seemed like good ideas. Whether anything would have been left of them in the cold light of dawn I do not know, but I had a powerful reinforcement. I woke up with a banging on the bed lid and the growly, grumbly voice of Nelson Rockwell, my two-to-ten roomie, telling me that he switched turns with Berg-holm and it was time for his turn.

Sleepy as I was, I saw at once that he was looking really bad, bruise like a crushed grape stain over his right cheekbone, limping as he backed away to let me get out of the bed box. "What *happened*, Nelson?"

He looked as though I'd accused him of a crime. "Little misunderstanding," he muttered.

"It looks like a damn *big* misunderstanding to me. You've been beaten up, man!"

He shrugged, and winced as his muscles objected to the movement. "I got a little behind in my payments, so San Jacinto sent a couple of collectors around to the grommet works. Say, Tenn, you couldn't let me have fifty till payday, could you? Because they said next time it's my kneecaps."

"I don't have fifty," I said—nearly true, too. "Why don't you sell some of your figurines?"

"Sell them? Sell some of my stuff? Why, Tenn," he cried, "that's the stupidest thing I ever heard of! These here are invest-ment-grade collectibles! All I have to do is hold onto them for market appreciation—and then, boy, wait'll you see! They're all limited editions! Twenty years from now I'll have my place in the Everglades, taking it easy, and they're what's going to pay for it . . . only," he added sadly, "if I don't get caught up on the payments they're gonna repossess. *And* kneecap me."

I fled down the hall to the bathroom because I couldn't stand hearing any more of that. Limited-edition collectibles! Good lord, that was one of the first accounts I ever worked on—limited edition to as many copies as we could sell, fifty thousand anyway; collectible meaning that once you had them there was nothing you could do with them *but* collect them.

So I cleaned up quick and got out of the room fast, and by seven A.M. I was up on the campus of Columbia A&P University, poring through the catalog readout and signing up for courses. There were plenty of electives that would count for credit toward the master's; I picked a sampling of the most interesting. History. Mathematics—that's sampling techniques, mostly. Even creative writing. I figured that that might be an easy credit, mostly, but I also had it in the back of my mind that if the copy job in Intangibles didn't come through there might be some use to it. If I weren't going to be allowed to write anything real, at least I could bang out a few novels. Admittedly, there's no big bucks there. But there's always a market, because there's always a few misfits in the world who can't get it together enough to watch sports or follow the stories on Omni-V, so they can't think of anything better to do than *read*. I'd tried it myself, a time or two, calling up some of the old classics on the tube. It's a little flaky, but the market is there and it's no disgrace to pick up some loose change catering to it.

That's the other funny thing about depression. When you're sunk in the middle of it everything looks so hard and there are so many things to worry about that it's pretty nearly impossible to make a move. But as soon as you take the first step, the second gets easier, and the third—in fact, that very day I decided I would have to do something about the Mokes I was swigging. Not quit cold turkey. Not even cut down right away. The first thing to do was to analyze the problem. So I began noting the time of every Moke. I kept it up for a week and, my God, do you know, I was averaging *forty* of the damn things a day! And not enjoying them all that much, either.

I decided to deal with it. I didn't want to kick the habit, because actually each Mokie-Koke in itself was a pretty good thing. They're actually rather a taste-tingling blend of really good chocolate-type flavoring, along with synthetic coffee extract and some of those cocaine analogues to give it zip. Makes a nice drink. The thing was not to *stop*, but only to *cut down*. Put that way, it was a simple problem in schedule making and logistics, like when you schedule an optimal mix of consumer impacts for your advertising spots. Forty Mokes a day was ridiculous. About eight, I reckoned, would be just enough. I'd keep that little lift you get every time, but I wouldn't jade my taste buds.

A Moke every two hours, I calculated, would do it just right. So I drew up a little chart:

6:00 A.M.
8:00 A.M.
10:00 A.M.

—and so on through the day until ten at night, when I could turn

64

Nelson Rockwell out of our bed box, take the last one for a nightcap and so off to sleep.

When I counted them up, it turned out that a Moke every two hours for the sixteen waking hours of every day added up to nine instead of eight—unless I wanted to give up either the one to wake up or the one to go to sleep. I didn't want to do that. Anyway, what the hell, nine wasn't too many. I was very pleased about my little chart. It was such a powerful and effective scheme that I couldn't understand why no one seemed to have thought of it before me.

And, by gosh, I stuck to it. For very nearly a whole day.

It took a little willpower to wait out that first two hours until eight A.M., but I dawdled over breakfast and hung in the shower until the other tenants began banging on the door. Then ten A.M. was a long way off, but I took my time walking to the Agency building, and then I worked out a little supplementary scheme. They sent me out on deliveries right away. I didn't even look at my watch while I was pedaling from one place to another—well, mostly I didn't—what I did was wait till I got to a stop, then look at the watch and calculate how many more stops it would be before the next Moke was due. So I'd say to myself, "Not at the graphics studio, not at the bank, not at the box office for Audrey Wixon's tickets—when I get to the restaurant to pick up Mr. Xen's glasses that he forgot there last night, that's about when the next one will be due." It worked all right. Well—pretty nearly all right. There was a little mishap right after lunch, when I read my watch wrong and had the two o'clock Mokie-Koke at one by mistake. That wasn't really serious. I just decided to stick to the odd hours instead of the even for the rest of that day. It was bad for a while in the afternoon, when they kept me waiting around the reception desk until 3:14 for a package that was slow in coming, but I got through the day all right.

The night, not so all right. The Moke at five was to celebrate the end of the working day; that was fine. Seven was harder to wait for, but I dragged out eating dinner as long as I could. And then back to the room, and then, dear heaven, nine o'clock was such a long time coming! About a quarter past eight I took a Moke out of the six-pack and held it in my hands. I had the Omni-V on, and it was showing one of those grand old historical epics about the early days of mail-order advertising, but I wasn't really following it very well. The place my eyes clung to was the clock. Eight eighteen. Eight twenty. Eight twenty-two . . . by eight fifty my eyes were glazing over, but I made it all the way to the tick of nine before I popped the tab.

I drank it down, enjoying it, and proud of the fact that I'd held out.

And then I faced the fact that it would be six A.M.—nine long hours!—before I could have another.

It was more than I could handle. By the time Charlie Bergholm scratched and yawned his way out of the bed box to make room for me I had killed a whole new six-pack.

Courses began. I made attempts now and then to cut down on the Mokes, but I decided that the important thing was to deal with the rest of my life. And one part of my life was taking on more importance than I had anticipated.

It's funny. It's as though a person has just so much love and tenderness to spend. I told myself that the Moke addiction wasn't that bad, really; didn't interfere with my work really; certainly didn't make me worth, really, any less. . . . I didn't believe it. The lower I fell in my own eyes, the more esteem I had left over, without a good place to invest it. Any more.

The life of a diplomat is full of complicated taboos and vacancies. There we were on Venus, surrounded by eight hundred thousand irreconcilable enemies. There were only a hundred and eight of us diplomats. In such circumstances, what do you do for friendship? More than that, what do you do about—well—love? You have a universe of perhaps fifty opposite-gender candidates to choose from. Probably a dozen are married—I mean faithfully married—and a dozen or more are too old, and about the same are too young. If you're lucky there may be as many as ten really eligible lovers in the pool, and what are the odds that even one

66

of those will turn you on, and be turned on in return? Not good. Dips are as inbred as the *Bounty* survivors on Pitcairn Island. When Mitzi Ku came along I lucked in. We liked each other. We had the same feelings about sex. She was an immense convenience for me and I for her—not just for the physical act of sex, but for all the pair-bonding things that go along with it, like pillow gossip and remembering each other's birthdays. It was nice having Mitzi there for such things. She was maybe the most valued accessory the Embassy furnished me. I appreciated the convenience. We were most candid and outspoken with each other, but there was a four-letter word neither of us ever spoke to the other. The word was "love."

And now there wasn't any good way for me to say it to her. Mitzi had risen as fast as I had fallen. I didn't even see her from one week to another, except fleeting glimpses. I hadn't forgotten that she promised to get me on as a copy trainee in Intangibles. But I thought she had—until I brought Val Dambois's lunch up to him and discovered Mitzi in his office. Not just there. Head to head with him; and when I opened the door they sprang apart. "Damn it, Tarb," yelled Dambois, "don't you know enough to knock?"

"Sorry," I shrugged. I dropped his soyaburger on the desk and turned to go. I had no desire to break up their little cozy time . . . or, if I did, I certainly didn't want to show it. Mitzi put out a hand to stop me. She looked at me with that special, birdlike interest in her bright eyes, and then nodded.

"Val," she said, "we can finish this up later. Tenny? I think they might be ready to do something for you in Intangibles. Come on, I'll go down there with you and see what we can get going."

It was lunchtime and so we had to wait for the elevator. I was feeling nervous—wondering, not very happily, why she hadn't called me if the job had opened up; whether she ever would have remembered it again if I hadn't turned up just then. They were not ego-inflating thoughts. I tried to make conversation. "So what were you two conspiring about?" I asked jokingly. The way she looked at me made me think my tone had been a touch too sharp.

67

I tried to smooth it over: "I guess I'm a little strung out," I apologized, assuming she would take that as natural from a Mokie-head. But it wasn't that at all. It might even have been jealousy. "It seems a long time since you were running your spy ring on Venus," I said wistfully. What I meant by that was that my perceptions of Mitzi had changed a lot since then. She seemed —I don't know. Soberer? Kinder? Of course, it couldn't be that *she* had changed. What was different was that, having lost her, I valued her more highly.

And, having lost her, I stood open-mouthed, gaping at her when, having stepped off the descending elevator and waiting for me, she called up, "If you're not busy tonight, Tenny, how about dinner at my place?"

I don't know what expression was on my face, but whatever it was it made her laugh. "I'll pick you up after work," she said. "Now, the man I want you to meet is Desmond Haseldyne, and that's his office right down there. Come along!"

If Mitzi had surprised me with unexpected warmth, Haseldyne was a shock in the other direction. While Mitzi was introducing us he was glaring at me, and the only reading I could give his expression was loathing.

Why? I couldn't guess. I'd seen the man around the Agency from time to time, of course. But I certainly couldn't think of anything I'd done to offend him. And Desmond Haseldyne was not a man you would specially wish to have dislike you. He was *huge*. He was six feet six inches at least, shoulders like a stallion, fists that swallowed my hand up without a trace when he deigned to shake it. Haseldyne was one of those freaky talents that Advertising fits into odd places in its great machine—a mathematician, they said; also a poet; also he had, curiously, had a very successful career in the import-export business before giving it up to turn to advertising. I got my first glimpse of a reason for his expression when he growled, "Hell, Mitzi! He's the geek that's always looking at his watch!"

"He's also my friend," she said firmly, "and a star-class copysmith who suffered from an accident that was not his fault. I want you to give him a chance. You can't blame a person for being a victim of unethical advertising, can you?"

He relented. "I guess not," he admitted—and didn't even cover himself by adding, *and thank heaven we at this Agency don't stoop to such practices,* as anyone else would have had the sense to do. You never know who's bugging you. He stood up and lumbered around the desk to get a better look at me. "I guess," he conceded, "that we can give him a try. You can run along, Mitzi. See you tonight?"

"No, I've got a date. Another time, Des," she said, and winked at me as she closed the door.

Haseldyne sighed and passed a hand over his face. Then he returned to his chair. "Sit down, Tarb," he boomed. "You know why you're here?"

"I think so—Mr. Ha—Des," I said firmly. I'd made up my mind that I was going to be treated like what I was, not just another trainee. It caused him to look at me sharply, but all he said was:

"This is the Department of Intangible Accounts. We've got about thirty main areas of exploitation, but there are two lines that far outweigh all the others. One is politics. The other is religion. Do you know anything about either one of them?"

I shrugged. "What I studied in college," I said. "Personally, I was always a commodity man. I sold *goods,* not airy-fairy *ideas.* "

He looked at me in a way that made me think it wouldn't be so bad, really, to go back to delivering packages, but he had made up his mind to give me a job, and give me a job he would. "If you don't care which," he said, "I guess the place we need help right now is religion. Maybe you don't realize what a valuable account religion is?" Well, I didn't, but I didn't say anything. "You talk about commodities. Goods. All right, Tarb, figure it out. If you sell somebody a jar of Coffiest they pay maybe a dollar for it. Forty cents of that goes to the retailer and the jobber. The label and the jar cost a nickel, and you have to spend maybe three cents for the contents."

"Nice margin of profit," I said approvingly.

"That's where you're wrong! Add it up. Nearly half your money goes to the damn *product*. It's the same with appliances, the same with clothes, the same with all those tangible things. But religion! Ah, *religion,*" he said softly, his face beaming with a reverential glow. "In religion the product doesn't cost a damn *cent*. Maybe we spend a few bucks on land and construction—it looks really good if you can show some cathedral or temple or something, though mostly we just use miniatures and process shots. Maybe we print a few pamphlets. Sometimes a couple of books. But you just look at the P&L statements, Tenny, and you'll see that the bottom line is *sixty per cent* profit! And most of the rest is promotion cost which, don't forget, is our money too."

I shook my head wonderingly. "I had no idea," I said.

"Of course you had no idea! You product people are all the same. And that's just religion. Politics, the same—even a bigger cash spin-off because we don't have to build any churches. . . . Although," he said, his expression suddenly wistful, "it's hard to get people to take an interest in politics these days. I used to think that could be the biggest of all, but—" He shook his head. "Well," he said, "that's the picture. Want to give it a try?"

Well, you bet I did. I charged into the copy console room with my adrenalin flowing, ready to meet the challenge—I'd forgotten that I was still a trainee. That meant that when they needed me to deliver a package they could still draft me, and Mr. Dambois's suits needed to be picked up at the cleaners, and there was a sample of a new package for Kelpos, the Krispy Snack, that had to get to Production . . . it was closing time when I got back to my console. And I didn't get to see Mitzi that night after all. Instead of my date there was a message on my machine: *Something came up. Sorry. Reschedule tomorrow?*

It was a jolt. I'd been prepping myself for a happy evening, and now it was taken away from me.

On the way home I hit the Mokes pretty hard, and when I finally got my turn in the bed box and fell asleep my thoughts

70

were not cheerful, in spite of the new job. Things had changed a lot! Back on Venus, Mitzi Ku had been happy enough to date a section head. Even flattered! Now the world for the two of us had turned upside down. I could whistle, but unless she happened to feel like it she wouldn't come. Worse than that, somebody else might have a louder and more compelling whistle. The hardest thing for me to reconcile myself to was that there were two other toms preening their plumage in her direction. Evidently what I was supposed to do was take a number and wait until called. And I didn't care much for the contest. Competition from Val Dambois I could understand—I didn't say *like*. Haseldyne was another matter. Who was this sumo blimp with all the muscles who had suddenly turned up in Mitzi's life?

On the other hand, other things had changed a lot, too. When I finally got to work the next morning—after only an hour of coffee/doughnut runs for the secretaries and the model pool—I realized that the state of the art I had left behind when I boarded the shuttle for Venus was like flintlocks and mainframe computers compared to what was going on now. That was demonstrated to me the first time I sat down at my copy console and reached to turn on the grid-resolution interlock. There wasn't any.

It took me all the rest of the morning to learn how to operate the console, and at that I had to get help from the office girl.

But you don't get to be a star-class copysmith for nothing, and I hadn't lost all my skills while I was on Venus. I made a quick search of the files and discovered, as I thought, that there were areas the Department of Intangibles hadn't explored. I couldn't compete right away in the latest technology. What I could do was go back to some tried and true procedures of the past—always good, sometimes overlooked by the new people—and by four that afternoon I had completed my rough. I pulled the spool out of the console and charged into Haseldyne's office. "Take a look, Des," I ordered, plugging it into his reader. "Of course this is only preliminary. It isn't fully interactive yet, so don't ask it any hard questions, and maybe the model I used isn't the best for the purpose—"

71

"Tarb," he rumbled dangerously, "what the hell are you talking about?"

"Door to door!" I cried. "The oldest advertising technique there is! A whole new campaign, based on the soundest, best-tested procedures there are!"

I hit the switch, and immediately the three-dimensional image sprang up, a grave, gaunt figure in a cowl, face shadowed but benign, gazing directly into Haseldyne's eyes. Unfortunately it was only about two feet tall, and there was a halo of blue sparks around its edges.

"I guess I didn't get the size match right," I apologized, "and there's interference to be cleaned up—"

"Tarb," he growled, "shut up, will you?" But he was interested as the figure advanced toward him and began to speak:

"Religion, sir! Yes, that's what I have to offer! Salvation! Peace of mind! The washing away of sins, or simply the acceptance of the will of a Supreme Being. I carry a complete line, Roman Catholic, C. of E., twenty-two kinds of Baptist, Unification, Scientology, Methodist—"

"Everybody has those already," snapped Haseldyne, glancing irritably at me. I gloated; it was the reaction I had programmed for. The little image glanced over its shoulder as though making sure no one could hear, and then leaned forward confidentially.

"Right you are, sir! I should have seen you weren't the kind of person to adopt what everybody else has. So how about a genuine antique? I'm not talking your Buddha or your Confucius. I'm talking Zoroaster! Ahura Mazda and Ahriman! The forces of light and darkness! Why, half the religions you get these days are just sleazy plagiarisms of Zoroaster—and, listen, there's no fasting, there's no dietary laws, no don't-do-this or don't-do-that. Zoroaster is a religion for persons of *quality*. And—you won't believe this—I can let you have the whole thing, conversion included, for less than the price of an ordinary retreat or bar mitzvah. . . ."

I could see that he was really hooked. He watched the figure run through to the close. As it faded away in another shower

72

of those blue sparks—these automatic grid-resolution devices weren't all they were cracked up to be—he nodded slowly. "Might work," he said.

"It's bound to work, Haseldyne! I admit it's still rough. I need to talk to Legal about the contract signing at the close, of course, and I'm not sure about the cowl—maybe a sort of Indian dancing-girl outfit with a female vendor instead?"

"Tarb," he said heavily, "don't knock your own work. It's good. Clean up the size and the interference, and tomorrow we'll call a staff meeting and get it started." And I took the spool out of his machine and left him staring into space. It struck me as funny that he didn't seem pleased—after all, he'd admitted it was good! But when I got back to my console there was a message on it that drove such worries out of my mind:

I've been called out of the office, so why don't you come right to my place? Expect you about eight.

When I went back to my place to clean up, Nelson Rockwell was waiting for me. "Tenny," he coaxed, "if you could just let me have a few bucks till payday—"

"No way, Nelson! You're just going to have to work it out one way or another with the San Jacinto Mint."

"Mint? Who said anything about the mint?" he demanded. "This is something brand new—take a look!" And he pulled out of his pocket a little scrap of a picture in a cheap plastic frame. "It's the Frameable Treasury Secretary Lithographed Portrait Series on Banknote-Quality Paper!" he declared proudly. "They're pure gold, and all I need's a hundred to get my subscription started. Make it two hundred and I can get in on the charter subscriptions for Cabinet-Sized All-Metal Renderings of Famous American Suspension Bridges—" I left him still talking while I headed for the bathroom to spruce up. Tikli-Talc on my chin, LuvMe in my armpits—it had been a long time between dates. I figured I ought to bring something, so on the way I stopped to pick up a couple of six-packs of Moke. Naturally the supermarket was crowded. Naturally the checkout lines were interminable. I took the shortest one I could find, but it just didn't move. I craned past the stout lady with the full cart in front of me and saw that the checkout person was deeply involved in endless computations of discount coupons, special offers, rainchecks, scratch-a-line lottery tickets and the like, and, worse than that, the matron before me had at least twice as many clutched in her plump little fist. I groaned, and she turned to me with sympathy. "Don't you just *hate* standing in these lines? Gosh, me too! That's why I never go to Ultimaximarts any more." She waved proudly at the holosigns: *Speedy Service! Ultrafast Checkouts! We do everything to make shopping with us a joy!*

"The thing is," I said, "I've got a date."

"Aw," she said sympathetically, "so you're in a hurry, of course. Tell you what. You help me sort out these coupons, and it'll go a lot faster when I get to the desk. The thing is, see, I've got this thirty cents off on Kelpy Krisps, but the coupon's only valid if I buy a ten-ounce tube of Glow-Tooth Double-Duty Dentifricial Analgesics, but they only had the fourteen-ounce size. Do you think they'll accept that?" They wouldn't, of course. That was a T., G. & S. promotion, and I knew we would never have issued those coupons except when the ten-ounce size was being discontinued. I was spared having to tell her that, though. A red light flashed, a klaxon sounded to chase her out of the way, the barrier slammed shut in her face and a display lit up to say:

> We regret this Speedy Service Ultrafast Checkout Line is now closed. Please take your purchases to another of our counters for prompt attention from our friendly cashiers.

"Oh, *hell,*" I groaned, staring unbelievingly at the sign. That was a mistake. It wrecked my timing.

One of the slogans I'd come across on the Religion account was "the last shall be first." In this case, my hesitation made it true enough. The whole long line behind me broke and scattered and I was caught staring. That's when the finely honed consuming skills that you've developed over a lifetime meet their test. The split-second decisions come on you without warning: which line to jump to? You've got a dozen independent variables to weigh, and not just the obvious ones. There are things like the number of persons in line, the number of items for each, the factor for number of coupons per item—that's what you learn while you're still hanging on the end of Mom's cart with your thumb in your mouth and the can of Sweetees you've bawled your lungs out for clutched in your grubby little fist. Then you've got to learn to read the individual consumer. You look for the nervous twitching of the fingers that suggests this one may be close to a credit overdraft, so the whole line will crash shut while the Wackerhuts come to take him away. Or that other one sneaked a magnetic pen through the detectors to try to change a bonus offer. You've got to assign a value to each and integrate them, and then there's the physical stuff you've practiced, feinting to the wrong line, pretending not to notice a shopping cart left to save a place, use of elbows—all that is standard survival stuff, but my skills were rusty from the years on Venus. I wound up at the tail end of a line longer than ever, and even Miss Fourteen-Ounce had squeezed in ahead of me.

Something had to be done.

I peered over her shoulder to study the baskets in the line ahead and worked out my tactics. "Oh, *darn*," I said as though to myself—but loud enough for all to hear, "I forgot the Vita-Smax." Nobody had any. They couldn't have. The line had been discontinued even before I left for Venus—some trouble about heavy-metal poisoning. Three steps ahead of me, an old man with a full double-decker cart glanced at me, nibbling at the bait.

I grinned at him and called, "Remember those grand old Vita-Smax commercials? 'The All-American Cheese, Bran and Honey Breakfast Treat'?"

Miss Fourteen-Ounce looked up from her frantic inventorying of coupons. " 'Keeps You Regular—Tantalizes Your Tongue —Builds Health, Health, Health in Every Bite!' " she quoted. "Gee! I haven't had Vita-Smax in a long time! We used to call it the milk and honey cereal." Besides the heavy metals, the simulated milk solids had caused liver damage and the synthetic sucrose syrup rotted the teeth, but naturally no one would remember a thing like that.

"Mom used to make them every morning," said another woman dreamily.

I had them on the tip. I chuckled ruefully. "Mine too. I could kick myself for not picking up a box or two from the stack in Gourmet Foods."

Heads turned. "I didn't see any Vita-Smax there," the old man argued querulously.

"Really? The big stack under the sign that said, 'Buy 1 Get 1 Free'?" The line quivered. "With the special double-allowance coupon reintroductory offer?" I added, and that was what did it. They broke. Every one of them pulled carts out of line, racing for Gourmet Foods. Suddenly I was face to face with the checker. She'd been listening too, and I had to beg her to take my money before she ran after them.

All the same I was late. I almost trotted the last couple of blocks to Mitzi's place. The smog and exertion had me gasping and sweating by the time I got there—good-by LuvMe.

When I got past the doorthing I was startled to see what kind of a pad Mitzi lived in. I don't mean that it was fancy—I would have expected that, considering her current credit rating. On the contrary, what hit me in the eye when Mitzi let me in was its starkness.

It certainly was not poverty that made it so peculiarly bare. You don't get a four-hundred-square-foot flat in a building with twenty-four-hour reflex-conditioned attack guards without paying through the nose for it—I would have known that even if I hadn't known about all that Veenie damage money. The surprising thing was that splurging had stopped with the pad itself. No RotaBath. No tanks of tropical fish. No—well, no anything at all to show her status. She didn't even have Nelson Rockwell's pathetic busts or commemorative medallions. A few pieces of furniture, a small Omni-V set in a corner—that was about it. And the decor was

76

peculiar. It was all hot reds and yellows, and on one wall there was a huge static mural—not even liquid crystal—which I puzzled over for a moment before I recognized it. Sure enough, it was a rendering of that famous scene in Venusian history when they put the first big Hilsch tube on top of the tallest mountain in the Freysa range, to blow the noxious gases out into orbit as they began reducing the atmosphere to something people could stand.

"Sorry I'm late," I apologized, staring at the mural, "but there was a long line at the supermarket." I held up the Mokie-Kokes as explanation.

"Aw, Tenny, we don't need that swill." Then she bit her lip. "Come on in the kitchen while I finish dinner, and you can tell me how things are going for you."

To my surprise, she put me to work while I talked. To a surprise bigger still, the work was peeling potatoes! I mean, raw *vegetable* potatoes—some of them still had dirt on them! "Where'd you get these things?" I asked, trying to figure out what I was supposed to do to "peel" them.

"Money will get you anything," she said, shredding some other raw unprocessed vegetables, orange and green colored ones this time. It wasn't exactly an answer, since I hadn't really wondered where, or even how, but why?

I was brought up polite, though. I really did eat quite a lot of her dinner, even the raw roots and leaves she called salad, and I didn't say anything critical at all. Well, not *critical*. I did, after a while, when the conversation seemed to be limping along, ask if she really liked that stuff.

Mitzi was chomping away with a faraway look in her eyes, but she collected herself. "Like it? Of course I like it! It's—" She paused, as though something had occurred to her. "It's *healthy*," she said.

"I thought it must be," I said politely.

"No, really! There are some new, uh, studies, not yet published, that show that. For example, did you know that processed foods may cause memory deficiencies?"

77

"Aw, come on, Mitzi," I grinned. "Nobody would sell consumers things that did them harm."

She gave me a quizzical look. "Well, not on purpose," she said, "maybe. But these are new studies. Tell you what. Let's test it out!"

"Test what out?"

"Test out whether your diet has screwed up your memory, damn it," she flared. "We'll try a little experiment to see how much you remember about something and, uh, I'll tape it so we can check it over."

It did not sound like a very fun game to me, but I was still trying to be polite. "Why not?" I said. "Let's see. Suppose I give you the annual billings of the Agency for the past fifteen years, broken down for—"

"No, nothing that dull," she complained. "I know! Let's see how much you remember about what was going on in the Embassy on Venus. Some particular aspect—I don't know—sure! Let's hear everything you remember about the spy ring I was running."

"Ah, but that's not fair!" I protested. "You were doing the actual running, all I know is bits and pieces."

"We'll make allowances for that," she promised, and I shrugged.

"All right. Well, for a starter, you had twenty-three active agents and about a hundred and fifty free lancers and part-timers —most of them weren't actual agents, at least they didn't know who they were working for."

"Names, Tenny!"

I looked at her in surprise—she was taking this pretty seriously. "Well, there was Glenda Pattison in the Park Department, she was the one who got the defective parts in the new power-plant. Al Tischler, from Learoyd City—I don't know what he did, but I remember him because he was so short for a Veenie. Margaret Tucsnak, the doctor that put anticonception pills in with the aspirins. Mike Vaccaro, the prison guard from the Pole—say, should I count Hamid or not?"

"Hamid?"

78

"The grek," I explained. "The one that I tricked old Harriman into taking as a bona-fide political refugee. Of course, you left before he got to make contact, so I don't know whether I should include him on the list. But I'm surprised you don't remember him." I grinned. "You'll be saying you don't remember Hay next," I ventured. Bafflingly, she looked puzzled even at that. "Jesus Maria Lopez, for God's sake," I said, exasperated, and she looked at me opaquely for a moment.

Then she said, "That's all back on Venus, Tenny. He's there. We're here."

"That a girl!" Things were looking up. I moved closer to her, and she looked at me almost invitingly. But there was still the ghost of a scowl on her face. I reached up and touched her frown lines; they seemed actually sculpted into her brow. "Mitzi," I said tenderly, "you're working too hard."

She flinched away almost angrily from my hand, but I persisted. "No, really. You're—I don't know. More tired. More mellow, too." She was; my brassy lady was bronze now. Even her voice was deeper and softer.

And, as a matter of fact, I liked her better that way. She said, "Keep going with the names, please?" But she smiled when she said it.

"Why not? Theiller, Weeks, Storz, the Yurkewitch brothers —how'm I doing so far?"

She was biting her lip—vexed, I thought, because my memory was pretty good after all. "Just go on," she said. "There's plenty more."

So I did. Actually I only remembered about a dozen names, but she agreed to accept my remembering some of the agents just by where they worked and what they did for her, and when I wasn't just sure of something she helped out by asking questions until I got it straight. But it went on so long! "Let's try something else," I offered. "For instance, let's see which of us can remember more about the last night we spent together."

She smiled absently. "In a minute, Tenn, but first, this person from Myers-White who spoiled the wheat crop—"

I laughed out loud. "Mitzi dear," I said, "the Myers-White agent was growing rice; it was at Nevindale that they messed up the wheat crop! See? If diet messes up memory, maybe you ought to switch to Kelpy Crisps!"

She was biting her lip again, and for a moment her expression was not friendly at all. Funny. I'd never thought of Mitzi as a sore loser. Then she smiled and surrendered, clicking off the recorder. "I guess you've proved your point, dear," she said, and patted the couch beside her. "Why don't you come over here and collect your winnings?" And so it turned out that we had a nice time after all.

III

The nice time didn't get repeated very rapidly, though. Mitzi didn't leave any more messages for me. I called her a few times —she was friendly enough, to be sure—she was also, she explained, *really* busy, and maybe some time next week, Tenn, dear, or anyway right after the first of the month—

Of course, I had plenty to keep me busy. I was doing very well on the Religion account, and even Desmond Haseldyne was flattering. But I wanted to see Mitzi. Not just for the sake of, well, you know, the things for the sake of which I'd got interested in her in the first place. There were other things.

A couple of times when I went into Haseldyne's office, he was making mysterious private calls, and I had the funny idea that some of them were to Mitzi. And I saw him, along with Val Dambois and Mitzi and the Old Man himself, in a huddle in a fast-food place a long way from the Agency. It wasn't a place where executives went for dinner. It wasn't even a place where junior copy trainees like me went for dinner very often, but it happened to be near Columbia Advertising & Promotion University. When they saw me it obviously shook them up. They were all in on something together. I didn't know what. None of my business, maybe—but it hurt me that Mitzi didn't tell me what it was. I went on to my Columbia class—that was the creative writing one—and that whole evening I'm afraid I didn't pay much attention.

That was the best of the courses I was taking, too. Creative writing is really—well—creative. At the beginning of the course the professor told us that it was only in our time that the subject had been taught in a reasonable way. In the old days, she said, creative-writing students would just sort of make things up themselves, and the teachers would have to try to distinguish how much of what was good, or bad, about a paper was the idea or how the ideas were expressed. And yet, she said, they had the example of art courses for hundreds of years to show them the right way to do it. Aspiring artists had always been set to copy the works of Cézanne and Rembrandt and Warhol in order to learn their craft, while all aspiring writers were urged to create was their own blather. Handy word-processors changed all that, and so the first assignment she gave us was to rewrite *A Midsummer Night's Dream* in modern English. And I got an A.

Well, from then on I was teacher's pet, and she let me do all sorts of extracredit themes. There was a good chance, she said, that I would pass her course with the highest mark ever attained, and you know that sort of thing can do you nothing but good when it comes time to add up your degree credits. So I took on some pretty ambitious projects. The hardest one, I guess, was to rewrite all of *The Remembrance of Things Past* in the style of Ernest Hemingway, changing the locale to Germany in the time of Hitler and presenting it as a one-act play.

That sort of thing was well beyond the capacity of any equipment I had in my little shared-time condo, not to mention that my roomies were likely to interrupt me, so I took to staying after work now and then to use the big machines in the copy consoles. I had set sentence length for not more than six words, dialed introspection down to 5 percent and programmed playscript format, and I was just getting set to run the program when I ran out of Mokes. The soft-drink machine had nothing but our own Agency brands in it, of course. I had tried them before; they didn't satisfy the craving. I had the idea that I'd seen a Mokie-Koke bottle in the wastebasket in Desmond Haseldyne's office once—I suppose it was just my imagination—so I wandered over in that direction.

Somebody was in his office. I could hear voices; the lights were on; the data processors had their hoods off and were running some sort of financial programs. I would have turned quietly away and gone back to my copy console, except that one of the voices was Mitzi's.

Curiosity was my undoing.

I paused to look at the programs running on the machines. At first I thought it was a projection for some sort of investment plan, for it was all about stock holdings and percentages of total shares outstanding. But it seemed to make a pattern. I stood up, deciding to get out of there—

And made the mistake of trying to leave inconspicuously through the darkened offices on the other side of the processors. They had been locked for the night. Nothing kept me from entering, but the break-in trap had been set. I heard a great, hollow hissing, like the sound of the Hilsch tubes around Port Kathy, and a huge cloud of white blew up around me. I'd been foamed! I could see nothing at all. The foam allowed me to breathe, but it did not allow me to see, not anything at all. I stumbled around for a moment, bashing into chairs, bumping over desks.

Then I surrendered to the foam and just stood there, waiting. And while I waited, I thought.

By the time I heard someone approaching I had figured it out.

It was Mitzi and Haseldyne, spraying the foam with a dispersant chemical as they came—I could hear the hiss. "Tenn!" Mitzi cried. "What the hell are you doing here?"

I didn't answer, not directly anyway. I wiped the last of the foam off my face and shoulders and grinned at her.

"I'm onto you," I said.

What I said had a curious effect on them. Naturally they were startled to see me there. Mitzi was holding the dispersant spray like a weapon, and Haseldyne was fondling a heavy tape dispenser as though he'd brought it along to bash someone's head in with it—not so very surprising, I suppose, since I had set off the burglar alarm and foam. But both of them went absolutely expressionless. It was as though their faces had become dead, and they kept that queer immobility for seconds.

Then Mitzi said, "I don't know what you mean, Tennison." I chuckled. "It's perfectly obvious. I saw the programs you're running. You're planning a takeover bid, aren't you?"

Still no expression. "I mean," I clarified, "the two of you, maybe Dambois too, are planning to take over control of the Agency with your investments. Isn't that right?"

Slowly, glacially, expression returned to Haseldyne's face, and then to Mitzi's. "I'll be darned," rumbled Haseldyne. "He's caught us fair and square, Mitzi."

She swallowed, and then smiled. It was not a very good smile —too much tension in the jaw muscles, too much narrowing of the lips. "It certainly looks that way," she said. "Well, Tenn, what are you going to do about it?"

I had not felt this good in a long time. Even Haseldyne looked like a harmless and friendly fat man to me, not a ravening monster. I said amiably, "Why, nothing you don't want me to, Mitz. I'm your friend. All I want is a little friendliness from the two of you."

Haseldyne glanced at Mitzi. Mitzi looked at Haseldyne. Then both of them turned to me. "I guess," said Haseldyne, choosing his words with care, "what we ought to do now is talk about just how friendly you want us to be, Tarb."

"Gladly," I said. "But first—have you got a Moke on you?"

IV

The next day at the Agency the climate had thawed. By mid-afternoon it was downright tropical, because Mitzi Ku had smiled on me. What made Mitzi Ku so suddenly great a power no one exactly knew, but the water-cooler gossip had made it clear that she was. There was no talk about putting me back on the pedicab run.

Even Val Dambois found me worthy of love. "Tenny, boy," he boomed, making the long trek down to my little cubicle in Intangibles, "why'd you let them put you in a hole like this? Why the hell didn't you *say* something?" I didn't say anything because I couldn't get past his sec³, was the answer, but there was no sense telling him what he already knew. Bygones could be bygones— for now, anyway. Forgiveness, no lingering grudges, a truly sales-fearing spirit, that was what Tennison Tarb was like these days. I grinned back at Dambois and let him throw his arm around me as he conducted me back to Executive Country. There would be a time, I knew, when his throat would be exposed to my fangs— until then it was forgive and forget.

They even, without saying a word about it, arranged to put a Moke dispenser in my office. There was no official ruling. It just appeared that afternoon.

And that made me do some hard thinking. Swigging Mokes was surely harmless enough—hell, I'd proved that!—but did it really suit the star-class image I ought to present to the world? It was such a consumer kind of thing to do—and a consumer, moreover, of a competing Agency's account. I pondered over it all the way home in my company car. When I tipped the pedaler the thought crystallized, because I got a look at the black resentment in his eyes before he covered it up and touched his cap to me. Three days earlier, we'd shared the same tandem pedicab run. I could understand his resentment. What that resentment implied was that if I got cast down into the lower depths again, he and the other sharks would be waiting.

So I marched in and rapped on the sleeping tank. "Rockwell," I shouted. "Wake up! I want to ask you something!"

He wasn't a bad guy, old Nelson Rockwell. He had nearly six more hours coming to him in the tank before it was my turn, and every right in the world to bite my head off when I dragged him out of it. But when he heard what I wanted he was kindness itself.

A little puzzled, maybe. "You want to go dry, Tenny?" he repeated, still half-asleep. "Well, sure, that's the smart thing to do, you don't want to screw up your big chance. But I don't honestly see what it's got to do with me."

"What it's got to do with you, Nels, is, didn't you tell me once you were in ConsumAnon?"

"Yeah, sure. Years ago. Gave it up, though, because I didn't need it once I straightened myself out and got into collectibles —oh!" he said, eyes lighting up. "I get it! You want me to tell you about ConsumAnon so you can decide if you want to try it."

"What I want, Nels, is to go to ConsumAnon. And I want you to take me."

He glanced wistfully at the warm, inviting sleep box. "Gosh, Tenny. It's open to anyone. You don't need to be taken."

I shook my head. "I'd feel better if I went with someone," I confessed. "Please? And soon? Tomorrow night, even, if there's a meeting—"

He laughed at that. When he was through laughing, he patted my arm. "You've got a lot to learn, Tenny. There's a meeting *every* night. That's how it works. Now, if you'll just hand me my socks. . . ."

That's the kind of guy Nels Rockwell was. All the time he was dressing I was thinking of ways to return the favor. I'd have to be moving out of this shared-time dump, of course. What was to stop me from, say, prepaying two or three months of my share and letting him have it, so he could pick his own time to sleep? I knew he had to take the lobster trick at the grommet works because of his sleep schedule; he could probably get a different shift, maybe even more money. . . .

But I got a grip on myself. It wasn't doing a consumer any favor, I told myself, to give them ideas above their station. He was getting along all right the way he was. I might mess him up badly by interfering.

So I kept my mouth shut about prepaying the rent, but in my heart I was truly grateful.

·· ◆ ··

85

ConsumAnon turned out to be a bad idea. I knew that in the first two minutes. The place Rockwell had taken me to was a *church*.

Now, that's not so bad in itself. In fact, it was kind of interesting—I'd never seen the inside of one before. Besides, you could look at it as a kind of research for my Intangibles work, which meant I could put in a chit for my and Rockwell's pedicab fare (even though he'd insisted we take the bus).

But—these *people!* I don't just mean they were consumers. They were the dregs of the consumer class, shriveled up little old men with facial tics; fat, frowning girls with the kind of complexions you get from solid soy and not much of that. There was a young couple whispering jitterily to each other, with a small child crying itself frantic unnoticed in the seat between them. There was a weasel-faced man skulking by the door as though he couldn't make up his mind, stay or run—well, I couldn't either, really. These people were *losers*. A well-trained consumer is one thing. They were all of that. They had been bred and trained to do what the world needed from them: buying what we Agency people had to sell. But, oh, what stolid and stunned faces! What made for a good consumer was boredom. Reading was discouraged, homes were no joy to be in—what else did they have to do with their lives but consume? But these people had made a travesty of that noble—well, fairly noble—calling. They were *obsessed*. I almost ducked out for a Moke to ease the jangly shudders they gave me, but as long as I'd come this far I decided to stay for the meeting.

That was my second bad mistake, because the proceedings rapidly became disgusting. First, they started with a *prayer*. Then they began singing *hymns*. Rockwell nudged me to join in, grinning and croaking away at the top of his voice, but I couldn't even look him in the face.

Then it got worse. One by one, these misfits stood up and sobbed out their tawdry stories. Talk about sickening! This one had blighted her life by popping NicoChews, forty packs a day, till her teeth came out and her bosses fired her because she couldn't handle her job—her job was phone operator. This other one was into deodorants and breath-fresheners, and had so thoroughly scoured away every trace of natural body exudates that his skin was chapped and his mucous surfaces dried out. The jittery young couple—why, they were Moke-heads like myself! I stared at them in amazement. How could they let themselves sink so low? Sure, I had a Moke *problem*. But just being here meant I was *doing* something about the problem. No way would I let myself turn into such raddled wrecks as they! "Go on, Tenny," muttered Rockwell, nudging me. "Don't you want to testify?"

I don't know what I said to him, except that it included the word, "Good-by." I squeezed past him and out the door, yearning for the open air. As I stood in the entrance, wheezing and clearing my lungs, the weasel-faced man crept out after me. "Gee," he said, grinning slyly, "I heard what your friend said. Sure wish I had your monkey instead of my own."

No one likes to hear that the trouble that blights his life is less awful than some stranger's. I was not cordial. I said stiffly, "My, ah, problem is bad enough to suit me, thanks." For some reason my mind was fluttering just then. I had half a dozen separate yearnings and loathings filling my head at once—the desperate need for a Moke, the contempt for those ConsumAnon dummies inside, the more acute dislike for Weasel-face himself, the itchy yearning for Mitzi Ku that came over me every now and then . . . and, under them all, something else that I couldn't quite identify. A memory? An inspiration? A resolve? I couldn't quite put my finger on it. It had something to do with what was going on inside—no, with something before that, something Rockwell had said?

Weasel-face, I suddenly realized, was hissing rapidly in my ear. "—What?" I barked.

"I said," he repeated behind his hand, glancing about, "I know a guy's got what you need. Moke-Eeeze pills. Take three a day, one each meal, and you'll never need a Moke again."

"My God, man!" I roared. "Are you offering me *drugs?* I'm no consumer. I'm Agency personnel! If I could find a cop I'd have you locked up—" And I actually looked around for a familiar

87

Brinks or Wackerhut uniform; but you know how it is, there's never a policeman when you want one, and anyway when I looked back Weasel-face was gone.

And so was my idea. Whatever it had been.

The human kidney is not meant to handle forty Mokie-Kokes a day. There were times over the next twenty-four hours when I wondered if Weasel-face hadn't had a good idea after all. Some cautious inquiries at the Agency clinic (oh, how sweet they were to me now!) solidified the vague notions I'd had. The pills were bad news. They worked, but after a time—maybe six months, maybe more or less—the stressed nervous system faltered and ultimately broke. I didn't want that. True, I was losing weight and the view in the mirror when I depilated showed new strain lines on my face every morning; but I was functioning well enough still.

No, hell, let's tell the truth: I was functioning *magnificently*. Every new set of hourlies showed that Religion was uptrending. Joss sticks, up 0.03; prayer candles, 0.02; exit polls from three hundred and fifty randomly chosen Zoroastrian temples showed a nearly one percent increase in first-time worshippers. The Old Man called me himself. "You've established a lot of credibility with the Planning Committee," he boomed. "Tarb, my hat's off to you! What can I do to make your work easier? Another assistant?"

"Great idea, sir!" I cried, and added carelessly, "What's Dixmeister doing now?"

So my old trainee was back on my team. Apprehensive, placatory, desperate to please—consumed by curiosity. Just the way I wanted him.

He wasn't the only one devoured by curiosity, because everybody in the Agency knew something big was going on, and none of them knew exactly what. The gravy was that none of them knew how little I myself knew. Account executives and copy chiefs, on the way from level nine to level fifteen, a dozen times a day decided to take the shortcut through my office. Common courtesy made them stop in to slap me on the back and tell me what a great job everybody knew I was doing . . . and tell me that we really ought to get together for lunch or a drink, or a round of bumper pool at the country club. I smiled, and accepted no invitations. I declined none, either, because if they pressed me too hard they'd find out how ignorant I really was. So, "Sure thing," I'd say, and, "Real soon!" And then if they lingered I'd pick up the phone and whisper into it until, smiling but eaten up inside, they went away. While Dixmeister, in his cubicle outside my office, would have his eyes on me, worried and glowering until he caught me looking at him, and then there'd be that hangdog, whimpery smile.

Ah, I loved it!

Of course, common sense reminded me not to push too hard. I was only a tiny cog in the takeover bid Haseldyne and Mitzi were putting together. I was tolerated more than needed. No. I wasn't needed at all, except that it was easier for them to cut me in than to shut me up.

All I had to do was keep on making it easier for them to cut me in than cut me down . . . and then . . . and then the time would come when the takeover would go through, and Mitzi and Haseldyne would be owners. And, with a little luck, Tenny Tarb would be right on their team. An account executive—no, I thought, swigging a Moke, better than that. A C.E.O.! And that was a dream of splendor. You know what a king is? I'll tell you what a king is. Compared with a Chief Executive Officer of a major ad Agency, a king is *nothing*.

And, then, I thought, opening another Moke, what about the future? What if Mitzi and I got back together again on a full-time basis? What if we even got *married?* What if I were not just C.E.O. but a community-property coowner of the Agency? Intoxicating dreams! They made my little Moke problem seem pretty small potatoes. With that kind of money I could afford the best detoxing in the world. I could even . . . wait a minute . . . what was it? The idea that had been poking around in my subconscious at the ConsumAnon meeting?

I sat up straight and almost dropped the Moke. Dixmeister came rushing in, scared. "Mr. Tarb? Are you all right?"

"I'm *fine*, Dixmeister," I told him. "Listen, didn't I see the Old Man going down the hall a minute ago? See if you can find him—ask him if he'd like to drop in for a minute."

And I sat back and waited, while the idea formed itself into perfect shape in my mind.

You don't get the Old Man without his gaggle of droogs, three or four of them tagging along and clustering in the doorways while he paid his calls. They all had big titles, and any one of them made four times as much a year as I did, but they were stooges. I ignored them. "Thanks a lot for dropping in, sir," I beamed. "Sit down, won't you? Here. Take my chair!"

You don't get the Old Man without five minutes of preliminary chitchat, either. He sat down and began to tell me about the old days and how he'd made his pile, averting his eyes from my Mokie-Koke dispenser as though it were false teeth I'd left on the dresser. I heard all over again the saga of how he'd come back from Venus with his lucky millions and bet it all on the forlorn hope of turning two dead Agencies into one towering success. "It worked, Tenn," he rasped, "because of product! That's what T., G. & S. is built on, *product*. I'm not saying anything against Intangibles, but it's *goods* that people need to be sold, for their own sakes and the sake of humankind itself!"

"Right, chief," I said, because no other response is allowed when power speaks, "but I've got a little idea I'd like to bounce off you. You know ConsumAnon?"

He gave me a frown like thunderclouds. His vertical lines were as deep as Mitzi's, and there were a lot more of them. "When I see ConsumAnon people," he declared, "I always think I'm looking at dupes of the Venusians. They're crackpots at best!"

"You bet they're crackpots, but there's a market potential there that I don't think we've tapped. You see, these Consum-Anon people have gone out of control. It's Coffiest fifty times a day, a Mementoes habit that would bankrupt a star-class time-buyer, every sort of mega-hypertrophy of normal, decent consuming. So they go to C.A. Then what happens? Why, most of them stay clean about two days. If that. Then they slip. In a week they're worse off than ever. They become institutional cases, as like as not, lost to consuming forever. And the successes are even worse. They're brainwashed into *economizing*. Even *saving*."

"I've always said," the Old Man announced gravely, "that C.A. is the next thing to Conservationism."

"Right! But we don't have to lose these people. All we have to do is redirect them. Not abstinence. Substitution."

The Old Man pursed his lips. Naturally all of the droogs followed suit. Not one of them had grasped the idea, and not one of them would admit it.

I let them off the hook. "We set up a self-help group for each kind of overconsuming," I explained, "and we train them to *substitute*. If they're Coffiest addicts, we switch them to Nic-O-Chews. Nic-O-Chews to the San Jacinto Mint—"

Clearing of throat from the doorway. "The San Jacinto Mint isn't one of our clients," said Droog No. 2.

I said stonily, "Then to someone who is our client, *of course* —we're a full-range Agency, we've got something for every consuming niche, don't we? I would estimate that a consumer who's five years into, say, a Coffiest habit and just about on the skids still has years of useful life with, say, Starrzelius Diet-Aids." The Old Man glanced once at his droog, who shut up instantly. I pressed on. "The next part," I said, "is where I think the real money is. What about these self-help groups? Why shouldn't they be actual clubs? Like lodges. They could charge dues. They could have to buy regalia and paraphernalia—watches, rings, tee shirts. Ceremonial robes. A different design for each degree as they move up, and so constructed that they can't be passed on as second-hand goods—"

"*Product,*" whispered the Old Man, and his eyes gleamed.

It was the magic word; I had won him over. The retinue knew it before I did, of course, and the air was thick with congratulations and plans. A whole new department within Intangibles. First a two-week crash feasibility survey, just to make sure there were no roadblocks and to identify the main profit areas. That would have to go to the Planning Committee, but then—"When it happens, Tenny," the Old Man beamed, "it's all yours!" And then he did the ritual act that generations of ad execs have done to show their whole-hearted admiration. He took off his hat and placed it on the table.

It was glory time. My heart was full. And I could hardly wait for them to get out of the office because it was a grand scheme that would benefit its inventor very little. Money, yes. Promotion and prestige, yes. But substitution could not cure Campbellian limbic compulsion . . . and, God, how I wanted a Moke!

I even got to see my brassy lady once in a while, though not very often. She did show up in my office in response to the memo I flashed her about my new project, looking around abstractedly while I apologized for going to the Old Man with it instead of waiting until, uh, *after.* "No problem, Tenny," she said cheerfully —and absentmindedly. "It won't affect our, uh, *plans.* See each other? Why, certainly—real soon—we'll be in touch—bye!" Real soon it was not. She wouldn't come to my place and didn't invite me to hers, and when I tried to get her on the phone she was either out or too rushed to talk. Well, that wasn't unreasonable. Now that I knew what she was up to I could see that there wasn't time in her life for everything just now.

But I still wanted to see her, and when I got a surprise call in my office just before quitting time I raced right up to her office, waited out the sec^3, breezed past the sec^2 and was allowed to call Mitzi herself from the sec^1's desk. "I was just on the phone with Honolulu," I said. "Your mother. I've got a message from her."

Silence from the other end of the line. Then, "Give me an hour, will you, Tenny? Then let's have a drink in the Executive lounge."

Well, it wasn't an hour, it was a lot nearer two, but I didn't mind waiting. Although I was well on the way to being a fair-haired boy, my official status had not yet improved to the point of full Executive privileges. I was glad to be admitted on Mitzi's invitation and sit with my Drambuie, gazing out over the cloudy, smoggy city with all its wonderful wealth and promise, in the company of my peers—well, almost peers. They didn't snub me, either. In fact when Mitzi at last appeared and frowned around the room, looking for me, I had trouble disengaging myself to find a quiet table for two.

She was frowning—she was always frowning these days—and she looked flustered. But she waited until I had ordered drinks, her favorites, Mimosas, with nearly real champagne and reconstituted orange juice, before she demanded, "Now, what's this about my mother?"

"She called me, Mits. She said she'd been trying to reach you ever since you got back, and no luck."

"I did talk to her!"

"Once, right," I nodded, "the day after you landed. She says for three minutes—"

"I was busy!"

"—and then you never returned her calls after that."

There were at least half a dozen of the frown lines warning me, and her voice was chilly: "Tarb," she snapped, "get straight. I'm a big girl. What's between my mother and me is none of your business. She's an interfering old busybody who's half the reason I left for Venus in the first place, and if I don't want to talk to her I don't have to. Got it?" The drinks arrived, and she grabbed for hers. Halfway to her lips she added, "I'll call her next week." And poured half the Mimosa down her throat.

"It's not really bad," she admitted grudgingly.

"I can make them better myself," I offered. Thinking: Damn it, I'd better get out of that shared-time condo fast, can't expect Mitzi to offer her place every time. And it was as though I'd spoken out loud. She leaned back in her seat, regarding me thoughtfully. Most of the frown lines had gone from her brow, bar the two that now seemed semipermanent, but her gaze was more analytical than I would have hoped for.

"Tenny," she said, "There's something about you that appeals very strongly to me—"

"Thank you, Mits."

"Your dumbness, I think," she went on, not paying attention to what I said. "Yes. That's it. Dumb and helpless. You remind me of a lost pet mouse."

I essayed, "Only a mouse? Not at least a kitten to cuddle?"

"Kittens grow up to be cats. Cats are predators. I think what I really like best about you is that you've lost your fangs somewhere." She wasn't looking at me now, staring past me out the window at the smoggy lights of the city. I would have given a lot to know what sentences were forming in her mind just then, that she had vetoed before they came out of her mouth. She sighed. "I'd like another of these," she added, coming back to the world I was in.

I signaled the waiter and whispered in his ear while she exchanged smiles and nods with a dozen others from Executive country. "I'm sorry I stuck my nose in about your mother," I said.

She shrugged absently. "I said I'd call her. Let's forget it." She brightened. "How's the job going? I hear your new project's looking good."

I shrugged modestly. "It'll be a while yet before we know if it will amount to anything."

"It will, Tenn. So until then are you going to stay with Religion?"

I said, "Well, sure, but that's pretty well in hand. I thought I'd take a few extra classes, see about speeding up that master's degree."

She nodded as though she were agreeing, but said: "Did you ever think of switching to Politics?"

That startled me. *"Politics?"*

She said thoughtfully, "I can't tell you much right now, but it might be useful if you got your feet wet in that."

There was a little tingle down my backbone. She was talking about *after!* "Why not, Mits? I'll turn Religion over to my Number Two tomorrow! And now—we've got the whole evening before us—"

94

She shook her head. "You do, Tenny, I've got something else I've got to do." She saw how my face fell. It seemed to depress her too. She watched the waiter bring the second round of drinks before she said: "Tenny, you know I've got a lot on my mind right now—"

"I understand perfectly, Mits!"

"Do you?" The thoughtful look again. "You understand, anyway, that I'm busy. I don't know if you understand how I feel about you."

"Good, I hope."

"Both good and bad, Tenny," she said somberly, "both good and bad. If I had any sense at all—"

But she didn't say what she'd do if she had any sense at all and, since I had a numbing suspicion that I knew what it would have been, I let the sentence hang in air. "To you," she said, examining the new Mimosa as though it were medicine before she sipped it.

"To us," I said, lifting my own drink. It wasn't a Mimosa. It wasn't an Irish Coffee, either, though it looked like one. On top was the regulation puff of whipped NeerKreme, but what was underneath it was what I had sent the waiter scurrying down to my office to get: four ounces of pure Mokie-Koke.

V

The next morning, first thing, I snapped my fingers. Dixmeister materialized in the doorway at once, waiting for either orders or an invitation to come in and sit down. I gave him neither. "Dixmeister," I said, "I've got Religion pretty straight now, so I'm turning it over to—what's his name—"

"Wrocjek, Mr. Tarb?"

"Right. I've got a couple days free, so I'm going to get Politics on the right track."

Dixmeister shifted position uncomfortably in the doorway. "Well, actually, Mr. Tarb," he said, "since old Mr. Sarms left I've been pretty much running Politics myself."

"That's exactly what we're going to straighten out, Dixmeister. I want all current sitreps and plan outlines fed to my monitor for approval and action, and I want them this afternoon. No, in one hour . . . no, come to think of it, let's do it now."

He stammered, "But—but—" I knew the problem; there were at least fifty separate stores of data to be tapped and digested, and preparing a decent synoptic was half a day's work. About that I cared little or not at all.

"Do it, Dixmeister," I said benignly, leaned back in my chair and closed my eyes. Ah, how good it felt!

I had almost forgotten I was a Mokie.

They say that Mokie-Koke gets you so wired up after a while that your decisions suffer. It isn't that you can't make the decisions. It isn't even that they're wrong when you make them. What it is, you're so hyper, so strung out, that one decision isn't enough for you. You make one, and then another, and then another, bing-bang-biff, and when the ordinary human being can't keep up with you, which is always, you lose your cool. Dixmeister probably would have thought that was going on with me, because I guess I gave him the sharp part of the tongue pretty often. But I wasn't worried. I knew that was *supposed* to happen, but I did not fear its happening to me. Oh, sure, maybe after a long time—ten years, five years—far enough in the future, anyway, so that I didn't have to worry about it, since I was going to give the stuff up any day. First chance I got. And meanwhile, actually, I was touching all bases and swinging the old home-run paddle. Even Dixmeister had to admit it. I spent two days on current projects and plans, and, man, how I made the old place hum!

The first thing I got into was the PAC department. You know what a Political Action Committee is. It's a group of people with a special interest who are willing to put up money to bribe—well, strike that, to *influence*—officials to enact laws and regulations that favor whatever it is they care about. In the old days the PACs belonged mostly to businessmen and what they called labor unions. I remembered seeing those great old historical romances

96

with the American Medical Association and the used-car dealers —eager young doctors winning tax exemption for conferences in Tahiti; antic car salesmen battling for the inalienable right to put sawdust in a transmission. That sort of show is fun when you're young, but as you get older and more cynical you stop believing people are so goody-goody. . . . Anyway, those battles are of course long won, but PACs are still around. They're almost as good as religion. You set them up and collect their money, and what do they spend it on? In the long run, advertising! Either their own, or for the campaign ads for the candidates they like. So in one long day I set up a dozen new PACs. There was an Objet-d'art PAC (I got the idea from Nelson Rockwell), a Swiss Army Knife PAC ("We need them to clean our nails—is it our fault that criminals use them for other purposes?"), a Pedicab-Pumpers PAC, a Tenants' PAC to legislate longer sleeping hours before the daytime users of the space moved in—oh, I was knocking them out!

It was almost too easy. I had more energy left at the end of a hard day than I knew what to do with. I could have gone on with school, but what was the point? How much higher in the world would a graduate degree get me? I could have moved to a better place, but the thought of hunting one out and moving into it depressed me . . . and there was one other thing. I *felt* secure. The way things were going I had every reason to *be* secure. But I had been real secure once before and out of a cloud no bigger than a man's hand Destiny had reached down to smite me. . . . I stayed in the shared-time condo. And talked with Nels Rockwell when we happened to be awake together, and watched the Omni-V until all hours when we were not. I watched sports events and soaps and comics, and most of all news. The Sudan had just been reclaimed for civilization, using the same Campbellian techniques that had been used on me—glow of pride at the world bettering itself every day; little nagging itch of resentment, because the Campbellian techniques had, after all, not bettered my own world a hell of a lot. A whale had been sighted off Lahaina, but further investigation showed it was just a lost tank

97

of jojoba oil. The spring Olympics were going on in Tucson, and there was a big upset in the unicycle event. Ms. Mitzi Ku, interviewed at the entrance to T., G. & S. Tower, denied reports that she was leaving the Agency—

And she looked so sweet and so tired on the little screen; and I wished for . . . No. I didn't wish "for" anything. I just wished. There was too much involved between me and Mitzi to wish for anything specific.

She didn't answer when I tried to call her at home.

The way to make all my wishes true with Mitzi, I told myself, was to do the best possible job on politics; and so I made the next morning hell for poor little Dixmeister. "The work's *wasted*," I yelled at him, "because Casting's lying down on the job!" He was directly responsible for Casting, of course.

"I do my best," he sulked, and I just shook my head.

"Candidate screening," I explained, "is one of the most important functions of a political campaign." He was still sulking, but he made the pretense of an eager nod. Well, of course, everyone knew that. It had been established way back in the mid-twentieth century that a candidate shouldn't sweat much; he had to be at least five per cent taller than average so he didn't need a box to stand on in a debate. His hair could be gray, but he had to have plenty of it. You didn't want him too fat (but not too skinny, either), and above all he had to be able to deliver his lines as though he really believed them.

"Absolutely, Mr. Tarb," Dixmeister said indignantly. "I always tell that to Central Casting, the whole list—"

"It isn't good enough, Dixmeister. From now on I'll do the first cut myself."

His jaw dropped. "Gee, Mr. Tarb, Mr. Sarms always used to let me handle that."

"Mr. Sarms isn't here any more. Casting call is nine A.M., in the big room. Fill it." And I waved him out of the room and closed the door, because I was half an hour behind on my next Moke.

· · ◆ · ·

98

Fill the big room he did, all nine hundred seats except for the first row. That was mine—mine and my secretary's and my makeup guy's and my director's. I came down the center aisle, not looking to the left or right, waved the entourage into seats and jumped up onto the stage. At once Dixmeister came bounding in from the wings. "Quiet!" he yelled. "Quiet for Mr. Tarb!"

I stood there, looking over them, waiting for the feel of the audience to reach me. Actually, they were quiet enough already, because they knew where they were. This hall was where the Old Man held his all-exec pep rallies, where major presentations were made and new accounts solicited us. Every one of the nine hundred seats had its own back, arm, cushion and phone jack—the Agency executives traveled first class! And the nine hundred people from Central Casting were nearly all consumer class in their origins.

So they were quiet with awe, and as I perceived their feelings I knew how to pitch to them. I waved an arm around the vast auditorium. "Do you like what you see here?" I demanded. "Do you want this sort of thing for your own lives? It's easy! *Just make me like you.* You're each going to be called up here on the stage and given ten seconds to make a presentation. Ten seconds! It's not much, is it? But that's all the seconds there are in a flash spot, and if you can't make it here in this auditorium you can't do the job for T., G. & S. in prime time. Now, what do you do with your ten seconds? That's up to you. You can sing. Tell a story. Say what your favorite color is. Ask for my vote—anything! But what you say doesn't matter, just so you make me care about you and want to help you get elected—make me *like* you!"

I nodded to Dixmeister. As the makeup guy helped me down to my seat Dixmeister sprang forward and barked: "First row! Start from the left! You on the end there—onstage!"

Dixmeister jumped down into the seat beside me, anxiously dividing his glances between my face and the actor before us. The actor was a big one, shaggy-haired, bright eyes under shaggy brows. A likeable face, all right. He'd thought about his bit, too. "I trust you all!" he boomed, "and you can trust Marty O'Loyre, because Marty O'Loyre *loves* you. Please help Marty O'Loyre with your vote on Election Day!"

Dixmeister stabbed the timer with his finger, and the result blinked up from the monitor: 10.0 seconds. Dixmeister nodded. "Great timing, and three name repetitions." He studied my face, trying to jump the right way at the right time. "Good sheriff candidate?" he guessed. "Solid, strong, warm—"

"Look at the way his hands are shaking," I said kindly. "Not a chance. Next!"

Tall outdoorsy blonde, with the forearm muscles you get from long hours of table polo: "Too upper-class. Next!"

Elderly black woman with plump, permanently pursed lips: "Maybe probate judge, but get her a haircut. Next!"

Twin brothers with identical heart-shaped birthmarks over their right eyes: "Sensational reinforcement there, Dixmeister," I lectured. "Have we got two alderman-at-large spots? Right. Next!"

Slim, pale, a faraway look in her eyes, no more than twenty-three. "I know what it is to be unhappy," she said—sobbed, almost. "If you help me I'll try my very best to take care of you too. . . ."

"Too sappy?" asked Dixmeister.

"There's no such thing as too sappy for Congress, Dixmeister. Take her name. Next!"

The find of the day was a callow, sharp-featured youth who grunted his lines while his eyes darted fearfully in all directions. Heaven knows how he got listed with Central Casting in the first place, for he was surely not a pro, and his "presentation" was a stumbling account of a boyhood trip to Prospect Park. Way over time, at that. Dixmeister cut him off in midsentence and glanced at me, eyebrows raised in amused contempt. As he was lifting a hand to wave the kid away I stopped him, for something was stirring in my mind. "Wait a minute." I closed my eyes, trying to recapture the vagrant image. "I see. . . . Yes. Got it! The unicycle races yesterday—one of the winners had just that look of eager stupidity. The jock look."

"Actually, Mr. Tarb," the kid called down, "I'm not much into sports. I'm a clip sorter in the Starrzelius mailroom."

"You're a unicyclist now," I told him. "Report to Wardrobe for costumes and Mr. Dixmeister here will find you a coach for the cycle. Dixmeister, take a copy theme note: 'My friends thought I was sort of peculiar for taking up the unicycle, but I don't see it that way. Stubborn, maybe. Willing to pay the price to do the hard job, whether it's on the unicycle or in the office of—' Let's see whether it's—".

"Congress, Mr. Tarb?" Dixmeister ventured, holding his breath.

I said generously, "Right, Congress. Maybe." Actually the wimp was too good for Congress; I was thinking of a lot higher, maybe Vice-President. But I could straighten out the casting later, and meanwhile it cost nothing to let Dixmeister feel good for a moment. "And, oh, yes," I said, remembering, "call up the unicycle club and arrange for him to win a couple of races."

"Well, Mr. Tarb," dithered Dixmeister, "I don't know if they'll want to go along with fixing a—"

"Tell them, Dixmeister. Tell them what a good tie-in promotion for unicycling this is going to be. *Sell* them. Got it? Good. Then next!"

And next. And next, and next. Nine hundred nexts. But we needed a lot of candidates. Although there were nearly a dozen Agencies with strong political divisions, there was plenty of work for all of us. Sixty-one state legislatures. Nine thousand cities and towns. Three thousand counties. And the federal government. Put them all together and, on the average, there were a quarter of a million elective posts to be filled a year. (Of course, only a fraction of them were important enough—by this I mean expensive enough—to warrant the time of T., G. & S.) About half the time we could recycle incumbents, but we still had to find every year five or ten thousand warm bodies to teach and dress and make up and rehearse and direct . . . and maybe elect. *Usually* elect. It didn't particularly matter who won any election in any real sense, but T., G. & S. had a reputation to protect as a can-do

Agency. So we battled for our candidates as hard as though winning or losing made some actual difference.

By the time we got to the end of the nine hundred the "coffee" thermos on my chair arm had been refilled twice with Mokes and my stomach was beginning to growl its first pangs of hunger. We had reduced the nine hundred to eighty-two possibles and sent the losers home. I mounted the stage again, beckoning to the survivors. "Come up front," I ordered. Briskly they obeyed; they knew they were on a streak. I reinforced that knowledge. "Let's talk about money," I said, and dead silence said they were listening intently. "The job of congressman pays as much as a junior copysmith. Even alderman pays not much less." There was a sound—not a gasp, but a sort of suspension of breathing as each one of them contemplated the kind of wage that would lift them right out of the consumer class in a single bound. "That's just *salary*. That's only the beginning. The gravy part is the retainers and the consultancies and the directorships—" I didn't have to say the bribes—"that go along with the position. They can be really big. How big? Well, I happen to know of two senators that sock away as much pay as an account executive." Thrill from the crowd, and this time the gasps were real. "I'm not going to ask you if you want that, because I don't think there are any crazy people in this room today. I'm going to tell you how to get it. Three things. Keep your noses clean. Work hard. Do what you're told. Then, if you're lucky—" I let the thought float in the air for a moment before grinning at them: "For now, go on home. Report at nine A.M. tomorrow for processing."

I glanced at my watch as they filed out. The whole thing had taken four hours and a bit, and Dixmeister was fawning all over me. "What a great day's work, chief! Sarms would have dawdled a week over this bunch. Now," he twinkled, "if I'm not being too forward, I know a place where they serve real meat and just about any kind of grain neutral spirits you can name. What would you say to a good old-fashioned three-martini—"

"Lunch," I finished for him, "will be a sandwich in my office and you're going to have the same in yours. Because I want this hall filled up again in ninety minutes!"

Well, it was, or just about, and we got seventy-one more candidate possibles. But when I ordered the same thing for the following morning, Central Casting could only send over about a hundred and fifty. We were eating up their pool faster than they could replenish it. And so I went out and roamed the streets, from one Mokie-Koke dispenser to the next, studying faces, walks, gestures. I eavesdropped on conversations. I started an argument, now and then, to see how the prospect would react. Then I went home or back to my office and watched the Omni-V news, looking for talent in a traffic victim or the weeping mother of someone who had just been mugged—someone who had just been doing the mugging, even, because I found one of my best New Jersey congressman candidate prospects in the police line-up after an attempted smash-and-grab. And I rode hard on Dixmeister to see that he kept the loose ends tied up. He made me up a tape of the Agency's present incumbents, and I cursored through the scenes to mark a good bit of business or a mannerism that they'd have to get rid of if they wanted us to run them again.

One gave me trouble. It was our President of the United States, a sweet-looking old man with turkey wattles strung from the point of his chin to his collarbone and the mummy of a face that three-quarters of the voters had grown up on. He'd played the daddy in the kiddyporn remake of *Father Knows Best*—you know, the one that's always stepping in the dog excrement or breaking wind when he bends down to pick up a dropped handkerchief. He'd been on the news interviewing the new High Chief Secretary of the Free-Market Republic of the Sudan. No more than a twenty-second clip, but the Sudanese managed to light two Verily cigarettes, drink a cup of Coffiest and spill half of it over his new Starrzelius suit while he coughed out, "Oh, yis, Mister Pres'nt, mony thoun thank-us for saving us!" I felt a warm rush of patriotism and love in the pit of my stomach as I thought of that little gook and all his people now blessed with a true mercantile society . . . but I felt something else, too. It wasn't the Sudanese. It was the President. He hadn't moved fast enough, and half the Coffiest had drenched his formal daywear short-suit . . . and I had the idea.

103

"Dixmeister!" I yelled, and in three seconds he was hanging in the doorway, waiting on orders. "The unicycle jerk. How's he doing?"

"Fell off five times this morning," said Dixmeister gloomily. "I don't know if he'll ever master it. If you want to go ahead with this—"

"Damn sure I do!"

He gulped. "No problem, Mr. Tarb, I've got that under control. We'll just take a couple of other unicyclists and matte his face in—"

"Ten minutes," I ordered, and it was even so. In nine minutes and thirty seconds he was back in my office to say that the clips were ready. "Display," I commanded, and proudly he keyed his selection of races.

They were all good, I had to admit. There were four of them. In each of them the winner was close enough to our jerk's appearance for a close simulation match, and in each of them the winner, grinning and gasping, came full-face into the camera so we could patch in our jerk's face delivering the commercial for his election. But one was better than the others, because it was just what I was looking for.

"Do you see it?" I asked. Of course he didn't. I shook my finger at him. "The crash," I said paternally. In one of the clips the fourth unicyclist at the finish had swerved desperately to miss colliding with the third. Yards short of the tape, he had come tumbling down in a splatter of arms and legs. The camera had zoomed in for a quick look at his face, sullen and humiliated, before whisking back to catch the winner.

And he still didn't see it. "We're going to run the wimp in the presidential primaries," I announced.

That took his breath away. "But he hasn't—He isn't—There's no way—"

"That's what we're going to do," I explained, "and there's something else. Notice the cyclist who fell down? Remind you of anybody?"

He zipped back, froze the image, stared. "No," he confessed.

104

"Not really, except—" He caught his breath. "The *President?*"
I nodded. "But—but he's *ours.* We don't want to defeat our own man—"

"What we don't want, Dixmeister," I snapped, "is to have our own man lose—whichever man it is. I said 'the primaries.' If the President wins out, fine, he gets another chance. But if this unicycle jerk can take him, why not? And we'll use this tape! Matte the President's face onto the one that falls down—just a flash—just enough to suggest him flopping at the finish line— then we go into the kid's commercial."

Dixmeister stared at me incredulously for a moment. Then it began to penetrate, and the expression melted into hero worship. "Subliminalwise," he glowed, "it's a masterpiece, Mr. Tarb."

Well, it was. Pedaling on both legs, I was.

And yet it didn't make me happy.

By Friday I was feeling very frayed. When Mitzi passed me in the hall she looked shocked. "You're losing weight, Tenny! Get more sleep. Eat more decent food—" But then Haseldyne tugged irritably at her elbow and she was gone into the downlift, peering worriedly up at me.

It was true that I was losing weight. I wasn't getting much sleep. I could feel that my temper was getting short, and even Nelson Rockwell didn't seem to want to talk to me much any more.

I should have been happy. The fact that I wasn't puzzled me very much, because never in my life had my prospects been so bright. Mitzi and Haseldyne were getting ready to make their move. I was proving every hour that I was the right stuff for them to take along in their takeover. I forced myself to daydream of the time when I'd be up there on the fifty-fifth floor, with a *window* in my *corner office,* and maybe a *stall shower* . . . and then, at last, they did it. They made their move. They made it that very Friday, at a quarter past four in the afternoon. I was out at a halfway house for recovering psychoneurotics, looking for an appellate court judge candidate, and when I got back to the Tower it was

105

in an uproar. Everybody was whispering to everybody else, and everybody's face was thunderstruck. On the way up I heard from the rungs below me the name "Mitzi Ku." As I got off I waited for the junior AE who'd been talking and smirked to her, "Mitzi's the new boss here, right?"

She didn't smile back, only looked at me strangely. "New boss, yes. Here, no," she said, and pushed past me.

Shaking, I finally made it to Val Dambois's office. "Val, baby," I begged, "what's happening? Was it the takeover?"

He frosted me with a look. "The hands," he said. "Get them off my desk. You're smudging the polish."

Yes, there had been a big change! "Please, Val, tell me!" I begged.

He said bitterly, "It was your girl friend Mitzi and that heavy-weight Haseldyne, all right, but it wasn't a takeover. Fooled everybody, though. It was the old Icahn maneuver."

"Icahn!" I gasped. He nodded.

"A textbook case, just like old Carl Icahn himself. Scared the Old Man into thinking it was a takeover bid—got the stockholders to buy them out at ten times what their stock was worth—took the money and bought another Agency!"

And I hadn't suspected a thing.

I reeled blindly toward the door, hardly aware of what I was doing, until from behind me Dambois said the magic words:

"One more thing. You're fired."

That turned me right around. I gasped. "You can't do that!" He sneered. "No, really! My ConsumAnon project—"

He shrugged. "In good hands. Mine as it happens."

"But— But—" Then I remembered, and brought it out as a drowning man might produce the only lifesaver in the ocean: "Tenure! I'm star class—I've got tenure—you can't fire me!"

He glared at me irritably, then pursed his lips. "Hmmm," he said, and sucked his teeth. He punched out my personnel code and studied the screen for a moment.

Then his expression cleared. "Why, Tarb," he said warmly, "you're a patriot! I had no idea you were in the Reserves. I can't fire you, no, but," he explained, "what I *can* do is furlough you to the services for a year or two—there's some kind of call-up going on—"

I got up, a hollow feeling in my stomach. "This is preposterous! I've still got tenure, you know. When this military call-up is over—"

He shrugged winsomely. "I always look on the bright side, Tarb," he told me. "After all, you may never come back."

Tarb's Downfall

·· ◆ ··

I

I knew I shouldn't have signed those Reserve papers in college, but who knew they'd take it seriously? When you're ten years old you join the Junior Copywriters. When you're fifteen it's the Little Merchandising League. In college it's the Reserves. Everybody does it. It's two course credits a semester, and you don't have to take English lit. All the smart students spotted it for a snap course.

But for somebody who'd got the bad breaks, somebody like me, it wasn't all that smart.

If I'd kept my wits about me I'd have seen a way to escape —maybe find Mitzi and grovel for a job—maybe find a friendly medic to help me fail the physical. Maybe suicide. What I actually did was closest to Option 3. I went on a Moke binge, lacing the stuff with Vodd-Quor, and woke up on a troop transport. I had no memory at all of reporting for duty, and not much of what turned out to be the forty-eight hours before that. Total blackout.

And total hangover. I didn't have time to appreciate the sordid miseries of traveling military style because I was too absorbed in the internal miseries of my own head. I was just beginning to be able to open the eyes without instant death when they dumped me, and five hundred others, at Camp Rubicam, North Dakota, for two weeks of the officers' refresher course. It consisted mostly of being told that we were doing society's most honorable work, plus close-order drill. Then it was pack your keyboard, sling your disk bag on your shoulder, all aboard for a field exercise.

Field exercise. I'd hate to get involved in the real thing.

The first troop transport had been plain hell. This one was nearly identical, except that it lasted many hours longer and I had to face it cold sober. No food. No toilets. No place to go outside the cocoon you were supposed to "rest" in. Nothing to drink but water—and the "water" was as close to purest ocean brine as you could get without actually breaking the law. The worst was we didn't know how long it was going to last. Some people thought it was all the way to Hyperion, to teach the gas miners a lesson. I might have thought so myself except that the transport had only wings and jets. No rockets. No space travel, therefore; so it had to be somewhere on Earth.

But where? The rumors that floated through the fetid air from bunk to bunk were Australia—no; Chile—no, positively; the watch officer had been heard to tell the flight engineer definitely Iceland.

We wound up in the Gobi Desert.

We piled out of the transport with our kits and our bursting bladders and lined up to be counted. The first thing we noticed was it was hot. The second thing was it was dry. I don't mean your average summer hot-spell dry, I mean *dry*. The wind blew fine white dust everywhere. It got between your fingers. If you kept your mouth closed it even got in between your teeth, and when you moved your jaw it crunched. They took an hour for the head count and then loaded us up into ten-trailer troop transports and dragged us along those dusty white roads to our billets.

The place is technically known as the Xinjiang Uygur Autonomous Region, but everybody called it the Reservation. It was where one of the last remaining batches of unconsolidated aboriginals lived, Uygurs and Hui and Kazak, the ones that never made the transition to the market society when the rest of China joined in. There's civilization all around them. There's RussCorp to the North, Indiastries South and all the China-Han complex at their gates. But the Eager Weegers just sit there and do their own thing. As we dragged along, coughing and choking, we'd see the men squatting in a circle in the middle of the side roads, never looking up at us. The squalor was shocking. Their mud houses were crumbling around them, with a stack of mud bricks in the backyard drying to be ready for building the next house when that one fell down. In the front there was a rusty old satellite dish that couldn't get a decent picture any more . . . and always there would be the kids, hundreds of them, laughing and waving to us—what did they have to be happy about? Not their housing, surely. Certainly not after we came along and requisitioned the best of it—what I guess had been a row of tourist motels (imagine anybody going there voluntarily?), with real air conditioners in the windows and a real fountain in the courtyard. Of course, the fountain was turned off. So, it turned out, were the air conditioners. So was all the power there was, so we ate (if you could call it eating—soy steaks and nondairy milkshakes!) by the light of *candles.* They promised the officers among us better quarters in the morning, after the commanders sorted us out, but for now, if we wouldn't mind—

Whether we minded or not made no difference, because there was nowhere for us to go but into the motel rooms. They might not have been so bad if the quartermaster had got mattresses onto the beds before we had to sleep on them. So we all spread out as much of our clothing as we could and tried to sleep, in the heat, in the dust, with everyone coughing around us and strange sounds coming from outside. The worst was a kind of mechanical honking noise—"Aaaah," and sometimes "Aaaah-*ee!*" I fell asleep wondering what sort of primitive machinery they kept going all night. Wondering what I was doing there. Wondering if I'd ever get back to the Tower, much less to the fifty-fifth floor. Wondering, most of all, what a guy's chances were of scoring a couple of Mokes around here in the morning, since the twelve-packs I'd put in my kitbag were just about running out.

"You Tarb?" grated a harsh voice in my ear. "Out of the sack!

110

Chow's in five minutes and the colonel wants to see you in ten."

I propped one eye open. "The what?"

The face leaning down to mine didn't retreat. "Up!" it roared, and as my eyes focused I perceived that it belonged to a dark, scowling man with major's stripes and a row of ribbons on his camouflage suit.

"Right you are," I mumbled, and managed to remember to add, "sir." The face didn't look pleased, but it went away. I edged myself to the side of the bed, trying to avoid the sharpest and rustiest of the springs—half my body was covered with punctures from where I had tossed and turned in the night—and attacked the problem of getting into my tee and culottes. That problem proved soluble, though I think I carried it out in my sleep. The problem of where "chow" was was no problem at all, because I only had to follow the slow migration of red-eyed, unshaved, blinking troops to what was marked Dining Hall A. At least there was Coffiest. Better than that, there were Mokes, though these were not government issue and I wasted precious moments wheedling change from the one or two slightly familiar faces doggedly attacking their Om'Lets and Bredd. Naturally the vending machine ate my first three coins without spitting out a Moke in return, but on the fourth try I got one—warm, to be sure—and faced the blinding outdoor sun a little more bravely.

Finding the colonel's office was a lot harder. None of the new replacements like myself seemed to have a clue. The wiser regulars were, it appeared, still happily asleep in their bunks, waiting out the press of new boys in the mess hall so that they could enjoy their breakfast in a more leisurely way later on. The couple of natives wandering around, bearing brooms or pails of gray, scummy water—though showing no signs of using either—were glad to give me directions; but as we had no language in common I had no notion of what they were directing me to. I found myself on the edge of the compound, passing through a gate, when a repellent odor filled my nostrils and, at the same moment, that raucous *Aaaah-ee!* blasted in my ear.

The mystery of the machine noises in the night was cleared

up. To my infinite disgust I discovered that the machines were no machines. These people had *animals.* Living animals! Not in a zoo or properly stuffed in some museum, but standing on the streets, pulling carts, even *defecating* right where people might walk. I had blundered into what was a kind of parking lot for the creatures. I tell you, for a minute there it was touch and go whether I would retain the hard-won Moke I had just swallowed.

By the time I finally found the colonel's office I was, of course, at least twenty minutes late, but I had learned some sobering facts about this new world I had been thrust into. The particular animals with the loud bray were called donkeys. A smaller, horned kind of donkey they called goat, but they also had chickens and horses and yaks. And each one smelled fouler, and had habits more disgusting, than the next. When at last I stumbled into the mud-brick structure marked 3d Bn Hq & Hq Cy I knew I was well on the way to earning my first reprimand, but I didn't care. It was air-conditioned, and the air conditioning actually worked, and when the first sergeant told me, scowling, that I would have to wait and the colonel would eat me out, I could have kissed him, for the air was cool, the sickening sounds from outside were muffled—and there was a Moke dispenser by the door.

The sergeant was a true prophet. The colonel's first words were, "You were late, Tarb! A bad beginning! I tell you true, you admen make me sick!"

In normal times that kind of talk would have had me up and fighting, but these were not normal times. I could read the colonel like a book: grizzled old campaigner, chest full of ribbons for the Sudan and Papua New Guinea and the Patagonian campaign. No doubt up from the ranks, with all the former consumer's hatred of the upper classes. I swallowed the words that rose to my lips, held the tightest brace at attention I could manage and said only, "Yes, ma'am."

She looked at me with the same sort of unbelieving dislike that, I am sure, I gave to the donkeys. She shook her head. "So what am I going to do with you, Tarb? You got any skills that don't show on your personnel record—cooking, plumbing, running an officers' club?"

I said indignantly, "Ma'am! I'm a copysmith, star class!"

"You were," she corrected. "Here you're just another casual officer that I've got to find a job for."

"But surely—my skills—my ability to create a promotional campaign—"

"Tarb," she said wearily, "all that stuff's done back in the Pentagon. We don't make strategy here in the field. We're just the dogfaces that carry it out." She flicked gloomily through the data stores—hesitated—went on—turned back and cursored one line in the Table of Organization.

"Chaplain," she said with satisfaction.

I goggled at her. "Chaplain? But I never—I mean, I don't know anything about—"

"You don't know anything about anything, Lieutenant Tarb," she said, "but chaplaining's easy work. You can get the hang of it in no time. You'll have an assistant who knows the ropes—and, as far as I can see, it's a place where you can't do much harm. Dismissed! And try to keep your nose clean till this campaign's over so you'll be somebody else's problem."

So I began my career as chaplain to the Third Battalion Headquarters and Headquarters Company—heavy limbic projectors and sky-screens—not the best duty in the world, but a long way better than going door-to-door with the infantry. The colonel had promised me an experienced chaplain's assistant, and I got one. Staff-Sergeant Gert Martels wore the ribbons of campaigns as far back as Kampuchea on her rather prominent chest.

She greeted me as I entered my domain for the first time with a sloppy salute but a fully accomplished smile. "Morning, Lieutenant," she sang out. "Welcome to the Third!"

I saw at once that S/Sgt Martels was going to be the best thing about my chaplaincy—well, the second best thing, anyway. The office itself was drab. It had been a laundry room in the motel, and you could still see the stains of bleach and soap powder outlining where the washing machines had been. Capped-off pipes were still present along the wall. But it was air-conditioned! It was located in that handsome motel with the fountains and shady arbors, only now the fountains were working—and we casuals had been moved out to "regular" housing, so that the space could become headquarters offices. I guess the air conditioning was the third best thing; the very best was a Moke vending machine, and the way it purred told me that the Mokes would be coming out ice-cold. "How did you know?" I demanded, and the handsome, scarred face lit up with another of those excellent smiles.

"It is," she said, "a chaplain's assistant's *business* to know such things. Now, if the lieutenant would care to sit at his desk I'll be glad to answer the lieutenant's questions. . . ."

It was better than that. I didn't even have to ask any questions, because S/Sgt Martels knew what the lieutenant needed to know better than the lieutenant did. This was the way to the officers' club. These were the blank passes I had the authority to sign. That on the wall was the intercom, used only by a friend in the colonel's office to warn us when the colonel was coming this way. And, in case the lieutenant didn't much care for the food in the mess hall, the lieutenant always had the privilege of declaring that he had been too busy with emergency duties during regular meal hours to get there, and so avail himself of between-meals "snacks" in the private dining room of the field-officers' mess. The lieutenant, she added innocently, had also the privilege of taking his assistant at such times if he cared to.

And why, I wondered starrily, had I been so reluctant to give up the Mad. Ave. rat race to come to this earthly paradise?

Well, paradise it was not. Nights were still hell. "Regular" housing turned out to be foam pop-ups, with slit trenches. The only "air conditioning" they had were tiny solar-battery fans, and the foam walls soaked up every calorie of the Gobi's blazing daytime sun to give back to us all night. There were also *bugs*. There was also the all-night braying of the animals in the stockades outside the walls. There were also the sleepless hours, miserably wondering what Mitzi was up to, who was taking over my job at Taunton, Gatchweiler and Schocken. There was also the fact that the desert heat was boiling the Mokes out of my body as fast as I could swallow them, and every day I got gaunter and shakier. On the second day Gert Martels looked at me in alarm. "The lieutenant," she said, "is working too hard." Palpable lie, of course; I had yet to see my first soldier coming in for solace or help. "I suggest the lieutenant write himself a pass and take the rest of the day off."

"Pass to where in this hellhole?" I snarled, and brought myself up short. Hadn't I had a conversation like this once before—on Venus—with Mitzi? "Well," I said, reconsidering, "I suppose that ten years from now I'll regret it if I don't see whatever sights there are. Only you come along."

So twenty minutes later we were sitting back-to-back on a sort of four-wheeled cart with an awning over our heads, clop-clopping along the white-dust road to the metropolis of Urumqi. Military trucks roared by, raising a six-foot wake of dust. What fun! Conversation was pretty nearly impossible, not only because we were facing away from each other but because we spent half our time coughing the dust out of our lungs until Gert produced some sort of white surgical masks to tie over our noses and mouths.

Fortunately Urumqi—they pronounced it "Oo-ROOM-chee," which tells you a lot about the Uygurs—wasn't far away. It also wasn't much when you got there. The main street had real trees, a double row of them, but there was nothing but bare yellow dirt under the trees. No grass. No flowers. What there was was about a dozen Uygurs with gauze masks of their own, sweeping leaves off the bare ground. You'd think there was already enough dust in the air for any normal person, but, no, there the Weegs were, sweeping great clouds up in case we might run out. "I wish I had a Moke," I gritted out, and Gert twisted around to say:

"Hang on, Lieutenant—"

"My name's Tenny."

"Hang on, Tenny, we're almost there. See it down the block? Divisional R&R, and they've got all the Mokes you want."

And so they did; and not only that, they had a bar, and an all-ranks coffee shop where you could get brand-name food, and an officers' lounge with satellite Omni-V. And flush toilets! And

—I'll give you an idea of what heavenly luxury this was after my forty-eight hours in the field—it wasn't until after I'd noticed all those things that I noticed that the whole building was air-conditioned. "How many passes can I give myself?" I demanded.

"All you want," said Gert gratifyingly, and we headed first for the coffee shop. When I said it was my treat she looked amused but didn't argue, and we washed down Turr-Kee salad sandwiches on real Bredd with half a dozen Mokes and sat comfortably at our windowside table, gazing disdainfully at the Weegs outside. "There's worse duty than this, Tenny," Gert announced, ordering another Coffiest.

I reached over and touched her ribbons. She didn't draw back. "I guess you've seen some, right?" I offered.

Her expression clouded. "I guess Papua New Guinea was about the worst," she said, as though the memory pained her.

I nodded. Everybody knew about Papua New Guinea, and the way hundreds of natives had died in the riots when the Coffiest and Reel-Meet ran out.

"It's good work, Gert," I said consolingly. "There aren't many abo reservations left. Cleaning up the holdouts has to be done— a dirty job, but somebody has to do it." She didn't answer, just took a sip of her Coffiest without meeting my eyes. I said, "I know what I've done isn't in the same league as you veterans. Still, I spent three years on Venus, you know."

"Vice-consul and morale officer," she nodded. She knew.

"Well, then you know that the Veenies aren't really much better than these Weegs. Salesless, bigoted, antiprogress—why, take away a little superficial technology and they'd fit right in on this reservation!" I waved my hand at the street outside. A bunch of enlisted personnel were loafing around the hotel steps, trying to tempt the Uygurs with Mokes and pocket viewers and Nic-o-Chews, but the tribesmen just smiled and shook their heads and moved on. "I doubt most of these aboriginals even know that civilization exists. They haven't changed for a thousand years."

She gazed out at the street, her expression hard to read. "More than that, Tenny. We're not the first invaders they've seen.

116

They've had the Manchus and the Mongols and the Hans and outlived them all."

I coughed—it wasn't dust in my throat. "*Invaders* isn't exactly the word I would have chosen, Gert. We're *civilizers,* you know. What we're doing here is an important mission."

"Important is right," she snapped, and there was an edge to her voice that caught me unaware. "The last one before the big push, eh? Did you ever think that there's a logical progression here, New Guinea, the Sudan, the Gobi? And then—" Suddenly she faltered and looked around the room, as though wondering who might have heard.

That I could understand, for she was saying things that would cost her if the wrong people were listening. I was sure she didn't mean them. Not deep down inside, that is. The combat troops at the spearhead of civilization couldn't be blamed if, now and then, strange ideas crossed their minds. Back in civilization that kind of talk could get you in a lot of trouble. Here—"Here," I said kindly, "you're under a strain, Gert. Have another Coffiest, it'll soothe you."

She looked at me in silence for a moment, then laughed. "All right, Tenny," she said, beckoning to the Weeg waitress. "You know what? You're going to make a *great* chaplain."

It took me a moment to respond to that—somehow it hadn't sounded like a compliment. "Thank you," I said at last.

"And in order to make you one," she said, "I guess I'd better fill you in on your duties. Now, you're going to get two kinds of people coming to you for help. The first kind will be the ones that are worried about something—they've received a Dear Jane letter or they think their mother's sick or they're convinced they're going crazy. The way you handle them is to tell them not to worry and give them a twenty-four-hour pass. The second kind will be the foul-ups. They're missing formations or oversleeping roll call or failing inspection. What you do with them is send a chit to the first sergeant cutting off their passes for a week, and you tell them they better *start* worrying. Now, sometimes there'll be somebody with a real problem, and what you do—"

So I listened, and I nodded, and, actually, I was quite enjoying myself. I didn't then know that there were two of those people with real problems in my company.

Or that both of them were sitting at my table.

Chaplaincy wasn't arduous. It left me plenty of time for long, late lunches in the field officers' mess and evening passes to Urumqi. It also left me time to wonder, rather frequently at first, just what I was doing there, because the operation that we'd all been hustled from hemisphere to hemisphere to perform didn't seem to be happening . . . whatever it was that was supposed to happen. When I asked Gert Martels, she shrugged and said it was just the good old tradition of hurry up and wait, so I stopped worrying about it. I took what each day offered. The old Urumqi hotel that had been commandeered for divisional R&R became as familiar to me as my official pop-up sleeping tent—in fact, the hotel was where I spent nights when I could, not only because of the air conditioning but because each of the tatty old guest rooms had its own flush toilet and tub and shower. Often all three of them worked. And in the officers' lounge there was the Omni-V.

That wasn't all joy. For one thing, what I really wanted was news. In order to get it I had to fight off the civilization-starved officers, most of them with more rank than I had, who were desperate for sports, variety shows, sitcoms and commercials— mostly commercials. The kind of news I wanted wasn't the usual thing—the goggling, blinking, grinning couple who'd won "Consumer of the Month" in Detroit, or the President's speeches, or the story of six pedicabs destroyed, with loss of eleven lives, when the spire fell off the old Chrysler Building and flattened half a block of Forty-second Street. I mean the *real* news, the "World of Advertising" report and the daily lineage and spot-time charts. That news came on at six o'clock in the morning, because of the fact that we were halfway around the world, and so I had no hope of seeing it unless I pressed my luck and took yet one more night in the divisional R&R—and, of course, managed to wake myself up in time to get down to the lounge. That wasn't easy. Every

118

morning waking up got harder and harder. The only thing that could get me out of bed, finally, was to not have any Mokes in the room, so as soon as my eyes opened I had to get up and out to find one.

And then what I saw wasn't all joy. There was a whole ten-minute spot, one morning, given to my ConsumAnon plan. It had been launched with a sixteen-megabuck promotion budget. It was a great success. But it wasn't mine.

For that I was prepared. What I wasn't prepared for was the commentator, with that sickly, covetous smile people get when somebody's pulled off a coup, finishing up by giving credit to that dynamic new agency that came from nowhere to challenge the giants . . . Haseldyne and Ku.

The captain who came into the lounge just then, swinging his weights and all ready for his morning setting-up exercises, didn't know how lucky he was. I let him live. If I hadn't startled him so with my blast of rage when he tried to change the channel he would surely have had me in for conduct unbecoming an officer, but I don't think he'd ever seen so much violence on a face. I clung to that channel selector. I didn't even look around when he slunk away, his weights hanging straight at his side. I was spinning that dial, hunting for news, starving for crumbs of information. With two hundred and fifty channels coming down from the satellites it was like looking for the winning boxtop in a trash can. I didn't care about the odds. Flick, and I was getting a Korean weather report; flick, a commercial jockey; flick, a kiddyporn audience-participation show; flick—I flicked on. I caught the tail end of the BBC's late-night wrap-up and RussCorp's early morning newscast from Vladivostok. I didn't get the whole story. I was not sure all the pieces fit together. But Haseldyne and Ku was news worldwide, and the outline was clear. Dambois hadn't told me all the truth. Mitzi and Desmond Haseldyne had taken their profits and started their own agency, right enough. But they hadn't taken just money. They'd taken the whole Intangibles department from T., G. & S. with them—raided the staff—pirated the accounts—

Stolen my idea.

The next time I knew what I was doing I was halfway back to headquarters along that mean, hot, dusty road, and I was walking.

I have never felt such fury. It was the next thing to madness —close enough, really, because what other than insanity would have gotten me walking through that inferno, where even the Weegs let their donkeys or yaks carry them from place to place? I was thirsty, too. I'd been hitting the Mokes hard—not just plain Mokie-Kokes, but spiking them with anything alcoholic the officers' lounge could supply. But it had all boiled out of me along the way, and the residue that was left was concentrated, crystalline rage.

How could I get back to civilization?—get back and get justice; get what I was owed from Mitzi Ku! There had to be a way. I was a chaplain. Could I give myself compassionate leave? If I couldn't do that, could I fake a nervous breakdown or get some friendly medic to supply me with heart-palpitation pills? If I couldn't do any of those, what were the chances of stowing away on the return flight of the next cargo plane that landed? If I couldn't do that—

And, of course, I couldn't do any of them. I'd seen what happened to the whimpering feebs who'd come into my office, with their cock-and-bull stories of errant wives or intolerable lower-back pain; there were no compassionate leaves given out from the Reservation, and no chance of stowing away.

I was stuck.

I was also beginning to feel really bad. Heavy drinking and sleepless nights hadn't done a thing to help my Moke-raddled body. The sun was merciless, and every time a vehicle went by I thought I'd cough my lungs out. There were plenty of vehicles, too, because the word was that our operation was going to come off at last. Any time now. The heavy attack pieces were in place. The troops had been given their designated assault targets. The support logistics were operational.

I stopped dead in the middle of the road, swaying dizzily as I tried to collect my thoughts. There was a meaning there, a hope

. . . of course! Once the operation was complete we'd all be rotated back to civilization! I'd still be in the service, sure, but in some stateside camp where I could easily wangle a forty-eight-hour pass, long enough to get back to New York to confront Mitzi and her nasty sidekick—

"Tenny!" cried a voice. "Oh, Tenny, thank heaven I found you—and, boy, are you in trouble!"

I squinted through the blinding dust and glare. A two-wheel Uygur "taxi" was pulling up alongside me, and Gert Martels was hopping off, the lean, scarred face worried. "The colonel's on the warpath! We have to get you cleaned up before she finds you!"

I staggered toward the sound of her voice. "Hell with the colonel," I croaked.

"Aw, please, Tenny," she begged. "Get on the taxi. Scrunch down so if any MPs come by they won't see you."

"Let them see me!" The funny thing about S/Sgt Martels was that she kept *blurring*. Part of the time she was a foggy figure of black smoke, opaque against the blinding sky. Part of the time she was in sharp focus, and I could even read the expression on her face—worry; revulsion; then, curiously, relief.

"You've got *heatstroke!*" she cried. "Thank heaven! The colonel can't argue with *heatstroke!* Driver! You savvy Army hospital, yes? You go there quick-quick, yes?" And I found myself being dragged aboard the cart by Gert Martels's strong arms.

"Who wants a hospital?" I demanded belligerently. "I don't need any damn hospital! All I need is a Moke—" I didn't get it, though. I didn't get anything. If I had I wouldn't have been able to do anything with it, because just then the sky darkened and wrapped itself around me in a black-wool cocoon, and I was out of it for the next ten hours.

II

They were not idle hours. The prescription for heatstroke was: rehydrate; keep cool; bed rest. Fortunately, it was the same prescription for acute hangover. I got what the doctor ordered. True, I didn't know it at the time, because I was unconscious at first, drugged asleep after that. I had hazy memories of the needles with saline and glucose going into my arm now and then, and of being coaxed awake to swallow immense doses of liquid. And of dreams. Oh, yes, dreams. Bad dreams. Dreams of Mitzi and Des Haseldyne pigging it in their deluxe penthouses and laughing themselves silly when they thought of poor, dumb old Tennison Tarb.

And when I did wake up at last I thought it was still a dream, because the first sergeant was bending over me, a finger to his lips. "Lieutenant Tarb? Can you hear me? Don't make any noise—just nod your head if you can—"

The mistake I made was in doing what he said. I nodded. The top of my head shook loose and rattled on the floor, exploding with pain at every bounce.

"I guess you've got a pretty bad hangover, right? Too bad . . . but listen, there's a problem."

The fact that there was a problem was not news to me. The only question was, which problem did he mean? Surprise; it wasn't any of the ones I was aware of. It was something brand new, and not so much my problem as Gert Martels's. One eye cocked for the floor nurse, whispering with his lips so close to my ear that his breath tickled my ear-hairs, he explained, "Gert's got this one bad habit, I guess you know—"

"What habit's that?" I asked.

"You don't know?" He looked surprised, then actually embarrassed. "Well," he said reluctantly, "I know it sounds real lousy, but a lot of the guys, you know, out in the field, exposed to all sorts of influences—"

Against all wisdom and desire, I pushed myself up. "Sergeant," I said, "I don't have clue one to what you're talking about. Spell it out for me."

He said, "She's off with the Weegs, Lieutenant. And she hasn't got her protective equipment. And it's T minus two hours and counting."

That got me. "You mean the operation's on tonight?" I yelled.

He winced. "Please, keep your voice down. But yes. It goes at midnight, and it's ten o'clock right now."

I stared at him. "Tonight?" I repeated. Where had I been? How had I missed the warning? Of course, it was technically secret information, but surely every trooper in the camp must have known hours before.

The first sergeant nodded. "They moved it up because the weather's perfect." Now that I knew what to look for I could see the polarized fabric hood slung over his shoulders and the huge sound-deadening earmuffs hanging down below his chin. "The thing is—"

Sound at the end of the ward. A door opening. A light.

"Oh, hell," he snapped. "Listen, I've got things to do. Go get her, will you, Lieutenant? There's a Weeg waiting for you downstairs, with protective gear for both of you—he'll take you to her —he—" Footsteps coming nearer. "Sorry, Lieutenant," he panted. "I've got to go."

And went.

So, as soon as the nurse had made her rounds and gone, I slipped out of bed, slid into my clothes, sneaked out of the ward. My head was hammering and I knew that the last thing I needed was to get an AWOL-from-hospital mark on my record to add to all the other black marks. The funny thing was, I didn't hesitate for a minute.

I didn't even hesitate long enough to realize that it was strange. Only later did it occur to me that there had been plenty of times in the past when someone or other had put his tail in a crack to save me from something. Never before had I had any trouble forgetting that when a chance came to pay the favor back.

123

All that was in my mind was that I owed Gert, and she needed me to bail her out. So I went . . . pausing only once, at the hospital door, to score a couple of Mokes from the vending machine. And I actually think that if the machine hadn't been right there and available, I might well have gone even without them.

The Weeg was waiting as advertised, not only with complete gear for two but even with a donkey and a two-wheel cart. The only thing missing was his knowledge of English. But, as he seemed to know where to go without any instructions from me, that didn't appear to be a problem.

It was a hot, dark night, so dark that it was almost scary. You could see the sky! I don't just mean a daytime sky, or even the night sky when the lights from below give it that dull reddish kind of glow, I mean *stars*. Everybody's heard of stars, but how many people have actually seen one? And here were *millions* of them, spanning the sky, bright enough to see by—

Bright enough, anyway, for the donkey to see by, because it didn't seem to have any trouble finding its way. We were off the main roads, heading for the nearby hills. Between us and the hills was a valley. I'd heard of it; it was kind of a curiosity in those parts, because it was fertile. What makes the Gobi a gobi—that is, a gravelly desert—is dryness and wind. Dryness turns the soil into dust. Wind blows the dust away, until all that's left is endless square miles of stony desert. Except that now and then in a few isolated places—a valley, the sheltered side of a hill—there's a little water, and those places trap the soil. Other officers had told me that this one was almost like an Italian vineyard, with trellised grapes and even murmuring streams. I hadn't thought it worth the trouble of visiting. I hadn't planned to visit it now, especially at night, especially when all hell was supposed to break loose in —I sneaked a look at my watch, brilliant in the dark night—about an hour and five minutes. And actually we didn't visit it this time. The Weeg took a path around the vineyard, stopped the cart, motioned me to get out and pointed up a hill.

In the starlight I could vaguely see a structure of some sort,

124

shedlike, all by itself. "You mean I should go up there?" I asked. The Weeg shrugged and pointed again. "Is Sergeant Martels in that shack?" Another shrug. "Hell," I said, turned around and, sighing, started up the hill.

The starlight was not quite enough to see by after all. I stumbled and fell a dozen times trying to climb that feeble excuse for a path—that damn, dirty, dusty path, so dry that when I slipped I was likely as not to slide a yard or two backward. I gashed myself at least twice. The second time as I clambered back to my feet something beyond the hills coughed *whump*, and a moment later *whump . . . whump . . . whump* came from all around the horizon, and in a score of places the stars were stained by slow, spreading clouds of darkness. I didn't have to be told what they were: sky screens. The operation was about to begin.

I smelled the shed yards before I reached it. It was used for drying grapes into raisins, and it was heavy with a winy stink. But over and above that sickening fruit stench there was something stronger—not just stronger. Almost frightening. It was a little like food—ReelMeet, maybe, or TurrKee—but there was something wrong with the smell. Not spoilage. Worse than spoilage. My stomach had been reminding me for some time that I'd given it a hard life recently; the smell almost pushed it into revolt. I swallowed and groped my way into the shed.

Inside there was a sort of light. They had built a fire—to see by while they ate stolen rations, I assumed. Wrong assumption. As wrong as the other assumption, which was that Sergeant Martels's "one bad habit" was something like shacking up with the natives, or maybe getting drunk on home-brewed popskull. How naive I had been! There were half a dozen troopers gathered around the fire in the shed, and what they were doing with the fire was desiccating an *animal* over it. Worse than that, they were *eating* the dead animal. Gert Martels stared up at me open-mouthed, and in her hand was a part of its limb. She was holding it by its skeleton—

That finished my stomach. I had to blunder outside.

I barely made it. When I had finished heaving everything I'd

125

swallowed for twenty-hour hours I took a deep breath and went back inside. They were scared now, looking at me with pale, fearful faces in the firelight.

"You're worse than gooks," I told them, my voice shaking. "You're worse than *Veenies*. Sergeant Martels! Put this on. The rest of you, get your heads down, put your fingers in your ears, don't open your eyes for the next hour. The operation's in ten minutes!"

I didn't wait to hear their anguished complaints, or even to see if Gert Martels was doing as I had ordered. I got out of that hellhole as fast as I could, slipping and skidding a dozen yards down the path before I paused long enough to put the earmuffs in place and the hood over all. Of course, then I could hear nothing at all, least of all Gert Martels coming up beside me. Conversation was impossible. That was just as well. There was nothing I wanted to say to her just then. Or hear. We picked our way down the hill to where the Weeg was waiting with his donkey, squeezed into the cart pointed back toward the encampment. The Weeg picked up the reins—

Then it began.

The first step was fireworks—plain, simple old pyrotechnics. Starbursts. Golden rain. Showers of diamond-bright waterfalls. They weren't quite bright enough to actuate the quick-response dimmers in our hoods, but they were bright enough to be startling —our Weeg driver almost dropped the reins, gazing pop-eyed at the sky—and all of it punctuated with bombs bursting in air, muffled and dim through our cutouts, but the sound rolling off the hills. The landscape was bright with the aerial bursts; and that was only the come-on. That was to wake the Weegs up and get them out in the open.

Then the Campbellian brigades went into action.

There weren't many blasts of sound now, but the ones there were sounded like a sonic boom happening between your shoulder and your ear. Incredibly loud. Even through the earmuffs, *painfully* loud—if we hadn't had the big cutouts half the troops would

126

have experienced hearing loss. For the Weegers, I suppose there was. I found out later that in those booms two glaciers on the distant mountains had calved, and an avalanche of loosened snow had caught the population of one Uygur village staring at the sky. But the noise was only half of it. The other half was *light.* It strobed in your eye—even through the quick-response hoods. Even through closed lids. There was never a show like it. Even protected, it shocked the senses numb.

And then, of course, the speaker balloons bellowed their commands and our projector battalion filled its vapor screens with the vivid, luscious, compelling images of steaming mugs of Coffiest and Cari-O candy bars and Nic-O-Chews and Starrzelius Verily pants suits and athletic supporters—and sizzling, juicy cubes of Reel-Meet with slices curling off them, so rich and rare that you could almost taste them—could in fact smell them because the Chemical Reinforcement Team from the 9th Battalion had not been idle, and their generators poured out whiffs of Coffiest and aromas of Reel-Meet Burgers and, worst of all for me, the occasional chocolaty tang of a Moke—and always and above all the deafening sounds, the blinding strobe lights. . . . "Don't look!" I shouted in Sergeant Martels's ear. But how could she help it? Even protected from the limbic stimuli by earpieces and hoods, the images themselves were so appetizing, so heart's-desire demanding, that my mouth watered and my hands reached as by themselves into my pockets for credit cards. Most of the basic compulsion of the campaign passed us by, of course. We were spared the Campbellian reinforcers. The verbal messages that boomed from hill to hill were in the Uygur dialect, which we did not understand. But our driver sat rapt, head thrown back, reins loose in his lap, eyes shining, and on his face a look of such unutterable longing that my heart melted. I reached in my pocket and found half a Cari-O bar; and when I gave it to him he responded with such a profusion of gratitude that, without understanding a word, I knew that I had earned his lifelong devotion. Poor Weegs! They didn't have a chance.

Or, to put it more properly, I corrected myself primly, at last they had entered the rich and rewarding comity of mercantile society. Where the Mongols and the Manchus and Hans had failed, modern cultural imperatives had triumphed.

My heart was full. All the worries and tragedies of the last few days were forgotten. I reached out for Gert Martels as we sat in that unmoving cart, with the last of the sky display fading and the echoes of the acoustics fading away, and put my arm around her shoulders.

To my astonishment, she was crying.

By eleven the next morning the trading posts were stripped bare. There were Kazaks and Uygurs and Hui begging at their empty shelves for the chance to buy Popsies and Kelpy Krisps. The entire operation was a flawless triumph. It meant a unit citation for everyone involved, and an Account-Exec citation for some.

It meant—it might even mean—a chance at a fresh start for me.

III

But, it turned out, it wasn't going to mean that right away. I got Gert, red-eyed and still mysteriously sniffling, back to her NCO quarters and sneaked back into the hospital with no trouble—half the patients, and nearly all the orderlies and medical staff, were still outside with their hoods thrown back over their shoulders, chattering excitedly about the attack. I mingled for a moment, worked my way through the crowd, found my bed and was asleep again; it had been a hard day.

The next morning replayed my first day, as the major came poking through the ward with the medics in tow to tell me that I was discharged from the ward and due at headquarters in twenty minutes. The only good thing was that the colonel wasn't there; she'd ordered herself to the fleshpots of Shanghai as soon as the exercise was over to report to General HQ. "But that doesn't let you off the hook, Tarb," lectured the lieutenant colonel who was

128

second in command. "Your conduct is *shocking*. You'd be a disgrace to the uniform even as a consumer, but you're an adman. Watch your step, because I'll be watching you!"

"Yessir." I tried to keep my face impassive, but I guess I didn't succeed because he snarled: "Think you're going home, do you, so you won't have to worry about this sort of thing any more?"

Well, that was exactly what I'd been thinking. The word was that troop redeployment would start that very day.

"No way," he said positively. "Chaplains are part of Personnel. Personnel get the job of getting everybody else out before they can go home. You're not going anywhere, Tarb . . . except maybe to the stockade if you don't straighten out!"

So I crept back to my office and my shamefaced S/Sgt Gert Martels. "Tenny," she began in embarrassment.

I snapped, "Lieutenant Tarb, Sergeant!"

Her face flushed dark red and she came to a hard brace. "Yes, *sir*. I only want to offer to apologize to the lieutenant for my, uh, my—"

"Your revolting behavior, you mean," I lectured. "Sergeant, your conduct is *shocking*. You'd be a disgrace to the uniform even as—ah—as a private, but you're a noncommissioned officer. . . ." I stopped, because there was an echo in the room. Or in my head. I stared at her in silence for a moment, then collapsed heavily into my chair. "Aw, hell, Gert," I said. "Forget it. We're two of a kind."

The flush drained out of her face. She stood there uncertainly, shifting from foot to foot. Finally she said in a low voice, "I can explain about that business on the hill, Tenny—"

"No, you can't. I don't need to hear it. Just get me a Moke."

Lieutenant Colonel Headley may have meant to keep an eye on me, but he only had two eyes. Redeployment took both of them. All the heavy limbic equipment was packed up and loaded onto transports and the assault troops marched into the bays after it and were gone. The returning transports weren't empty, though. They were full of Services of Supply troops and, most of all,

129

merchandise. And the merchandise melted like the snow. Every morning you'd see the Weegs lined up at the trading posts waiting for them to open, and staggering away to their yurts with their arms full of candy bars and food snacks and Thomas Jefferson Pure Simulated Silver amulets for the wives and kiddies. The operation had been a total triumph. You never saw such a dedicated bunch of consumers as the Eager Weegers, and I would have taken pride in my participation in the great crusade if my spirit had any pride left in it. But that commodity the Services of Supply could not provide.

If I had had anything to do it might have been easier. The chaplain's office was the quietest place on the Reservation. The old troops had nothing to come and complain about because they were on their way home anyway; the Supply forces were too busy. Gert Martels and I, without ever spelling it out, worked out an ad hoc division of labor. Each morning I would sit alone in the empty office, guzzling Mokes and wishing I were—anything—anything but what and where I was. Even dead. And in the afternoon she would take over and I would be off to the officers' lounge in Urumqi, squabbling over what channels to watch on the Omni-V and waiting fruitless hours in my endless attempts to get a call through to Mitzi, or Haseldyne, or the Old Man . . . or God. I even dared the lieutenant colonel's office a couple of times, trying to get myself turned loose. The time to go home a hero is before everybody forgets what you were being heroic about, and already the Gobi operation was disappearing from the Omni-V newscasts. No luck. And it kept on being *hot*. No matter how many Mokes I swilled I seemed to sweat them out faster than I could pour them down. I didn't weigh myself any more, because the numbers that were coming up were beginning to be scary.

Fridays were the worst, because we didn't even try to keep the chaplain's office open. I fought my way up to Urumqi through the masses of Weegs in their wagons and carts and bicycles, all with the consumer light glowing in their eyes as they headed for the bazaars of the big city, reserved a room, stocked up on Mokes, headed for the officers' lounge and my unending squabbles about Omni-V and phone calls—

130

But Gert Martels was waiting for me outside the lounge. "Tenny," she said, glancing around to make sure no one was near enough to listen, "you look like hell. You need a weekend in Shanghai. So do I."

"Out of my pass authority," I said gloomily. "Go try with Lieutenant Colonel Headley if you want to. He might let you go, maybe. Not me. I'm sure." I stopped, because she held up two pass cards before my eyes. Over the magnetic striping was Headley's signature.

"There's no use," she said, "in being friends with the first sergeant if he can't slip a couple of passes into the colonel's signature box when he wants to. The plane leaves in forty minutes, Tenny. Want to be on it?"

Shanghai! Jewel of the Orient! By ten o'clock that night we were in a floating bar along the Bund. I was getting down the tenth, or maybe it was the twentieth, well-spiked Moke, checking out the dark-haired little bar girls with their flapper haircuts, wondering if I ought to try connecting with one before I got too paralyzed to do anything about it. Gert was drinking straight GNS, and with every shot getting more and more upright and careful in her speech, and glassy-eyed. That was a funny thing about Gert Martels. She was not a bad-looking woman, not counting the scars that slashed down the left side of her face, from ear to jawbone. But I had never come on to her, nor she to me. A lot of it had to do, I guess, with the military code and the trouble you could get into fraternizing between officers and enlisted personnel, but lots of other Os and EPs had taken their chances and gotten away with it. And it had been a long, long time since Mitzi. "How come?" I asked, waving to the waitress.

She hiccoughed in a ladylike fashion and turned her eyes on me. It took a second or two; she seemed to be having trouble focusing. "How come exactly what, Tennison?" she asked with careful articulation.

I would have answered her question except that the waitress came by and I had to order another Moke-and-Djinn and a grain neutral spirits for the lady. It took a moment for me to remember.

"Oh, yeah," I said, "what I wanted to ask was how come you and I never made it."

She gave me a dignified smile. "If you want to, Tennison."

I shook my head. "No, I don't mean if I want to, I mean how come we've never, you know, sort of, like, *emanated* to each other." She didn't answer right away. The drinks came, and when I finished paying the waitress and handed the GNS to Gert I saw that she was crying.

"Aw, listen," I said, "I wasn't pulling rank or anything. Was I?" I demanded, looking around the table for confirmation. I didn't remember exactly how it had happened, but there seemed to be four or five other people who had joined us. They all smiled and shook their heads—meaning maybe no I wasn't and maybe no, we don't understand English. But one of them did, anyway. The civilian. He leaned across and shouted over the noise of the bar:

"You let me buy next lound, okay?"

"Why not?" I gave him a thank-you smile and turned back to Gert. "Excuse me, but what did you say?" I asked.

She reflected over that for a moment, and the civilian leaned back to me:

"You guys from Ooloomoochee, light?" It took me a moment to realize he was trying to say Urumqi, but then I admitted he was right. "Can always tell! You guys tops. I buy two lounds!" And the sailors from the Whangpoo River Patrol all grinned and applauded; that much English they knew too.

"I guess," said Gert reflectively, "I was going to tell you the story of my life." She accepted the next drink, nodded courteously and knocked it back between sentences without missing a beat. "When I was a little girl," she said, "we had a happy family. What Mom could do with Soya-tem and CelloWheet and a couple pinches of MSG! And then on Christmas we'd have Turr-Kee—real reconstituted meat, and cranberry-flavored Jellatine Dessert and all."

"Chlistmas!" cried the civilian in delight. "Oh, you guys *tops* with you Chlistmas!"

She gave the man a polite but distant smile and reached out for the next drink. "When I was fifteen Daddy died. They said it was bronchio-something. He coughed himself to death." She paused to swallow, and that gave the plump old civilian a chance.

"You know I went to missionary school?" he demanded. "Had Chlistmas there, too. Oh, we owe you missionary guys big debt!"

It was not easy for me to follow one life story, much less two. The bar had gotten a great deal noisier and more crowded and, although the old excursion steamer was moored tightly to the Bund pilings, I could have sworn it was swaying in the waves. "Go on," I said in general.

Gert was faster on the uptake. "Did you know, Tenny," she asked, "that once factories had smoke-scrubbers in their stacks? They scrubbed out the sulfur and fly ash. The air was clean, and the average life expectancy was eight years longer than it is today."

"Here, too!" cried the civilian. "When I young boy in missionary school—"

But she rode right over him. "Do you know why they stopped? Death. They wanted more death. There's big money in death. Partly it's the insurance-company accounts—the actuaries figured out it cost less to pay off life policies than annuities. Then there's all the dollar volume from hospitalization insurance, and a fifty-year-old who's lived all his life in smog knows he's going to spend a lot of time sick, so he has to buy—then, if he dies quickly, it's nearly all profit. Of course, there's the morticians, too. You wouldn't *believe* the profits in burying the dead. But mostly—" she looked around the table, smiling gently—"mostly, well, hell. When a consumer gets to be past working age how much money does he have to buy things? Damn little. So who needs him?"

I said nervously, "Gert, honey, maybe we ought to get some fresh air." The old civilian was grinning and bobbing his head; he'd had enough to drink himself that he didn't care what anybody said. But one of the Whangpoo sailors was frowning as though he understood a little English after all. It didn't seem to faze Gert.

"If there was any fresh air," she explained, "probably Daddy wouldn't have died that way, would he?" She extended her empty glass with a sweet, little-girl smile. "Could I have just a little more, please?" she asked.

God bless the old civilian. He had the waitress there with another round in a minute, and the Whangpoo sailor's face relaxed as he got his refill.

I was a long way from sober, but not so far that I didn't realize Gert was in worse shape than I was. I made an effort to change the subject. "So you like the missionaries, eh?" I offered genially to our benefactor.

"Oh, damn good guys, yes! Owe them plenty."

"For bringing Christianity to China, you mean?"

He looked puzzled. "What Chlistianity? For *Chlistmas*. You know what Chlistmas mean? I tell you! My business—wholesale dless goods, all kinds—Chlistmas sales mean fi'ty-four percent annual letail volume, almost fi'ty-eight percent of net. *That* what Chlistmas mean! Buddha, Mao, they never give us anything like that!"

Unfortunately he had set Gert off again. "Christmas," she said dreamily, "wasn't the same after Daddy died. Fortunately he had an old gun. So I'd go out in the garbage dumps—we were living in Baltimore at the time, down by the harbor—and I'd shoot seagulls and sneak them home. Of course, they weren't like TurrKee, but Mom—"

I almost spilled my drink. "Gert," I cried, "I think we'd better go now!" But I was too late.

"—Mom would cook up those seagulls so you'd think they were ReelMeet and we'd just eat ourselves sick, and—"

She never finished. The Whangpoo sailor leaped to his feet, his face working in rage and disgust. I didn't understand the words he said, but the meaning was clear enough. *Animal eater.* And that was when it all hit the fan.

I don't remember the fight very clearly, only the MPs pouring in along about the second time I pulled myself out from under the table. Adrenalin and panic had boiled a lot of the booze out of me, but I thought I was still drunk, hallucinatory drunk, DTs drunk, when I saw who was leading them. "Why, Colonel Heckscher!" I murmured. "Fancy seeing you here."

And that was when I passed out.

Well, it was one way of getting home. Almost home. Arizona, anyway. That was where Colonel Heckscher was going and, as we were still nominally members of her command, she had no difficulty getting us transferred along with her for the court-martial.

So I went from one dusty desert to another. It seemed like half the assault troops from Urumqi had gotten there before me. From my lonely room in the BOQ—Gert was in the stockade but, being an officer, I was just under house arrest—I could see their pop-ups in neat rows stretching to the horizon, and at the very edge of the camp a line of space shuttles. I didn't spend much time looking at them. I spent most of my time with the law officer the court had assigned me for defense. Defense! She was no more than twenty, and her principal credential was that she'd served in the Copyright & Trade Mark Division of a minor Houston agency while waiting to be accepted to law school.

But I had a powerful friend. The Chinese civilian didn't forget his old drinking buddies. He wouldn't testify against us, and it appeared he'd paid off the whole Whangpoo fleet, because when they were called on the person-to-person video for depositions they one and all testified that they didn't speak English, didn't know what if anything Gert or I had said, wasn't even sure we were the Westerners who'd been in the bar that night. So all they could get me for was conduct unbecoming an officer and that meant no more than a dishonorable discharge.

It meant no less, either. Colonel Heckscher saw to that. But I was lucky. Gert Martels got the same DD, but as she was enlisted personnel and a career noncom they had a long file on her; and just to make the dishonorable discharge a little nastier in her memory they gave her sixty days' hard first.

Tarb in Purgatory

·· ◆ ··

I

When I went to Taunton, Gatchweiler & Schocken to ask about getting my old job back I was afraid Val Dambois wouldn't even see me. I was wrong about that. He saw me. He was glad to. He laughed all the way through the interview. "You poor fool," he said, "you poor, shaking, demoralized wreck. What makes you think we need pedicab pushers bad enough to take you on?"

I said, "My tenure—"

"Your tenure, Tarb," he said with pleasure, "ended with your dishonorable discharge. Terminated for cause. Get lost. Better still, kill yourself." And, walking down forty-three flights of stairs to the back exit—Dambois hadn't seen fit to give me an elevator pass—I wondered how long it would be before that seemed a logical option.

There was a body of opinion which said that was what I was doing already, for at my final separation physical from the service the medic had read her dials and gauges with an increasingly worried look until she punched up my discharge papers and saw I was a DD. "Ah, well," she said then, "I guess it doesn't matter. But I'd say you're headed for total physical and mental collapse in the next six months." And she scribed in great red letters across the long list of my deteriorating physical traits the legend *Not Service Connected,* so that not even the Veterans Administration was likely to take an interest in what became of Tennison Tarb. Would Mitzi? Pride kept me from asking—for five days. Then I sent her a message, bright and positive, how about a drink for old time's sake? She didn't answer that. She also didn't answer the less bright and far from positive messages of the tenth day, the twelfth, the fifteenth. . . .

Tennison Tarb didn't have any friends any more, it seemed.

Tennison Tarb didn't have a whole lot of money any more, either. Dishonorable discharge included forfeiture of all pay and allowances, which meant, among other things, that all my bar bills from the officers' lounge in Urumqi got passed on to a collection agency. The rest of the world had forgotten I was alive, but the knee-breakers had no trouble finding me and what remained of my bank account. By the time they went away with the amount due plus interest plus collection fees plus tax—plus tip!—because they explained that customers *always* tipped the collectors, swinging their hard-rubber batons as they explained—there wasn't much more left of Tennison Tarb financially than in any other way.

And yet I still had my bright, original, creative mind! (Or had my mind so deteriorated with the rest of me that trivial insights and dumb ideas seemed brilliant?) I read *Advertising Age* every time I got a chance to pick an Omni-V channel, waiting in some hiring hall for interviews for jobs I never got. I nodded approvingly over some campaigns, frowned with disgust at others—I could have done them so much better!

But nobody would give me the chance. The word was out; I was blacklisted.

Even the cheapest shared-time rental was more than I could afford, so I took a futon with a consumer family in Bensonhurst. They'd advertised space to share and the price was right. I took the long subway ride, found the building, climbed down the steps to the third sublevel and knocked on the door. "Hello," I said to the tired, worried-looking woman who answered, "I'm Tennison Tarb," and at the end of the sentence I took a breath. Oh, wow!

I had forgotten! I had forgotten how consumers lived, and most of all I had forgotten what a consumer diet turned into in the digestive system. It is true that textured vegetable protein does resemble meat—a little like meat—like the ReelMeet from the cell cultures, anyway—but even if the taste buds are deceived the intestinal flora are not. They know what to do with the stuff. Get rid of it—a lot of it as gas. The best way I can describe the atmosphere of that suburban consumer household is like when you're caught short in a bottom-class neighborhood and have to use the communijohn, and it's in the last half hour before the morning or evening flush. Only now I had to live in it.

They weren't all that happy to see me, either, because my little shoulder bag of Moke containers added a new worry to the lines on the woman's face. But they needed the money, and I needed the space to sleep. "You can have meals with us, too," she said hospitably, "just eat right with the family, and it wouldn't cost you much."

"Maybe later," I said. They'd already put the kids to sleep in their over-the-sink cribs. With their help I tugged the furniture around to make space to roll out my futon, and as I fell asleep, my bright, original, creative mind was finding inspiration even in adversity. A new product! Antigas deodorizers to put in the food. The chemists could cook something up in no time—whether it actually worked or not, of course, mattered very little, just so we had a strong theme campaign and a good brand name. . . .

When I woke up in the morning the campaign was still clear in my mind, but something was wrong. Where was the pong? I didn't smell it any more! And I realized that consumers don't perceive their own stink.

Of course, I told myself that only meant they had to be told about it. That's the glory of advertising—not just to fill needs, but to *create* them.

I learned something that morning on my way to the next employment agency. I learned that brilliant ideas aren't worth a snake's sneeze if the wrong people get them. Back at T., G. & S., when I had easy access to the Old Man's office and the planning committee, that brainstorm would have turned into a ten-megabuck account in ninety days. Hanging onto the subway car en route to a job interview, unemployed, nearly broke, all my network of associates and connections evaporated, it wasn't a brainstorm. It was a fantasy, and the sooner I stopped fantasizing and reconciled myself to my new station in life the better, or anyway the less worse, it was going to be.

But, oh! Pride or no pride, how I missed my brassy lady, Mitzi Ku.

That night I made a decision. I didn't go back to my consumer family for dinner. I didn't eat dinner at all. I sat outside Nelson Rockwell's shared-time condo, swigging Mokes and waiting for him to wake up. A tired old man with a tray of Kelpy-Krisp samples traded me snacks for Mokes; a nasty young Brinks beat cop moved me on twice; a thousand hurrying consumers scowled their way past, ignoring me even when they tripped over me— I had plenty of time to think, and not much pleasant to think about. I was a long way from Mitzi Ku.

When at last Rockwell came out and spotted me leaning against the garbage disposal his jaw dropped—not far, because it was wired shut. And his head was covered with bandages; as a matter of fact he looked like hell. "Tenny!" he cried. "Gee, it's good to see you! But what've you been doing to yourself; you look like hell!" When I returned the compliment he gave an embarrassed shrug. "Aw, nothing serious, I just got a little behind in my payments. But what're you doing out here? Why didn't you come right in and wake me up?"

Well, actually the reason was I didn't want to see whoever it was that had taken over my ten-to-six shift in the sleepy box. I passed the question by. "Nels," I said, "I want to ask you another favor. Well, I mean the same favor over again. Would you take me to that ConsumAnon place again?"

He opened his mouth twice, and closed it twice without saying anything. He didn't have to. The first thing he was going to say was that I could go by myself, but he'd already said that.

The second thing, I was pretty sure, was that maybe I'd left it a little too late for ConsumAnon to do me any good; maybe a hospital was a better idea right then. On the third try the censor passed what he wanted to say: "Well, gee, Tenny, I don't know. The group's kind of fallen apart—there's this new self-help franchise deal, see, and a lot of the members are into substitution instead of abstinence." I kept my mouth closed and my face expressionless. "Still," he said—and then, sunnily, "Well, hell, Tenny, what are friends for? Sure I'll take you!" And, this time, he insisted on a tandem pedicab, and insisted on paying the pullers himself.

See, I hadn't looked for that sort of kindness from Nelson Rockwell. All I wanted from him was one little favor, so little that he wouldn't even know exactly what it was. Consideration, tact, generosity—they were more than I wanted, and more than I really cared to accept; if you take more kindness than the giver can afford there's a debt that I didn't want to repay. So I let him spend his tact on a blank wall—smiling, cordial, reserved, off-handed; and I turned away his generosity. No, thanks, I didn't need twenty until I got myself straightened out. No, really, I'd just eaten, no sense stopping for a quick soyaburger anywhere. I gave polite but dismissive answers to his overtures, and all I volunteered was comments on how the neighborhoods we were passing through had run down, or how the off-puller was limping in her left leg as she struggled up a not very steep hill. (And wondering inside of me if she'd have to quit the job, and if so whom to apply to for the vacancy.)

The church was as dismal as before, and the congregation far more sparse; my little scheme had obviously cut into their membership. But my luck wasn't entirely out. The one person I had hoped to find there was there. After ten minutes of exhortations from the pulpit and fevered vows of abstinence from the wimps, I excused myself for a moment, and when I came back I had what I needed.

All I wanted then was to get away. I couldn't do it. I hadn't voluntarily incurred the debt of courtesy to Nelson Rockwell. But there it was on the books.

So I stayed with him to the grisly, tedious end, and even let him buy the soyaburgers when it was over. I guess that was a mistake. It emboldened him to offer help all over again. "No, honestly, Nels, I don't want to borrow any money," I said, and then something made me add, "especially since I don't know when I could pay it back."

"Yeah," he said gravely, licking burger juice off his fingers. "Good jobs are hard to get, I guess." I shrugged as though the problem was in making up my mind which offer to accept. There'd been only one. Attendant in a custodial-care institution for the brainburned, and I hadn't had any problem turning *that* down—who wants to change the diapers of a forty-year-old contract-breach criminal? "Listen," he said, "I maybe could get you in at the grommet works. Of course, it's not such good pay, I mean, for somebody with your background—"

I smiled in a forgiving fashion. He looked abashed. "I guess you've got Agency prospects, hey, Tenny? That girl friend of yours. I hear she's got her own Agency now. I guess now that you're into CA and getting that problem under control, pretty soon you'll be right up there again."

"Of course," I said, watching him dunk the last crust of his soyaburger roll into his Coffiest. "But for now—what kind of money, exactly, do they pay in grommets?"

And so by the time I was in the subway on my way back to Bensonhurst I had the promise of a job. Not a good job. Not even a passable job. But the only job in sight.

In the dim light from the flickering subway tunnel lamps, I pulled out the flat plastic box I'd bought from the weasel-faced man outside the church. The wind was streaming through my hair, and I opened it carefully. The contents had cost too much to let them blow away.

With them, I probably did have that problem under control, I thought. At least for a while.

141

I looked at the little green tablet for a long time. They said in six months you went psycho, in a year you'd be dead.

I took a deep breath and popped it down.

I don't know what I expected. A rush. A feeling of liberation. A sense of well-being.

What I got was very little. As best I can describe it, it was like novocaine all over my body. Faint tingle, then a total absence of feeling. Although I was three hours past my last Moke, I didn't want one.

But, oh, the world was gray!

"We make grommets *cheap,*" said Mr. Semmelweiss. "That means *no rejects.* That means we can't take chances on stumblebums in this industry, there's too much at stake." He glared disapprovingly at my personnel record. I couldn't see the screen from where I stood, but I knew what it said. "On the other hand," he conceded, "Rockwell's one of my best men, and if he says you're all right—"

So I had the job. For that reason, and for two others. Reason 1: The pay was lousy. I would have done better with the brain-burned, financially speaking, although in the grommet plant of course I didn't have to risk my fingertips spoon-feeding the patients. Reason 2: It gave Semmelweiss a thrill to point out his adman employee to visitors. I'd be lugging away full boxes and sliding empties into place, and I'd see him inside his glass-enclosed cubicle at the end of the floor pointing toward me. And laughing. And the people with him, customers or stockholders or whatever, grinning incredulously at what he said.

I didn't care.

No, untrue, I did care, cared a lot. But not as much as I cared about holding onto the job, any job, until I could figure out how to get back to my life. The little green pills were maybe a first step. Maybe. True, I didn't swig Mokes any more. That was all you could say. I didn't gain back any weight, didn't get rid of that hair-trigger tension that made my fingers want to twitch and kept me tossing and turning on my futon until, sometimes, I woke one

142

of the kids and the parents glowered and muttered to themselves. But most of that was inside, where it didn't show, and my mind was busier, quicker than ever. I dreamed up great slogans, campaigns, product categories, promotions. One by one I went down the list of Agencies, printing up résumés, begging for interviews, calling on personnel managers. The résumés drew no answers. The phone calls were hung up. The visits ended when they threw me out. I tried them all, the big and the little. All but one.

I came close. I got as far as the sidewalk outside the rather undistinguished little building near the old Lincoln Center that held the brand-new Agency of Haseldyne & Ku. . . .

But I didn't go in.

I'm not sure what kept me going, because it certainly wasn't ambition and it was positively not the rewarding quality of my life. The gray numbness kept pain and want out, but it was just as good against pleasure and joy. I slept. I ate. I worked on my résumés and sample books. I pulled my trick at the grommet works. One day followed another.

There certainly was nothing inspiring about the grommet works. The job was dull, and the industry appeared to be dying. We never saw the finished product. We turned out the grommets and they were shipped to places like Calcutta and Kampuchea to be used in whatever they were used in—it was cheaper for the Indians and Kampucheans to buy from us than to make them locally, but not *much* cheaper, so business was not thriving. My first week there they closed down the wire-plastic division, though extruded-aluminum and enamel-brass were still going well enough. There was lots of unused space on the upper floors of the plant, and when things were slow I went poking around. You could see the history of industry written in the stratigraphy of the old plant. Bolt holes in the floor where once the individual punch presses had stood . . . overlaid by the scars of the high-speed extrusion lines . . . buried under the marks of the microprocessor-controlled customized machines . . . and now again outmoded by the individual punch presses. And covered all by dust, rust and must. There were lights on the upper floor, but when I pressed the switch only a handful came on, old fluorescents, most of them flickering wildly. A regiment of stair-sleepers could have found homes here, but Mr. Semmelweiss was pursuing the fantasy of "more desirable" tenants . . . or the even more fantastic hope that somehow grommets would boom again and all the old space would be bustling.

Fantasies, I sneered—enviously, for the little green pills had not only taken away my Moke-hunger, they had punctured my own fantasies as well. It is a terrible thing to wake up in the morning and realize that the day just dawned will be no better than the last.

II

What changed things? I don't know. Nothing changed things. I made no resolve, settled no unanswerable questions. But one morning I got up early, changed trains at a different station, got out where I had not been in a long, long time and presented myself at Mitzi's apartment building.

The doorthing opened its jaw to sniff my fingertips and read my palm print. Medium success. It didn't admit me, but it didn't clamp down to hold me until the cops came either. In a minute Mitzi's sleepy face appeared on the screen. "It really is you," she said, thought for a minute and then added, "You might as well come on up."

The door opened long enough for me to squeeze through, and all the way up on the hang-on lift I was trying to figure out what had been odd about the way she looked. Hair tousled? Sure, but obviously I'd got her right out of bed. Expression peculiar? Maybe. It was clearly not the look of someone glad to see me.

I pushed that question to the corner of my mind where the growing mountain of unanswered questions and unresolved doubts was locked away. By the time she let me in to her own place she'd washed her face and thrown a kerchief over her hair. The only expression she wore was polite curiosity. Polite *distant* curiosity. "I don't know why I'm here," I said—"except that, really, I've got nowhere else to go." I hadn't planned to say that. I hadn't planned anything, really, but as the words came out of my mouth and I heard them I recognized them as true.

She looked at my empty hands and unbulging pockets. "I don't have any Mokes here, Tenny."

I brushed it aside. "I'm not drinking Mokes any more. No. I haven't kicked them; I'm just on replacements."

She looked shocked. "Pills, Tenny? No wonder you look like hell."

I said steadily, "Mitzi, I'm not mad and I don't think you owe me anything, but I thought you'd listen to me. I need a job. A job that'll use my skills, because what I'm doing now is so close to being dead that one morning I just won't wake up because I won't be able to tell the difference. I'm blacklisted, you know. It's not your fault; I'm not saying that. But you're my only hope."

"Aw, Tenny," she said. The polite curiosity face broke, and for a minute I thought she was going to cry. "Aw, *hell*, Tenny," she said. "Come on in the kitchen and have some breakfast."

Even when the world is all gray, even when the circumstances are so wildly unlike anything you've ever done before that part of your mind is chasing its tail in baffled circles, your habits and training carry you through. I watched Mitzi squeeze oranges (real fruit oranges! *Squeezed* them!) for juice, and grind coffee beans (real coffee beans!) to make coffee, and all the while I was pitching her as confidently and strongly as ever I'd done for the Old Man. "Product, Mitzi," I said. "That's what I'm good at, and I've worked out major new product campaigns. Try this: Did it ever occur to you that it's a lot of trouble to be using disposable pocket tissues, razors, combs, toothbrushes? You have to keep a supply on hand. Whereas if you had permanent ones—"

She wrinkled her brow, the frown lines very deep and very conspicuous. "I don't see what you're getting at, Tenny."

"A permanent replacement for, say, pocket tissues. I've researched it; they used to be called handkerchiefs. A luxury item, don't you see? Priced for prestige."

She said dubiously, "There's no repeat business, though, is there? I mean if they're permanent—"

I shook my head. "Permanent's only as long as the consumer wants to keep it. The key is fashion. First year we sell square ones. Next year triangular, maybe—then with different designs, prints, colors, maybe embroidery; the numbers say there's bigger grosses in that than in disposables."

"Not bad, Tenny," she conceded, putting a cup of this peculiar coffee in front of me. Actually it didn't taste bad.

"That's only one little one," I said, swallowing my first sip. "I've got big ones. *Very* big ones. Val Dambois tried to steal my self-help substitution groups from me, but he only got part of it."

"There's more?" she asked, glancing at her watch.

"You bet there's more! They just never let me work it all out. See, after the groups are formed, each member goes out and digs up other members. He gets a commission on the new ones. You get ten new members at fifty dollars a year each, and you get a ten percent commission on each one—that pays your dues."

She pursed her lips. "I suppose it's a good way to expand."

"Not just expand! How do you recruit these new members? You have a party in your condo. Invite your friends. Give them food and drinks and party favors—*and we sell them the favors.* And then—" I took a deep breath—"the beauty part, the member that signs up new members gets promoted. He becomes a Fellow of the group, and that means his dues go up to seventy-five a year. Twenty members, he becomes a Councilor—dues, a hundred. Thirty he's a, I don't know, Grand Exalted Theta-Class Selectman or something. See, we always stay ahead of them, so no matter how many memberships he peddles he pays half of it back—and we go on selling him the merchandise."

I sat back with my coffee, watching the expression on her face. Whatever that expression was. I had thought it might be admiration, but I could not really tell. "Tenny," she sighed, "you are one hell of a true-blue huckster."

146

And that broke through the well-trained reflexes. I set the coffee cup down so hard that some of the coffee spilled into the saucer. Once more I listened to the words coming out of my mouth and, although I had not planned to say them, I recognized they were true. "No," I said, "I'm not. As far as I can tell I'm not a true-blue anything. The reason I want to get back into the ad business is that I have a notion I *ought* to want it. What I really want is only—"

And I stopped there, because I was afraid to finish the sentence with the word "you" . . . and because the other thing I noticed was that my voice was shaking.

"I wish," I said despairingly, and thought for a minute before going on: "I wish this was a different world."

Now, what do you suppose I meant by that? That's not a rhetorical question. I didn't know the answer to it then and don't now; my heart was saying something my head hadn't considered at all. I guess the meaning of the question isn't that important. The feeling was what counted, and I could see that it reached Mitzi. "Oh, hell, Tenny," she said, and her eyes dropped.

When she raised them again she stared at me searchingly for a moment before she spoke. "Do you know," she said—funny, but as much to herself, I thought, as to me, "that you keep me awake at night?"

Shocked, I began, "I had no idea—" But she pressed on.

"It's foolish," she mused. "You're a huck. True, you're down right now, and you're thinking things you wouldn't have let yourself think a few weeks ago. But you're a huck."

I said—not quarrelsomely, just making my point, "I'm an adman, yes, Mitzi." It wasn't like her to use that kind of language.

She might as well not have heard. "When I was a little girl Daddy-san used to tell me that I'd fall in love and I wouldn't be able to help myself, and the best and only thing for me to do was to stay away from the kind of man I wouldn't be able to help myself with. I wish I'd listened to Daddy-san."

My heart swelled inside me. Hoarsely I cried, "Oh, Mitzi!"

147

And I reached out for her. Didn't touch her though. Easily, not hurrying a bit, she stood up, just fast enough for my reaching hands to miss her, and stepped back. "Stay here, Tenny," she ordered calmly and disappeared into her sleep room. The door slid locked behind her. In a minute I heard the shower begin to run, and there I sat, studying Mitzi's queer ideas of interior decoration, trying to see what anybody would like about the painting of Venus on the wall—trying to make sense of what she had said.

She gave me plenty of time. I didn't succeed, though, and when she came out she was fully dressed, her hair was neat, her face was composed, and she was somebody else entirely. "Tenny," she said directly, "listen to me. I think I'm crazy and I'm sure I'm going have trouble over this. But still, three things:

"First, I'm not interested in your product ideas or your ConsumAnon scams. That's not the kind of Agency I'm running.

"Second, at this moment I can't do a thing for you. Probably I shouldn't even if I could. Probably in a day or two I'll come to my senses and then I won't see you at all. But right now there's no space for another adman in our offices—and no time in my life, either.

"Third—" she hesitated, then shrugged—"third, there *might* be something for us to talk about later on. Intangibles, Tenny. Political. A special project. So hush-hush I shouldn't even be saying it exists. Maybe it never will. It won't unless we can get a lot of things straight—we even need a place to house it, out of sight, because it's *really* hush-hush. Even then maybe we'll decide the time isn't ripe and we shouldn't go ahead with it now anyway. Do you hear how iffy all this is, Tenn? But if it does happen, then maybe, just maybe, I can find a place for you in it. Call me in a week."

She stepped briskly toward me. With my heart in my eyes I reached out for her but she sidestepped, leaned forward to kiss me chastely and firmly on the cheek and then went to the door. "Don't come with me," she ordered. "Wait ten minutes, then leave."

And she was gone.

148

Although those little, flat green tablets seemed to be clarifying my thoughts, they didn't make what I was trying to think about Mitzi clear at all. I rehearsed every word of our conversation in my mind, tossing on my futon while the babies whimpered and the parents snored or bickered softly between themselves in the same room. I could not make sense of it. I couldn't figure out what Mitzi felt about me (oh, she'd all but said the word "love"—but surely she never acted it!). I could not square the Mitzi I had known so casually and carnally on Venus, her only secrets Agency ones, with the increasingly mysterious and unpredictable one on Earth.

I couldn't understand anything at all—except for one thing that rang clear in my memory. And so I finished my shift at the grommet works, cleaned myself up, combed my hair and presented myself at the glass cubicle at the end of the floor. Semmelweiss wasn't alone; the man with him was there at least once a week, staying for hours sometimes, going out to lunch with him and coming back with that three-martini lurch. I knew what they talked about: nothing. I coughed from the doorway and said: "Excuse me, Mr. Semmelweiss."

He gave me the exasperated can't-you-see-I'm-in-conference growl: "In a minute, Tarb!" And went back to his friend. The conference was about their pedicars:

"Acceleration? Listen, I had an old Ford with the outside pushoff, first pedicar I ever owned, secondhand, real clunker—but when I'd be waiting for a light to change I'd just stick that old right foot outside and *zoom!* I'd cut right in front of the pedicabs and all!"

I coughed again. Semmelweiss cast a despairing glance at heaven and then turned to me: "Why aren't you at your machine, Tarb?"

"My shift's over, Mr. Semmelweiss. I just wanted to ask you something."

"Tchah," he said, glancing at his friend, eyebrows raised in scorn—scornful of me, who had once owned a battery-powered bike! But he said, "What the hell is it, then?"

149

"It's about that extra space, Mr. Semmelweiss. I think I know someone who might rent it. They're an Agency."

His eyes popped. "Hell, Tarb! Why didn't you say so?" And then everything was all right. It was all right for me to show Mitzi and Haseldyne the space. It was all right to take off work the next day to bring them there. It was all right to interrupt him, hell, Tarb, sure it was, any time! Everything in the world was all right . . . except maybe me, and all the worries and fears and puzzles that I couldn't even put a name to.

III

When I finally got Mitzi on the phone she was very irritable, exactly as though she was mad at herself for encouraging me at all—which, I was sure, was exactly the case. She demurred, and hesitated, and finally admitted that yes, she had said they needed hideout space. She'd have to check with Des Haseldyne, though.

But when I called her back, on her instructions, ten minutes later, she said, "We'll be there." And so they were.

When I met them on the filthy sidewalk outside the grommet plant Haseldyne looked far more irritated than Mitzi had sounded. I put out my hand. "Hello, Des," I said civilly.

Uncivilly he ignored my hand. "You look like hell," he said unsympathetically. "Where's this rathole you're trying to sell us?"

"This way, please," I said, usherlike, and bowed them in. I didn't tell them to watch out for the dirt. They could see the dirt themselves. I didn't apologize for it, or for the coughing, barking, sometimes machine-gun noise of the machines spitting out their million grommets an hour; or for Semmelweiss waving greasily to us from his cubicle; or for the smells; or for the neighborhood. Or for anything. It was their decision to make. I wasn't going to beg.

Once we got upstairs it was a little better, anyway. Those ancient buildings were put together solidly; you could hear the machines below, but only as a distant and not unpleasant mutter. The lights were still flickering madly, and the dust made Mitzi wheeze and sneeze. But they didn't seem to notice. They were more interested in the back stairs and the freight elevator and all the unused ratholes marked Exit that no one had opened in decades. "Plenty of ways in and out, anyway," said Desmond ungraciously. I nodded, but I hadn't actually heard him. I was adrift in my own head. Funny. With Mitzi actually in the same room with me I seemed farther away from her than ever. I supposed I was just strung out. The pills were not without cost, and although my weight loss had slowed, it had not stopped, nor had my insomnia come to an end. And yet there was something very strange—

"Tarb!" Haseldyne called crossly. "Are you nodding off on us? I asked you about transportation."

"Transportation?" I counted off on my fingers. "Let's see, there's two subway lines, all the north-south buses, the crosstown buses, the crosstown pedstrip. And pedicabs, of course."

"And power availability?" Mitzi put in, sneezing.

"Sure, there's power. That's how they make the grommet machines go," I explained.

"No, damn it, I mean is it *reliable?* No interruptions?"

I shrugged. I hadn't really noticed. "I guess not," I said.

I hadn't realized she was more on edge than I. "You *guess?*" she flared. "God, Tenny, even for a Moke-head you're—ah, ah— you're pretty stupid—ah—"

When the *choo* came it was violent. She clapped her hands to her face. "Oh, *hell!*" she growled. Down on her hands and knees, scrabbling at the dusty floor, she looked up ferociously, and one of Mitzi's blue eyes was brown.

I suppose that if I hadn't been a Moke-head I would have figured it out long before. Eating salads. Contact lenses to hide her eye-color. Dodging the mother who desperately wanted to see her daughter. Calling me a "huck" when she got mad. A dozen different incongruous things.

And only one explanation to fit them all.

I suppose if I hadn't been first a Moke-head, then a pill-

151

popper, I would have reacted in a different way entirely. Called the cops, I guess. Or tried to, even though that might easily have cost me my life. But I'd been through the wringer. What she was doing might be terribly wrong. But I hadn't anything left that I was sure was right.

I seemed to have all the time in the world. I pulled my notepad out of my pocket, wrote swiftly, then ripped out the page and folded it over. "Mitzi," I said, stepping forward, careless of her lost contact lens, "you're not Mitzi, are you?"

Freeze-frame. She stared up at me with one brown eye and one blue eye.

"You're a fraud, aren't you?" I asked. "A Veenie agent. A double for the real Mitzi Ku."

And Haseldyne exhaled a long, slow breath. I could feel him move toward me, tensing to act. "Read this!" I said, and shoved the note into his hand.

He almost didn't stop, but then he glanced at it, frowned, looked startled and read it aloud:

" 'To Whom It May Concern; I can't face life as an addict any longer. Suicide's the only way out.' Signed, Tennison Tarb. What the hell's this, Tarb?"

I said, "Use it if you want to get rid of me. Or let me help you. I'll help the best I can, every way I can, whatever you're doing. I don't care what it is. I know you're Veenies. It doesn't matter."

And I added:

"Please."

The False Mitsui Ku

·· ◆ ··

I

Once upon a time there was this man Mitchell Courtenay, the one half the streets on Venus seem to be named after. They think he is a hero, but when my grade school teacher told us about him in history class she spat his name with loathing. Like me, he was a star-class copysmith. Like me, he got caught up in a crisis of conscience that he never wanted and didn't know how to handle.

Like me, he was a traitor.

That's the kind of a word that you don't want to hear, when it is you it is applied to. "Tennison Tarb," I yelled at the top of my voice—into the thunder of the subway tunnel as I took the late local to my Bensonhurst flop, where no one could hear the word, not even me—"Tennison Tarb, you are a traitor to Sales!"

Not even an echo answered. Or if it did it was drowned in the subway roar. I felt no pain from the word, though I knew it was fair, and damning.

I suppose it was the long green pills that dulled that pain, along with all the other pains I didn't feel any more. That was my good fortune; but if you flipped that coin, the other side was that I felt no joy at being an adman again, either. Up, down. Up, down. How long I would stay up this time I could not guess, but there I was. I would have exulted—if the world had not been so gray.

153

And, if the world had not been so gray, I might still have been shaking with fear, too, because it had been a very close thing, there in the loft over the grommet works. I could see the plans coming up, one after another, in Desmond Haseldyne's card-sorter mind: Bash his head in and stick him in a grommet press to hide the evidence. Drug him and toss him out of a high window. Get some Moke extract and OD him—that would have been the easiest and surest of all. But he didn't do it. Mitzi choked out that she wanted to give me my chance, and Haseldyne didn't overrule her.

He also didn't give me the "suicide" note back, though.

When I looked at the life ahead of me I could see two yawning chasms. On the one side, Haseldyne would, after all, use the suicide note and that would be the end of Tennison Tarb forever. On the other, discovery, arrest, brainburning. Between the two was a narrow knife-edge that I might hope to walk—leading to a future in which my name would forever be reviled by generations of schoolchildren to come.

It was a great blessing that I had the long green pills.

Since I was committed to the knife-edge, I went ahead with it. I shaved and pressed and spiffed up as far as I could manage on the money I had left and the facilities available in my Bensonhurst pad—when I could get past sleepwalking parents and cranky kids to get to them. The long, steamy subway ride soaked the new press out of my shorts and blew soot into my washed hair, but all the same I was reasonably presentable when I reported to the lobby of the Haseldyne & Ku building. There a Wackerhut cop checked my palm prints, pinned a temporary visitor's magnetic badge on my collar and whisked me up to Mitzi's office. To the door of Mitzi's office, anyway, where her new sec^2 stopped me. He was a stranger to me. I was not to him, for he greeted me by name. I had certain formalities to go through. The sec^2 had Personnel all primed; an employee-contract fax was ready for my thumbprint, and as soon as I had officially signed on he presented me with a permanent Agency I.D. and a two-week salary advance.

So it was with money in my credit store that I finally made

it through the door into Mitzi's office. It was a first-class brain-room, as opulent and formidable as the Old Man's at T., G. & S. It was furnished with desk and conference couch, with a wet bar and vidscreen, with *three* windows and *two* visitors' chairs. What it wasn't furnished with was Mitzi Ku. In her place Des Haseldyne sat glowering behind the desk, and he never looked bigger. "Mitzi's busy; I'm handling this for her," he announced.

I nodded, though being handled by Des Haseldyne was not among my dearest dreams. "Can we talk here?" I asked.

He sighed patiently and waved a hand at the windows. Sure enough, windows and door all sparkled with the faint glimmer of a privacy curtain; no electronic buggery would go out of this room while it was on. "Fine," I said. "Put me to work."

He was oddly hesitant. "We don't really have a place for you," he grumbled at last.

That was obvious enough. I hadn't been any part of their calculations until I dumped myself on them. I didn't think anything I might offer would seem like a good idea to him; he might listen to Mitzi, but never to me. Still, I tried to make the pill easier to swallow. "Mitzi mentioned Politics—I can sell the hell out of that," I offered.

"No!" The bark was loud, angry and definite. Now, why did that upset him so? I shrugged and tried again.

"There are other Intangibles—say, Religion. Or any kind of product—"

"Not our line of work," he growled, the huge head shaking. He raised his hand to cut off any more useless suggestions from me. "It will have to be something a lot more significant than that," he said definitely.

Enlightenment! "Ah," I said, "I see. You want an overt act. You want me to put my neck on the line to prove loyalty. Commit an actual crime, right? So I can't turn back again? What is it you want me to do, murder somebody?"

I said that so easily! Maybe it was the grayed-out numbing of everything the pills had given me, but once I took his meaning the words came out without a qualm. Haseldyne had been taking no pills, though. The huge face assembled itself into a granite look of total revulsion. "What the hell do you think we are?" he demanded, loathing me. I shrugged. "We're not doing anything like that!" I waited for him to come down from the dudgeon. It took a while, because he seemed to be having trouble assembling his thoughts.

"There is one possibility," he said at last. "You were part of the limbic forces in the Gobi action."

"Chaplain, right," I agreed. "They fired me out with a DD."

"That's easy enough to reverse," he said impatiently. That was true enough, for somebody with the clout of an Agency partner. "Suppose we got you back in. Suppose we put you in a place where you had Campbellian equipment under your command—you do know how to use the stuff, I suppose."

"Not thing one, Des," I told him cheerfully. "That's technician stuff. You don't learn that, you hire it."

He said stubbornly, "But you could direct the technicians?"

"Of course. Anybody could. For what purpose?"

If I had been in any doubt that he was improvising as he went along, and not very well, he dispelled it then. "To promote the Venusian cause!" he roared. "To make the damn hucks leave us alone!"

I looked at him in real astonishment. "Are you serious? Forget it!"

Rumble lower and more dangerous: "Why?"

"Ah, Des, I can see now that you had to be a Veenie agent, for you certainly aren't an adman. Limbic stimulation isn't a technique in itself. It's only an intensifier. An expediter."

"So?"

"So it has to obey the basic laws of all advertising. You can only make people *want* things, Des. You can train knee-jerk buying patterns into them or create hungers, but you can't use advertising to make people *kind*, for God's sake!" I'd put my finger on the truth. Advertising-wise, the man was an ignoramus. How he'd kept his ignorance secret for so long at a major Agency was a miracle—although what I had just said was true: You didn't need to learn what you could hire from others. He glowered resentfully as I went on to explain, "For that kind of thing you need B-mod if you're in a real hurry, and that's out of the question except with small, captive audiences. You don't really want advertising at all, Des."

"I don't?"

"Publicity," I explained. "Word of mouth. You want to create an image. You start stories about the 'good Veenies' for openers. Get a couple of Veenie characters in sitcoms, and gradually change them from villainous clowns to sweet eccentrics. Do some tie-in commercials with a Venusian background—the 'Venus Loves Cari-Os' sort of thing."

"Venus damn it to hell *doesn't*," he exploded.

"The exact details could be different, of course. Of course, you'd have to be supercareful of how you did it. You're tampering with deep-down prejudices, you know, not to mention maybe even bending the law. But it can be done, given the money and the time. I'd say five or six years."

"We don't *have* five or six years!"

"I didn't think you did, Des," I grinned. It was funny, but I found myself enjoying his aggravation just as much as though the thorn tearing his flesh wasn't me—and as though he didn't have the easy and obvious way to remove it that my "suicide" note had given him. It came down to the fact that I simply didn't care what happened to me. The whole thing was out of my hands. Mitzi was the only friend I had in the world. Either she would save me . . . or she wouldn't.

I left the glowering Des Haseldyne feeling as close to at ease as I'd been in many months, and that night I went out and spent a big chunk of my credit balance on new clothes. I picked them out as happily and carefully as though I were confident of being alive to wear them.

When the next morning's summons to Mitzi's brainroom came along, Mitzi herself was in it—red-eyed, looking as though she hadn't slept well, the frown lines deeper than ever between her eyes. She silently pointed to a chair, flicked on the secrecy screen and sat with her elbows on the desk and her chin in her elbows staring at me. At last she said, "How did I get into this with you, Tenny?"

I tipped her a wink. "I'm just lucky, I guess."

"Don't make jokes!" she snapped. "I didn't *ask* for you. I didn't want to fall in l— . . . in l—" She took a deep breath and forced it out: "In love with you, damn it! Do you know how dangerous all this is?"

I got up to kiss the top of her head before I said seriously, "I know exactly, Mits. What's the use of worrying about it?"

"Sit down where you belong!" Then, relenting as I retreated to my chair, "It's not your fault that my glands are messing me up, I guess. I don't want you hurt. But, Tenn, if it ever comes to a point where I have to choose between you and the cause—"

I raised my hand to stop her. "I know that, Mits. You won't ever have to do that. You'll be glad to have me aboard because, honestly, Mitzi, you clowns don't know what you're doing."

Hard stare. Then, sullenly, "It's true all this stuff revolts us too much for us to be really good at it. If you could supply some expertise—"

"I can. You know I can."

"Yes," she said reluctantly, "I guess I do. I told Des that limbic stuff was hopeless, but he didn't want to let you in on the real plan. All right. I'm taking the responsibility. What we're doing is political, Tenny, and you're going to do it for us. You'll run the whole campaign—under my direction and Des's."

"Fine," I said heartily. "Here? Or—"

She dropped her eyes. "For the beginning, anyway, here. Now are there any questions?"

Well, to begin with, there was the question of why it was going to be here instead of in the loft over the grommet works, but that didn't seem to be one of the ones she wanted to answer. I said slowly, "If you could just start by filling me in on what's going on—"

"Yes, of course." She said it as though I had asked directions

158

to the men's room. "The big picture is, we're going to wreck Earth's economy, and the way we're going to do it is by taking over the governments."

I nodded, waiting for the next sentence that would make that all clear. When there wasn't any next sentence I asked, "The what?"

"The governments," she said firmly. "Surprises you, doesn't it? So obvious, and yet none of you hucks have ever had the wit to see it, not even the Conservationists."

"But Mits! What would you want to take over the government for? Nobody pays any attention to those dummies. The real power's right here in the Agencies."

She nodded. "So it is, de facto. But, de jure, the government still has eminent domain. The laws have never been changed. It's just that the Agencies own the people who write the laws. They get their instructions. No one ever questions them. The only difference is *we* will own them. The dummies will go right on taking our orders, and what we order will plunge this planet into the damnedest, worst depression the human race has ever seen— *then* let's see if they can still screw around with Venus!"

I goggled at her. It was about the craziest idea I had ever heard. Even if it worked, and all conventional wisdom swore to me it couldn't work, was that what I wanted? An economic depression? Mass unemployment? The destruction of everything I had been taught to revere. . . .

And yet—humility said—who was I, failure and addict, to criticize? Heaven knew my principles had been rocked and shaken so many times in the past few roller-coaster months that I couldn't pretend to know anything. I was floundering—and Mitzi seemed so sure.

I said, feeling my way, "Listen, Mits, since some of our Earth ways are so unfamiliar to you—"

"Not unfamiliar!" she flared. "Rotten! Criminal! *Sick.*"

I spread my hands, meaning, "No argument"—especially since I seemed to be changing sides in that argument. "The question is, how can you be sure this will work?"

159

She said fiercely, "Do you think we're illiterate barbarians? It's all been gamed and dry-run a hundred times. We've had input from the top brains on Venus—psychologists, anthropologists, poli-sci think tanks and war-plans strategists . . . hell," she finished glumly, "no. We don't know that it will work. But it's the only thing we've come up with that might."

I sat back and gazed at my brassy lady. So this was what I had committed myself to—an immense and lethal conspiracy, planned by eggheads, conducted by zealots. It was comically hopeless, baggy-pants farce, except that it wasn't very funny when you thought of what it meant. Treason, Contract Breach, unfair commercial practices. If it went sour, the best I could hope for was a return trip to the Polar Penal Colony, this time on the wrong side of the bars.

The expression on Mitzi's face might once have belonged to Joan of Arc. She seemed almost to glow, eyes lifted to the sky, the brassy-lady face transmuted through bronze to pure, warm gold, the twin frown lines harsh between her eyes. . . .

I reached across the desk and touched them. "Plastic surgery, I guess?" I inquired.

She came down fast, glowered at me (the frown lines reinforced now with real ones), pursed her lips. "Well, hell, Tenny," she said, "of course there had to be some plastic surgery. I only looked a *little* like Mitsui Ku."

"Yeah," I said, nodding, "I thought that was it. So the idea was," I added conversationally, "you'd kill both of us in the tram station, right? And then you'd announce that through Herculean efforts and the skill of Veenie surgeons you'd pulled at least Mitzi through? Only it would really be you?"

She said harshly, "Something like that."

"Yeah. Say," I inquired interestedly, "what's your real name, anyway?"

"Damn you, Tenn! What difference does that make?" She sulked for a minute, and then said, "Sophie Yamaguchi, in case it matters."

160

"Sophie Yamaguchi," I repeated, tasting the name. It didn't taste right. "I think I'll go on calling you Mitzi, if you don't mind."

"Mind? I *am* Mitzi Ku! I spent *seven months* practicing to be her, studying the surveillance tapes, copying her mannerisms, memorizing her background. I even fooled you, didn't I? Now I hardly remember Sophie Yamaguchi at all. It's like Sophie died instead of—"

She stopped short. I said, "I guess Mitzi's dead, then."

The false Mitzi said unwillingly, "Well, yes, she's dead. But she wasn't killed by the tram. And believe me, Tenny, I was glad! We're not assassins, you know. We don't want to hurt anybody, unnecessarily. It's just that the objective realities of the situation . . . Anyway, they hustled her away for, ah, retraining."

"Ah," I nodded. "The Anti-Oasis."

"Sure she went there! And she would have been all right there, too. Either she would have come around to our way of thinking or, at least, been kept there alive and out of sight. But she tried to escape. Ran out of oxygen or something in the desert. Tenny," she said earnestly, "it was nobody's *fault.*"

"Well, whoever said it was?" I asked. "Now, about what you want me to do . . ."

When you come right down to it, I guess nothing is ever anybody's fault, or anyway nobody ever thinks it is. You have to do what you have to do.

Yet, going back to Bensonhurst that night, I looked around me at the tired, sad-faced commuters hanging to their harnesses as the filthy tunnel walls flew past, the smoggy wind blowing us around, the lights flickering. And I wondered. Did I really want to make the hard life of these consumers harder? Wrecking Earth's economy wasn't an abstraction; it meant concrete things, a concrete loss of a job for a file clerk or a Brink's cop. A concrete downgrading for an adman. A concrete cut in the food budget for the family I lived with. Well, sure, I now believed that Earth was wrong in trying to sabotage and overpower Venus, and it was right to join forces with Mitzi, the false Mitzi, that was, and put a stop

161

to that wickedness. But what degree of wickedness was appropriate to achieve that nonwicked end?

To all my troubles and worries and dilemmas I did not want to add the only one I hadn't much suffered from yet: guilt.

Nevertheless . . .

Nevertheless I did the job Mitzi had given me. Did it damn well, too. "What you're going to do, Tenny," she had ordered, "is *elect.* Don't try anything complicated. Don't try to get *principle* into the campaigns. Just do your huck damnedest to make our people win."

Right, Mitzi. I did—my damnedest, and tried not to let myself feel damned. One of the people she'd stolen from Taunton, Gatchweiler and Schocken was my old flunky, Dixmeister; he'd been jumped up to take my job and was gloomy, but resigned, to be jumped down again. He brightened when I told him he could have more authority this time; I let him set up all the casting calls, even let him pick possible candidates from the first screenings. I didn't tell him that I was keeping an eye on the screenings through the closed-circuit TV to my office, but then it wasn't necessary—left on his own, having had the benefit of my training, the kid was doing all right.

And I had more important things to do. I wanted *themes.* Slogans. Combinations of words that might or might not mean anything (that wasn't important) but were short and easy to remember. I put the Research Department to work, digging up all the themes and slogans that had ever been used in political campaigns, and presently my monitor was flooded with them. "The Square Deal." "54-40 or Fight." "The Moral Majority." "The Forgotten Man," "Mink, Stink and Pink." "Get Government off the Backs of the American People." "Cuba 90 Miles Away." "I Will Go to Korea." "Truth in Advertising"—well, no, that one didn't have the right ring. "I Am Not a Crook"—that one hadn't worked. "The War on Poverty." Better, though that one, it seemed, hadn't won the war. There were hundreds of the damned things. Of course, most of them had no bearing on the

162

world we lived in—what could you make of "Tippecanoe and Tyler Too"?—but, what I used to tell my copy cubs, it isn't what a slogan says that matters, it's what people can read into it that somehow touches the subconscious. It was hard, slogging work, not made easier by the fact that I had lost something. What I had lost was the feeling that winning was an end in itself. It *was,* in this case—Mitzi had told me so. But I no longer *felt* that.

All the same I came up with some beauties. I called Dixmeister in to see them, all beautifully calligraphed and ornamented by Art, with theme music and multisensual background by Production. He gaped at the monitor, puzzled.

" 'Hands Off Hyperion'? That's truly superb, Mr. Tarb," he said by reflex, and then, hesitating, "but isn't it really kind of the other way around? I mean, we don't want to let go of Hyperion as a market, do we?"

"Not *our* hands off, Dixmeister," I said kindly. *"Veenies'* hands off. We want them left alone by *Veenies."*

His expression cleared. "A masterpiece, Mr. Tarb," he said raptly. "And this one. 'Freedom of Information.' That means no attempts at censoring advertising, right? And 'Get Government Off the Backs of the People'?"

"Means abolishing the requirement to post warnings at Campbell areas," I explained.

"A work of genius!" And I sent him off to try the slogans on that day's crop of candidates, to see which of them could say them without stumbling or looking confused, while I got busy setting up a spy system to check out the other Agencies' candidates. So much to do! I was working twelve, fourteen hours a day, losing weight slowly but consistently, sometimes almost falling asleep and losing my grip on the hang-on in those long subway trips to Bensonhurst. I didn't care. I had made my commitment and I was going to see it through, whatever it cost. At least the pills were still working; I hadn't had even the desire for a Moke in a long time.

I hadn't had much of a desire for anything else, either—for almost anything else—for anything but the one thing, anyway, and that one thing was not the sort of famished physical craving the green pills anesthetized so well. It was a head-yearning. It was a memory-desire, a longing to feel again the sweet touch of bodies as we slept and the sound of breathing that came from a warm, soft body wrapped in my arms. It was Mitzi I wanted.

I didn't get much of her. Once a day I would report to her brainroom. Sometimes she was not there and it was Des Haseldyne who shifted his huge body irritably in the chair and scowled through my sitrep, never complete enough or fast-moving enough to please him, because Mitzi was off at some other meeting. Sometimes the meetings were far away. I knew there was much going on that I was not privy to, as they tried to patch and shore up the rickety scheme that I had committed myself to. It was just as well I was anesthetized. The pills didn't keep away entirely the sweaty nightmares about Fair Commercial Practices hit squads storming my office or Bensonhurst pad, but they let me live through them.

Even when Mitzi was there we didn't touch. The only difference between reporting to Mitzi and reporting to Des was that once in a while she called me "dear." The days went on. . . .

And then late one night I was rehearsing one of our candidates in the traditional moves of debate: the cocked eyebrow of humorous skepticism; the clenched jaw of resolution; the indignant thundercloud frown of disbelief—the sudden glance of astonishment and the edging away, as though the opponent had just, grossly and unforgivably, broken wind. As I was coaching the dummy in the various demeaning possible mispronunciations of his opponent's name, Mitzi came in. "Don't let me interrupt, Tenny," she called as she entered. And then, coming closer, she said softly in my ear so that the dummy couldn't hear: "But when you're through— Anyway, you're working too hard to take that long trip to Bensonhurst every night. There's plenty of room at my place."

It was what I would have prayed for, if I had prayed.

Unfortunately, it wasn't very satisfactory. The pills had not

164

only grayed down the environment, they had grayed *me* down. I didn't have the passion, the zest, the overwhelming hunger; I was glad we were doing what we did, but it didn't really seem to matter all that much, and Mitzi was nervous and strained.

I guess old married couples go through times when both are tired or fretful—or, like me, strung out—and what they do, they do because they don't have anything better to do at the moment.

Actually, it seemed we did have something better to do. We talked. We talked a lot, pillow talk but not *that* kind of pillow talk. We talked because neither of us was sleeping very well and because, after some seldom very satisfactory sex, it was better to talk than to pretend to be asleep and listen to the person next to you pretending the same.

There were things we didn't say, of course. Mitzi never mentioned the secret bulk of the iceberg, the mysterious meetings I was not allowed to attend or know about. For my part I never again mentioned my doubts. That the Veenie conspirators were floundering in a ramshackle plan was clear. I'd known that from the moment Des Haseldyne began asking about limbic compulsion. I didn't discuss it.

I did, now and then, think about brainburning. When Mitzi cried out and twitched in her sleep, I knew she was thinking about it too.

What I talked about mostly was confidences I could betray. I told Mitzi everything I could think of that might help the Veenies out, every Agency secret I'd ever heard, every Embassy covert operation, every detail of the Gobi Desert strike. Each time she'd sniff and say something like, "Typical merciless huck tyranny," and then I'd have to think of some other highly classified datum to betray. You know Scheherazade? That's what I was, telling a story every night to stay alive the next morning, because I hadn't forgotten how expendable I was.

Naturally it handicapped me in more intimately important areas.

But it wasn't all like that, really. I told her about my childhood, and how Mom made my uniform with her own hands when

165

I joined the Junior Copysmiths, and my school days and my first loves. And she told me—well, she told me everything. Well, at least everything about herself. Not so much about what my coconspirators were up to, but then I didn't expect that. "My Daddy-san came to Venus with the first ship," she would say, and I would know that she was telling me these things to avoid the risk of telling me something more risky.

It was interesting, though. Mitzi had a thing about her Daddy-san. He'd been one of old Mitchell Courtenay's gang of self-righteous revolutionary Conservationists that so hated the brainwashing and people-manipulating of the mercantile society that they jumped from the frying pan of Earth into Venus's pure hellfire. When she told me about Daddy-san's stories of the early days, it sounded like a clone of hell itself, all right. And her father hadn't been any big wheel. Just a kid. His main job appeared to be digging out holes for them to live in with his bare hands, and carrying slop outside of the ship to bury between work shifts. While the construction crews were putting together the first huge Hilsch tubes to tap the biggest asset Venus had—the immense energy in its hot, dense, wild winds—Daddy-san was changing diapers for the first generation of kids in the nurseries. "Daddy," she said, wet-eyed, "wasn't just an unskilled kid, he was also a physical wreck. Too much junk food when he was little, and something wrong with his spine that never got fixed—but he never let that keep him from doing his best!"

Along about the time they began nuking tectonic faults to make volcanos, he took time enough to get married and have Mitzi. That's when he got promoted, and subsequently died. The whole idea of the volcanos, of course, was that they were the best way the Veenies had of getting the underground oxygen and water vapor out where they could use them. That's where all the Earth's oceans and air came from, but Venus couldn't squander them the way the early Earth did because they couldn't afford to wait four billion years for the results. So the volcanos had to be capped. "That was hard and dangerous work," said Mitzi, "and when something went wrong and one of the caps blew, it blew my Daddy-san along with it. I was three years old."

Strung out, exhausted, worn as I was, she touched my heart. I reached out for her.

She turned away. "That's what love is," she said into the pillow. "You love somebody and you get hurt. After Daddy-san died I used up all my love on Venus—I never wanted to love another *person!*"

After a moment I got up unsteadily. She didn't call me back.

Dawn was breaking; might as well get into this next bad day. I put some of her "coffee" on and stared out the window at the smoggy, huge city, with its teeming hucks, and wondered what I was doing with my life? Physically the answer was easy; I was wrecking it. The faint reflection in the glass showed how every day my face got thinner, my eyes brighter and more hollow. From behind me she said, "Take a good look, Tenny. You look like hell."

Well, I was getting tired of hearing that. I turned. She was sitting up in bed, eyes fixed on me. She hadn't put her contacts in yet. I said, "Mits, honey, I'm sorry—"

"I'm getting tired of hearing *that!*" she snapped, as though she'd been reading my mind. "You're sorry, all right. You're about the sorriest specimen I've ever seen. Tenny! You're going to die on me!"

I looked out of the window to see if anybody in the dirty, old city was going to offer me an answer for that. Nobody did. Since what she said actually seemed like a likely possibility, the best plan appeared to be to let her remark alone.

Mitzi wouldn't let it alone. "You're going to die of those damn pills," she said furiously, "and then I'll have goddam *grief* to go with my goddam *worry* and goddam *fear.*"

I moved back to the bed to touch her bare shoulder soothingly. She wasn't soothed. She glared up at me like a trapped feral cat.

The anesthesia was wearing thin.

I reached for my morning pill and popped it down, praying that this once it would give me a lift instead of a numbness, that

167

it would give me the wisdom and compassion to answer her in a way that would ease her pain. Wisdom and compassion didn't come. I did the best I could with what I had to work with; I said, placatingly, "Mits, maybe we better get dressed and go to work before we say something we shouldn't. We're both pretty ragged, maybe tonight we'll get some sleep—"

"Sleep!" she hissed. "Sleep! How can I sleep when every fifteen minutes I wake up thinking the Department of Fair Commercial Practices goons are breaking the door down!"

I winced; I had had the same nightmares; I thought about brainburning a lot. I said, my voice unsteady, "Isn't it worth it, Mits? We're really getting to know each other—"

"I know more than I want to, Tenny! You're an addict. You're a physical wreck. You're not even good in bed—"

And she stopped there, because she knew as well as I did what that meant. That was the mortal word. There was nothing to say after it but, "We're through." And in the special circumstances of our relationship there was only one way to terminate it.

I waited for the next words, which had to be, "Get out of here! Get out of my life!" After she threw me out, I thought abstractedly, the best plan would be go straight to the jetport, fly as far as my money would take me, lose myself in the seething mass of consumers in Los Angeles or Dallas or even farther. Des Haseldyne might not find me. I might just sit out the next few months, while the coup either succeeded or didn't. After that, of course, it got nasty—whichever side won, the winners would surely come looking for me. . . .

I noticed that she hadn't said those words. She was sitting up in bed, listening intently to a faint sound from the door. "Oh, my God," she said despairingly, "look at the time, they're here!"

Somebody was indeed at the door of Mitzi's apartment. It wasn't being broken down. It was being opened with a key, so it wasn't the Fair Practices stormtroopers.

It was three people. One of them was a woman I had never seen before. The others were two people who, I would have bet everything I owned, would be the last possible people to come

168

into Mitzi's apartment in that way: Val Dambois and the Old Man.

When I saw them I was only startled. They were thunderstruck and, besides, furious. "Damn it, Mits!" raged Dambois, "you've really torn it now! What's that Moke-head doing here?"

I could have told him I wasn't a Moke-head, exactly, any more. I didn't try. I was spending all my shocked and horrified thoughts on what their presence here meant. I wouldn't have had a chance to tell him, anyway, because the Old Man held up a hand. His face was like granite. "You, Val," he ordered. "Stay here and keep an eye on him. You others, come with me."

I watched them go, Mitzi and the Old Man and the woman with them—short, dumpy, and what she had muttered when she saw me seemed to have had an accent. "She's RussCorp, isn't she?" I asked Dambois, and he gave me the answer I expected. He snarled:

"Shut up."

I nodded. He didn't have to confirm it. Just the fact that he and the Old Man were sneaking into Mitzi's apartment that way told me all I needed to know. The conspiracy was a lot bigger than Mitzi had admitted. And a lot older. How had the Old Man got his stake? From Venus. From a "lottery" that he had "happened" to win. How had Mitzi got hers? From a "damage settlement" for the "accident." How had Dambois? From "trading profits." All from Venus. All uncheckable by anyone on Earth.

All used for the same purpose.

And if RussCorp was in it, it wasn't just America; I had to assume it was worldwide. I had to assume that for every little crumb of information Mitzi had so reluctantly leaked out there was a whole hidden loaf behind. "There's some evidence you can trust me," I mentioned to Dambois. "After all, I haven't said a word to anybody so far." And, of course, he only replied with:

"Shut up."

"Yeah," I said, nodding. "Well, do you mind if I get myself some more coffee?"

"Sit still," he snapped, then thought it over for a moment. Reluctantly he added, "I'll get it for you, but you stay there." He went over to the pot, but he never took his eyes off me—heaven knows what he expected. I didn't move. I sat still, as ordered, listening to the rise and fall of furious voices from Mitzi's bedroom. I couldn't make out the words. On the other hand, I didn't have to; I was pretty sure I knew what they were discussing.

When they came out I searched their faces. They were all serious. Mitzi's was impenetrable. "We've made a decision," she said gloomily. "Sit down and drink your coffee and I'll tell you about it."

Well, that was the first ray of hope in a sunless situation. I listened carefully. "In the first place," she said slowly, "this is my fault. I should have got you out of here an hour ago. I knew they were coming for a meeting."

I nodded to show I was listening, glancing around to gauge their expressions. None of them were informative. "Yes?" I asked brightly.

"So it would be wrong, morally wrong," she said, every word coming out at spaced intervals, as though she were weighing each one, "to say that any of this is your fault." She paused, as though looking for a response from me.

"Thank you," I said, nervously sipping my coffee. But she didn't go on. She just went on watching me and, funny thing, the *expression* on her face didn't change, but her *face* did. It blurred. The features ran together. The whole room darkened and seemed to shrink. . . . It took me all that time to realize that the coffee had tasted just a tiny bit odd.

And, oh, how I wished I had never written that suicide note. I wished it hard and with all my being, right up to the point where my wishes stopped functioning entirely and so did my eyes, and so did my ears, and so—in the middle of a silent scream of terror, pleading for one more chance, begging to live one more day—so did my brain.

The world had gone away and left me.

170

II

Even then Mitzi must have fought hard for me. What they slipped into my coffee hadn't been lethal after all. It had only put me to sleep, deeply and helplessly asleep for a long time.

In my dream somebody was shouting, "First call—five minutes!" and I woke up.

I wasn't in Mitzi's apartment any more. I was in a tiny, Spartan cell with a single door and a single window, and outside the window it was dark.

Once I had come to believe in the odd fact that I was alive I looked around. I wasn't tied up, I found to my surprise, nor did I appear to have been recently beaten. I was lying quite comfortably on a narrow cot, with a pillow and a light sheet thrown over my somehow undressed body. Next to the bed was a table. On the table was a tray with some kind of cereal and a glass of Vita-Froot, and between them was an envelope like the tricky kind you use for top-secret Agency messages. I opened it and read it fast, working against the time limit. It said:

> Tenny, dear, you're no good to yourself or us as an addict. If you live through the detox we'll talk again. Good luck!

There wasn't any signature, but there was a P.S.:

> We've got people in the center to report on how you're doing. I ought to tell you that they're authorized to take independent action.

I mulled over what the words "independent action" might mean for a moment—a moment too long, because the trick paper scorched my fingers as it did what it was supposed to do and began to self-destruct. I dropped the smoldering ash hastily and glanced around the room.

There wasn't much information there. The door was locked. The window was shatterproof glass, and sealed. Evidently this center didn't want me walking away from this detox thing. It was all pretty ominous, and there wasn't any long green pill to numb the feelings. Still, there was food and I was starving. Evidently I had been asleep past a couple of mealtimes. I reached for the Vita-Froot just as all hell broke loose. The screaming voice from my dream was no dream. Now it was yelling, "Last call—everybody out!" It wasn't alone. There were sirens and klaxons to make sure I heard; the door lock snicked open, and running feet in the corridors accompanied a banging on every door. "Out!" yelled some individual live human being, glaring in and jerking a huge thumb.

I saw no reason to argue with him about it, since he was at least two sizes bigger than Des Haseldyne.

He was wearing a blue jogging suit. So were about a dozen others, the ones doing all the yelling. I had found a pair of shorts and grabbed them at the last minute, feeling desperately underdressed—but not alone; besides the jogging-suit tyrants there were a couple dozen other human beings streaming out of the building, all as inadequately clothed as myself and looking at least as unhappy. They chased us out into the sweaty, smoggy air, still dark although now there was a discouraging reddish glow in one corner of the sky, and we huddled there, waiting to be told what to do. It was, I thought, like the worst of basic training.

That was wrong. It was a lot worse than any basic training. Basic training at least usually starts with fairly healthy raw meat for its processing. There was nothing like that in sight among my compeers. They came in all shapes and sizes but good. There was one woman who had to weigh over three hundred pounds, and a couple of others, both sexes, who probably weighed less but made up for it by being a lot shorter, so that they billowed grossly over their belts. There were scarecrows skinnier than me and at least as frazzled. There were elderly men and women who looked not hopelessly inhuman except that they had tics they couldn't control—hand to the mouth, hand to the mouth, over and over in endlessly repeated gestures of smoking, eating, drinking. But they had nothing in their hands. And, oh, yes, it was raining.

The joggers shoved and nagged us into a disorderly sort of clump in the middle of a wide cement quadrangle, surrounded by low barrackslike buildings. Over the door to the building we had just come out of was a sign:

Acute Addiction Facility
Detox Effort Division

One of the instructors blew a whistle close by my right ear. When the sound had stopped bouncing around inside my skull I saw that an Amazon in the same jogging suit as the others, but with a gold badge sewn to the jacket, was strutting toward us. She looked at us with revulsion. "God," she observed to the lunatic with the whistle, "every month they get worse. All right, you!" she bawled, climbing on a box to see us better and emphasizing her orders with a blast on her own whistle that neatly severed the top of my head and sent it spinning off over the barracks. "Pay attention! See that sign? 'Detox Effort Division.' The crucial word is *effort*. We'll make the *effort*. You'll make the *effort*, too, I promise you that. But in spite of all of our best *efforts* we're usually going to *fail*. The stats tell the story. Out of ten of you four will go out clean—and then readdict themselves within a month. Three will develop incapacitating physical or psychoneurotic symptoms and require extended treatment—extended has been known to mean the rest of your lives, which are often short. And two of you won't make it through the course." She grinned kindly—I guess she thought it was kindly. I was six hours behind my last pill and the Madonna wouldn't have looked kind to me just then.

Another shattering blast on the whistle. She had paused for a moment, and she didn't want us daydreaming. "Your treatment," she said, "comes in two phases. The first phase is the unpleasant one. That's when we cut you back to minimum dose, feed you up to build resistance, exercise you to develop muscle

173

tone, teach you new behaviors to break up your body-movement patterns that reinforce your habit—and a few other things—and that starts right now. Down on your bellies, everybody, for fifty push-ups—and then it's clothes off and into the showers!"

Fifty push-ups! We stared at each other incredulously in that dark, sultry dawn. I had never in my *life* done fifty push-ups, and I didn't think it was possible . . . until I found out that there were no showers, no breakfast, no leaving the drill ground—above all, no pills—until they were done.

It became possible, even for the three-hundred-pounders.

The lady hadn't lied. Phase One was unpleasant, all right. The only way I could force myself through every miserable hour was by thinking about the blessed green pill that would come at the end of the day. They didn't take the pills away; they only made me earn them. And the horror was that the better I got at earning, the less the reward; by the third day they had begun to shave the end of the pills; by the sixth they were cutting them in half. Three of us had pill habits from Moke addiction. The others had every imaginable addiction. The fat lady, whose name turned out to be Marie, was junk-food; she wheezed like a calliope going over the obstacle course but she always went, because there was no other way to the mess hall. A dark little man named Jimmy Paleologue had been a Campbellian technician himself, borrowed from his Agency by the services to help teach the New Zealand Maoris civilized ways. He was far too sophisticated to be caught by Campbellian stimuli himself, but had inexplicably fallen for a free trial sample of Coffiest. "It was a lottery-ticket tie-in," he explained sheepishly as we lay on the muddy ground, panting between knee-bends and rope-climbing. "First prize was a three-room apartment, and I was thinking of getting married. . . ." Palsied and pitiful, barely dragging himself at the tail end of the three-mile runs, he wasn't thinking of it any more.

The center was in one of the outer suburbs, a place called Rochester, and it had once been a college campus. The buildings still had the old lettering carved into the cement walls—Psychology Department, Economics Section, Applied Physics and so

174

on. There was a sludgy body of liquid lapping at the foot of the campus, and as far as physical surroundings were concerned that was the worst part. They called it Lake Ontario. When the wind was from the north the stench would knock you down. Some of the old buildings were barracks, some therapy rooms, a mess hall, offices; but there were a couple at the edge of the campus that we were not allowed in. They weren't empty. Now and then we would catch glimpses of creatures as miserable as ourselves being shepherded in and out, but whoever they were, we did not mix. "Tenny," gasped Marie, leaning on me as we headed past them toward afternoon therapy, "what do you suppose they *do* in there?" A woman in a pink jogging suit—even their instructors were separate from ours—leaned out the door of one of the buildings to glare at us as she tossed something in the refuse bin. When she went back inside I tugged Marie over.

"Let's take a look," I said, glancing around to see that no blue suit was near. I didn't *think* there would be any discarded green pills among the trash, and I'm sure Marie didn't expect to dig up any extra morsels of food. Disappointingly, we were right. All we came up with was a couple of gold-colored booties and a cracked pseudoivory-handled toy gun. They meant nothing to me, but Marie let out a sudden squawk.

"Oh, my gosh, Tenny, they're *collectibles!* My sister had these! Those are from the Miniature Authentic Replicas of Bronzed Baby Shoes of Twentieth Century Gangsters—that one's Bugs Moran, I think—and I'm nearly sure the other is from the Lone Star Scrimshaw Handgun Collection. That's aversion therapy they're doing in there—where first they make you stop needing it, then they make you hate it! Could that be Phase Two?"

And then the instructor's bellow from behind us: "All right, you two goof-offs, if you've got time to stand around and gossip you've got time for a few extra push-ups. Let's have fifty, now! And make it quick, because you know what happens if you're late for therapy!"

We knew.

When I wasn't doing jumps and jerks or having my head

rebent I was eating—every ten minutes, it seemed. Plain food, healthy food, like Bredd and ReelMeet and Tangy-Joose, and no argument. I cleaned off my plate every time, or it was, you guessed it, another fifty push-ups for dessert. Not that fifty extra push-ups made that much difference. I was doing four or five hundred a day, plus squats and sit-ups and bendings-and-touchings, and forty laps a day in the pool strip. There was only room for three of us to swim abreast, and they handicapped us so we three were pretty even in skill—guess what the loser got? Of course he did. The forty of us dropped to thirty-one, to twenty-five, to twenty-two. . . . The one that hit me hardest was Marie. She'd actually lost forty pounds or so, and was beginning to be able to eat her "meals"—vitamins and protein bars, and not much of them—without whimpering, when on the twelfth day, scrambling up the nets, she gasped and choked and rolled to the ground. She was dead. She wasn't permanently dead, because they wheeled out the heart shocker and whisked her off in a pneumatic three-wheel ambulance, but she was too dead to come back to our group.

And all the time my nerves were crawling inside my skin, and what I wanted to do more than anything else was to conk the medication nurse over the skull, take away his keys and get into the locked cabinet of long green pills.

But I didn't.

The funny thing was that, after two weeks, down to one quarter-strength cap a day, I actually began to feel a little bit better. Not *good*. Just less bad, less strung out, less Jesus-I'd-*kill*-for-a-cap. "False well-being," Paleologue panted wisely when I said as much to him, just out of the pool, waiting to start our two-mile run. "You'll hit these temporary plateaus, but they don't mean anything. I've seen you Campbellian-syndrome people before—"

And I laughed at him. I knew better; it was my own body, wasn't it? I could even spare time for thinking about something beyond long green pills—even got as far as the line for the one public phone, once, with every intention of calling Mitzi. And would have, too, if one of those nausea fits hadn't driven me to

176

the communijohn, and then there wasn't time to sweat the line again.

And two more weeks passed, and it was the end of Phase One. The unpleasant part.

Silly me. I hadn't asked our instructor what the second part was going to be like. I had happily, hopefully, assumed that if Phase One was described as *unpleasant* then Phase Two would be described best as something like at least *okay.*

That was before I encountered aversion therapy and final withdrawal, and found out that Phase Two certainly was not anything you would call *unpleasant.* It was way beyond unpleasant. The best term I can think of for it was just your ordinary plain hell.

I guess I don't want to talk any more about Phase Two because, every time I do, I start to shake; but I got through it. As the poisons got out of my body they seemed to get out of my head, too. By the time the director shook my hand and put me on a rocket back to the world—conscious, this time—I felt—still not good—more sad than good—more angry than sad—but, for the first time maybe in my life, *rational.*

The True
Tennison Tarb

·· ◆ ··

I

You lose track of the seasons in Phase Two, because one is as bad as the next. When I got back to the city I was surprised to find that it was still summery, though the tree in Central Park had begun to turn. Sweat streamed down the back of my pedicab pusher. The ear-shattering traffic din of yells and squeals and crunches was underlaid with the pusher's hacking, sooty cough. There was a smog alert, of course. Of course my pedaler wasn't wearing a face-filter anyway, because you can't get enough air through a filter to keep your speed up in heavy traffic. As we rounded the Circle into Broadway, a six-man armored bank van swerved right in front of us; dodging them, the pedaler slipped on the greasy fallout and for a moment I thought the whole rig was going over. She turned a scared face to me. " 'Scuse it, mister," she panted. "Those damn trucks don't give you a chance!"

"As a matter of fact," I called, "it's such a nice day that I'm thinking of walking the rest of the way anyway." Of course she looked at me as though I were insane, especially when I ordered her to pace me empty in case I should change my mind about walking. When I paid her off with a big tip at the Haseldyne & Ku Building she was sure I was insane. She couldn't wait to get away. But the sweat had dried on her back and she was hardly coughing at all.

I had never done anything like that before.

178

I waved absently at the colleagues I recognized as I entered the building. They were looking at me with varying degrees of astonishment, but I was busy being astonished at myself. Something had happened to me at the Detox Center. I had come back with more than the bruises from the jabs of vitamin spray and the distaste for long green pills. I had come back with some new accessories inside my head. What they were exactly I didn't yet know, but one of them seemed to want to answer to the name "conscience."

When I walked into my office Dixmeister was as pop-eyed as anyone. "Gosh, Mr. Tarb," he marveled, "you look so *healthy!* That vacation sure must have done you a lot of good."

I nodded. He was only telling me what the scales and the mirror had been telling me the last few mornings. I'd gained back twenty pounds. I didn't shake. I didn't even feel shaky; even the flashing commercials and glitter-bang posters hadn't awakened any cravings on the way to the office. "Carry on," I told him. "I've got to report to Mitzi Ku before I take over here."

That was not easy. She wasn't there the first time I tried. She wasn't there the second, and when I caught her at last on the third round trip between her office and mine she was there all right, but just on the point of leaving. "Mr. Haseldyne's waiting," her sec[3] warned, but Mitzi tarried. She closed the door. We kissed. Then she stood back.

She looked at me. I looked at her. She said to me with wistful surprise, "Tenny, you are looking *fine.*"

I said to her, "Mitzi, you are looking fine, too," and added for truth's sake, "to me." For in fact Mitzi's morning mirror would not have been as kind as mine. She was looking terribly worn, in fact, but the subjective fact behind those facts was that I didn't care how she looked as long as she was there. With her complexion, the circles under her eyes were not emphatic. But they were there: she'd missed sleep, maybe even had missed some meals . . . and she still looked to me quite splendid.

"Was it awful, Tenny?"

"Middling awful." There had been a lot of throwing up, a lot of scrabbling around frantically to find something to cut my throat with. But I hadn't succeeded in that, and I'd only had the convulsions twice. I dismissed it. "Mitzi," I said, "I've got two important things to tell you."

"Of course, Tenny, but this is the damnedest busiest time right now—"

I cut her off. "Mitzi. I want us to get married."

Her hands clenched. Her body froze. Her eyes opened so wide that I feared her contacts would pop out.

I said, "I had plenty of time to think things over in the Detox Center. I mean it."

From outside came Haseldyne's peevish rumble: "Mitzi! Let's get going!"

Silently, automatically, she came to life again, picking up her bag, opening the door, staring at me the whole while. "Come *on,*" barked Haseldyne.

"I'm coming," she called; and to me, heading toward the lift, "Dear Tenny, I can't talk now. I'll call you."

And then, two steps away, she turned and came back to me. And there, in the full view of God and everybody, she kissed me. Just before she disappeared into the descending lift she whispered, "I'd like that."

But she didn't call. She didn't call me that day at all.

Since I had never proposed marriage to anybody before, I had no personal experience to tell me if that was a reasonable response. It didn't feel like one. What it felt like was the way Mitzi herself had felt—well, not Mitzi herself; not *this* Mitzi, but the brassy other one back on Venus—the way *that* Mitzi had told me she felt when we first got it on together and I finished ahead of her, and she let me know that I'd damn well have to do better next time around or else. . . . Anyway, it felt bad. I was left hanging.

And I hadn't told her the other important thing.

Fortunately there was plenty to keep me busy. Dixmeister had kept things going as well as you could expect, but Dixmeister wasn't me. I kept him late that night, reviewing his mistakes and ordering changes. He was looking shop-soiled and grumpy by the time I let him go home. As to me, I flipped a coin about where I would spend the time and lost. I holed up in a private-drawer hotel a few blocks from the office and got to work early the next morning. When I went to Mitzi's office her sec[3] said her sec[2] had told her Ms. Ku would be out all morning, along with her sec[1]. I spent my lunch hour—all twenty-five minutes of my lunch hour, because one day hadn't been enough to get things turned around and moving right—sitting in Mitzi's anteroom, using her sec[1]'s phone to keep Dixmeister on the hop. Mitzi didn't show. The all-morning engagements had been protracted.

That night I went to Mitzi's condo.

The door thing let me in, but Mitzi wasn't there. She wasn't there when I arrived at ten, nor at midnight, nor when I woke at six, and waited a while, and dressed, and went back to the office. Oh, yes, Mr. Tarb, her sec[3] told me, Ms. Ku had called in during the night to say that she'd been called out of town for an indefinite stay. She would be in touch with me herself. Soon.

But she wasn't.

Part of my head filed that fact without comment and went on with what it was doing. That was to carry out the orders given. What Mitzi wanted me to do was to elect candidates. It was already September and the "election" only weeks away. There was much to keep me busy, and that part of my head took advantage of every minute it had. It took advantage of every minute Dixmeister had, too, and everybody else in the Intangibles (Politics) department. When I stalked the halls people from other departments averted their eyes and stayed out of my path—for fear I'd draft them to twelve-hour days, I suppose.

The other part of my head, the new one that I'd seemed to discover at the Detox Center—that wasn't doing so well. It was hurting—not just for Mitzi, but for the pain of that other thing it was carrying that I hadn't told her. Then the interoffice mail-person darted into my office long enough to drop a flash-paper envelope on my desk and whisk away.

The note was from Mitzi. It said:

Dear Tenny, I like your idea. If we get through this alive I hope you'll still want to, because I will, very much. But this isn't a time to talk about love. I'm under revolutionary discipline, Tenny, and so are you. Please hold that thought. . . .

With all the love I can only tell you about now—

Mitzi

Again it flared and scorched my fingers before I dropped it. But I didn't mind. It was an answer!—and the right answer, too.

There remained the question of the other thing I needed to say.

So I kept badgering the sec³, and when at last she told me that yes, Ms. Ku was back in the city that morning but going directly to an urgent meeting elsewhere, I couldn't wait.

Besides, I thought I knew where I could find her.

"Tarb," cried Semmelweiss—"I mean, Mr. Tarb, good to see you! You're looking really well!"

"Thanks," I said, looking around the grommet factory. The presses were chugging and rattling and thumping out their millions of little round things. The noise was the same, the dirt was the same, but something was missing. "Where's Rockwell?" I asked.

"Who? Oh, *Rockwell,*" he said. "Yeah, he used to be here. He got in some kind of accident. We had to let him go." His grin got nervous as he saw my expression. "Well, he really wasn't able to work any more, was he? Two broken legs, and then the way his face looked— Anyway, I guess you want to go upstairs? Go right ahead, Mr. Tarb! I guess they're up there. You never know, with all those entrances and exits—still, I always say if they pay their rent right on time, who needs to ask questions?"

I left him there. There was nothing else to say about Nelson Rockwell, and nothing I cared to say to satisfy his curiosity about his tenants. Poor Rockwell! So the collection agency had finally

182

not been willing to wait any more. I vowed I would have to do something about Nelson Rockwell as I pushed open the door—

And then I didn't think about Nelson Rockwell for a while, because the door that once had opened into the dirty old loft now opened into a thieflock. Behind me the stair door slammed shut. Before me was a barred door; around me were steel walls. Light flooded over me. I could hear nothing, but I knew I was being observed.

A speaker over my head rumbled in Des Haseldyne's voice, "You'd better have a damn good reason for this, Tarb." The door before me slid open. The one behind me heaved me out of the cubicle with a thrust bar, and I was in a room full of people. They were all looking at me.

There'd been changes in the old loft. High-tech and luxury had come in. There was a telescreen monitor spitting out situation reports along one wall, and the other walls were draped more handsomely than the Old Man's office at T. G, & S. The center of the huge room was filled with an immense oval table—it looked like genuine wood veneer—and in armchairs around the table, each one with its own decanter and glass and scribe-screen and phone, were more than a dozen human beings, and what human beings they were! Not just Mitzi and Haseldyne and the Old Man. There were people there I'd never seen before except on the news screen, heads of Agencies from RussCorp and Indiastries and South America S.A.—German, English, African—half the might of the world's advertising was creamed off and poured into this room. At every step I had been dazzled by the constant revelations of grander scope, greater power to the Veenie moles organization. Now I had taken the last step and penetrated its core. It felt an awful lot like one step too many.

Mitzi must have thought so. She jumped up, face working in shock: "Tenny! Damn you, Tenny, why did you come here?"

I said steadily, "I told you I have something you need to know. It affects you all, so it's just as well I caught you. Your plan is down the tube. You don't have time. There's going to be a huck fleet heading for Venus any time now, with full Campbellian ordnance."

There was a vacant chair near Mitzi at the head of the table. I plumped myself down in it and waited for the storm to break.

It came, all right. Half of them didn't believe me. The other half might have had an opinion one way or the other on that, but the big thing on their minds was that I had entered into their most secret place. There was fury by the megaton in that loft, and it wasn't all aimed at me. Mitzi got her share—more than her share, especially from Des Haseldyne: "I warned you to get *rid* of him," he yelled. "Now there's no choice!" The lady from S.A.[2]: "I theenk you have got big problem here!" The man from RussCorp, pounding the table with his fist, "Is no question, problem! Is only question, how do we solve? Your problem, Ku!" The man from Indiastries, palms together and fingers upthrust: "One wishes not to take life, to be sure, but in certain classes of predicaments one can scarcely find alternatives which—"

I had had enough. I stood up and leaned into the table. "Will you listen?" I asked. "I know your easy way out is to get rid of me and forget what I said. That means Venus is gone."

"You be quiet!" grumped the woman from Germany, but she was alone. She looked around the table, a dozen human beings frozen in positions of rage, then said sulkily, "So tell then what you want, we will listen. A short time we will listen."

I gave them a big smile. "Thank you," I said. I wasn't feeling particularly brave. I knew that, among other things, I was on trial for my life. But my life no longer seemed all that valuable. It was not, for example, equal to the session at the detox farm; if ever I faced the need of that again, knowing now just what it was like, I would surely have Xed myself first. But I was fed up. I said:

"You've seen the news over the last few years, mopping up aboriginal areas to bring them into civilization. Have you noticed where the last few were? The Sudan. Arabia. The Gobi Desert. Does anything strike you about those places?" I looked around the table. It hadn't; but I could see that it was beginning to. "Deserts," I said. "Hot, dry deserts. Not as hot as Venus and not as dry—but the closest thing to Venus there is on the surface of the Earth, and so the best place to practice. That's point one."

I sat down, and made my voice conversational. "When they court-martialed me," I said, "they kept me in Arizona for a couple of weeks. Another desert area. They had ten thousand troops there on maneuvers; as far as I could tell, they were the same troops they had had in Urumqi. And out in the boonies they had a fleet of rockets. Right next to the rockets were stockpiles: Campbell ordnance. Now, let's see if we can figure it out. They've been practicing in simulated Venus conditions; they've got trained combat troops rehearsing invasion tactics now; they've got Campbell heavy weapons ready to be loaded into shuttles. Add it up. What do you come out with?"

Total silence in the room. Then, tentatively, the woman from S.A.[2]: "It ees true, we have been told of very many shuttles formerly based in Venezuela now transferred for some purpose. We had assumed perhaps Hyperion was the target."

"Hyperion," sneered RussCorp. "One shuttle alone—plenty for Hyperion!"

Haseldyne snapped, "Don't get panicked by this pillhead! I'm sure he's exaggerating. The hucks are a paper tiger. If we do our job they won't have any time to worry about Venus—they'll be too busy sucking their thumbs and wondering what went wrong with the Earth."

"I am glad," said RussCorp gloomily, "that you are sure. I myself have doubts. Have been many rumors, all reported to this council—all dismissed. Wrongly, I now think."

"I personally suggest—" began the German, but Haseldyne cut her off.

"We'll talk this over in private," he said dangerously, and glared at me. "You! Outside! We'll call you back when we want you!"

I gave them a shrug, and a smile, and went out the door the man from Indiastries held open for me. It was no surprise to me to find that it led only to a short stairway and to an outside door —which was locked. I sat on the steps and waited.

When at last the inner door opened again and Haseldyne called my name I didn't try to read the expression on his face. I just politely slid past him and took the empty seat at the table. He didn't like it much; his face was reddening and his expression lethal, but he didn't say anything. He didn't have the right to. He wasn't the person in charge.

The person in charge now was the Old Man himself. He looked up to study me, and the face looked the same as it always had, pink and plump and wool-framed, except that it wasn't at all genial. The expression was bleak. And, wholly out of character for the Old Man I had known so long, he offered no small talk. He offered nothing at all for a long moment, just looked up at me, then back at his table-top screen, and his fingers busy tapping out new queries and getting bad answers. From the stairs I had heard a lot of noise—agitated rumbles and peremptory shrill squeals— but now they were silent. The stifling aroma of real tobacco came from the place where the RussCorp man was silently smoking his pipe. The SA^2 woman absently stroked something in her lap— a pet, I could see; possibly a kitten.

Then the Old Man slapped his board to clear his screen and said heavily, "Tarb, that's not good news you brought us. But we have to assume it's true."

"Yes, *sir*," I cried, out of old reflex.

"We have to act swiftly to meet this challenge," he declared. His pomposity had not gone the way of his good humor. "You will understand, of course, that we can't tell you our plans—"

"Of course not, sir!"

"—and you'll understand, too, that you have not yet proved yourself. Mitzi Ku vouches for you," he went on, his cold stare drifting across the table to focus on her. She was gazing at her fingertips and didn't look up to meet it. "Provisionally, we are accepting her guarantee." At that she winced, and I had a quick understanding of what the alternatives they had been discussing might be, *provisionally.*

"I understand," I said, and managed to omit the sir. "What do you want me to do?"

"You are ordered to continue with your work. That is our

186

major project and it can't be stopped. Mitzi and the rest of us will now have to be doing—other things—so you'll be on your own to some extent. Don't let that make you sloppy."

I nodded, waiting to see if there was more. There wasn't. Des Haseldyne led me to the door and escorted me through. Mitzi hadn't spoken at all. At the foot of the stairs Haseldyne pushed me into another thieflock. Before he closed the door he snapped, "You looking for thanks? Forget it! We thanked you by letting you live."

As I waited for the outer door to open I heard the furious rumbles and squeaks begin again as they went at it once more. What Haseldyne had said was true: they'd let me live. What was also true was that they could reverse that decision at any time. Could I prevent that? Yes, I decided, but in only one way: by doing such a good job for them that I would become indispensable . . . or more accurately, by making sure they *thought* I was.

Then the outside door opened.

Des Haseldyne must have been operating the controls. That lock had thrust-bar capacities too; the door behind me hurled me out into the street. I stumbled and fell, skidding across the sidewalk under the feet of hurrying pedestrians. "You all right, mister?" quavered one old consumer, gaping at me with alarm.

"I'm fine," I snapped as I picked myself up. I don't think I have ever told a bigger lie.

II

It is a bad and worrisome thing to have lined yourself up with a bunch of felons as accomplice to brainburning crimes. It's a lot worse to realize that they're inept. That circle of Venusian master spies and saboteurs might, among the lot of them, have summoned up enough skill and villainy to sneak a bunch of forged discount coupons past a supermarket checker. For the task of preserving their world against the might of Earth they simply were not up to it.

Dixmeister had an easy time of it that afternoon. When I

limped back into my office I snarled at him to go about his business and leave me alone until ordered otherwise. Then I locked my door and thought.

Without Mokes or little green pills to hide behind, what I saw when I opened my eyes was naked reality. It was not an attractive sight, for it was full of problems—three in particular:

First, if I didn't convince the Veenies that they needed me, and could even trust me, good old Haseldyne would know what to do about it. After that I wouldn't have any worries at all.

Second, if I did as I was told the future looked bleak. I hadn't been consulted in planning their great strategic campaign; the more I thought of it, the less sure I was that it would work.

Third and worst, if it didn't work, then we were all cooked. We would spend the rest of our lives living in playpens, wearing diapers, spoon-fed by attendants who didn't like us much and getting our chief intellectual stimulation from watching the pretty lights go by. All of us. Not just me. The woman I loved as well.

I didn't want Mitzi Ku brainburned.

I didn't want Tennison Tarb brainburned, either. My recently acquired clarity of thought soberly pointed out that there was a way out of that part of the fix, anyway. All I had to do was pick up the phone to the Fair Commercial Practices Commission and turn the Veenies in; I'd probably get off with the Polar Penal Colony, maybe even just reduction to consumer status. But that wouldn't save Mitzi. . . .

Just before the close of business Mitzi and Des called a top-level staff meeting in the boardroom. Mitzi didn't speak, didn't look at me, either. Des Haseldyne did all the talking. He said there were some, uh, unexpected expansion opportunities opening up and he and Mitzi would have to be out of the office to investigate them. Meanwhile, they had bought Val Dambois's contract from T., G. & S. and he would be coming in as temporary general manager; Intangibles (Political) would be directed independently by Tennison Tarb, that was me, and he was sure we'd carry on with full efficiency.

It was not a convincing performance. It wasn't received well, either. There were sidelong glances and worried looks in the audience. As we all got up to go I managed to get close to Mitzi long enough to whisper in her ear: "I'll stay on at the condo, all right?" She didn't answer that, either. She just looked at me and shrugged.

I didn't have a chance to pursue it, because at that point Val Dambois came up from behind and grabbed my shoulder. "A word with you, Tenny," he gritted, and led me to Mitzi's office —his office now. He slammed the door, slapped the privacy screen on and said: "Don't get too *independent*, Tarb. Remember I'll be right here, watching you." I didn't need to be reminded of that. When I didn't answer he looked at me closely: "Can you handle it?" he demanded. "Are you feeling all right?"

I said, in order, "I can handle it," which was a lot more hope than conviction, and, "I feel like somebody who's got two whole planets resting on his shoulders," which was true.

He nodded. "Just remember," he said, "if you have to let one of them drop, make sure it's the right one."

"Sure thing, Val," I said. But which was the right one?

Since Mitzi hadn't said I couldn't stay at the condo, I did. I didn't expect her to be there that first night, and she wasn't. I wasn't quite alone, though. Val Dambois made sure I had a certain amount of company. As I hailed a pedicab outside the office I noticed a muscular male type dawdling after me, and the same man was lounging around across from Mitzi's condo when I left in the morning. I didn't care. They left me alone in the office, although I might not have noticed if they hadn't. I was *busy*. I wanted that weight of two worlds off my shoulders, and the only way to do it was to win their war for them . . . somehow.

There were a dozen major theme commercials to prepare for the election and only days to do them in. I turned Dixmeister loose on lining up channel time and riding herd on the production department. I took over talent and script completely.

Now, normally when a project head says he takes over talent

189

and script, what he means is he has about half a dozen headhunters searching out talent for him and at least that many copysmiths generating the scripts; what he does is mostly kick tail to make sure they're doing their jobs. With me it was a little different. I had the staff, and I kicked their tails. But I also had plans of my own. They weren't very clear in my mind. They were a long way from satisfactory, even to me. And there wasn't anybody I could bounce them off to see how high they climbed. But they were what kept me in the office for sixteen hours a day instead of the mere ten or twelve I might otherwise have spent. It wasn't so bad; what else did I have to do with my time?

I knew what else I *wanted* to do with my time, but Mitzi was —was—what shall I say? Out of my reach? Not really; we bedded together every night she was in the city. Out of my grasp, though, because the bed was the only place I saw her, and not often there. I'd set the whole Veenie hive buzzing with my news, and they were zinging in all directions. When Mitzi was in the city she was at high-level, secret meetings every minute; when she wasn't in meetings here, she was somewhere else in the world. Or off it, because for a solid week she was on the Moon, trading furtive, coded messages with a freight-forwarder in Port Kathy on Venus.

One night I'd given up hope of her and gone to sleep when, in the middle of a really rotten dream about a Fair Commercial Practices strong-arm man creeping into the bed next to me, I woke to find someone really was, and it was Mitzi.

It took me a long time to get wholly awake because of exhaustion, and when I accomplished it, Mitzi was already asleep. I could see by looking at her that she was a lot more exhausted than I. If I'd had any compassion at all I'd have put my arms around her silently and let the two of us sleep through the night. I couldn't. I got up, and made some of that funny-tasting real coffee for her, and sat down on the edge of the bed until she smelled it and stirred. She didn't want to wake up. She was burrowed down under the blanket with just the top of her head and enough of her nose for breathing still visible, and there was a warm smell of sweet sleeping woman to mingle with the aroma of the coffee.

She tossed herself petulantly over to the other side of the bed, muttering something—all I could understand were some words about "changing fuses." I waited. Then the rhythm of her breathing changed and I knew she was awake.

She opened her eyes. "Hello, Tenny," she said.

"Hello, Mitzi." I extended the coffee cup, but she ignored it for a moment, looking bleakly at me over it.

"Do you really want to get married?"

"You bet, if—"

She didn't expect me to finish that sentence. She nodded. "So do I," she said. "If." She put herself up against the pillows and took the cup. "Well," she said, postponing that subject for the duration, "how's it going?"

I ventured, "I've got some pretty hot new commercial themes. Maybe I should check them out with you."

"What for? You're in charge." That subject was dismissed too. I reached over and touched her shoulder. She didn't move away, but she didn't respond, either. There were a lot of other subjects I would have liked to discuss. Where we were going to live. Whether we wanted to have any kids, and what genders. What we would do for fun and, that subject always dear to the newly engaged, how much and in what particular ways we loved each other. . . .

I didn't say any of those things. Instead, I asked: "What did you mean about 'changing fuses,' Mitzi?"

She sat bolt upright, slopping coffee into the saucer, glaring at me. "What the hell are you asking, Tenn?" she snapped.

I said, "It kind of sounds to me as though you're talking about sabotaging equipment. Campbellian projectors, right? You're probably infiltrating people into the limbic units to screw up the machinery?"

"Shut up, Tenn."

"Because if you are," I went on reasonably, "I don't think that will work. See, they've got a long flight to Venus and there'll be standby crews kept awake in rotating shifts. They won't have anything to do but to keep checking and rechecking the equip-

191

ment. Anything you bust, they'll have plenty of time to fix."

That shook her. She set the cup down by the side of the bed, staring at me.

"The other thing that worries me about that," I continued, "is that when they find out there's been sabotage they'll start looking for who did it. Sure, the huck intelligence services are fat, dumb and happy—they haven't had anything to worry about for a long time. But you just might wake them up."

"Tenny," she flared, "*butt out.* You do your own damn job. Let us worry about security!"

So I did what I should have done in the first place. I turned the light off and slipped into bed beside her and took her in my arms. We didn't talk any more. As I was drifting off to sleep I realized that she was weeping. I wasn't surprised. It was a hell of a way for a newly engaged couple to be spending their time, but it was the only way we had. We simply couldn't talk easily, for she had her secrets that she was obliged to protect.

And I had mine.

On the sixteenth of October the statutory ten-week-warning Christmas decorations appeared in the store windows. Election Day was getting very close.

It's the last ten days of a campaign that count. I was ready for them. I had done everything I had thought to do and done it real well. I was real well all over these days, barring a slight tendency to get the shakes when a can of Moke was in the room (that was aversion therapy for you), and a considerable loss of weight. People stopped telling me how well I looked. They didn't have to; I was looking as well as anybody could be expected to look when every night's sleep was maimed by dreams about brainburning. Dixmeister danced in and out of my office, thrilled by his new responsibilities, awed by the new themes I was unveiling. "They're really powerful stuff, Mr. Tarb," he told me uneasily, "but are you sure you're not going too far?"

"If I were," I smiled at him, "don't you think Ms. Ku would have stopped them?" Maybe she would have, if I had told her

192

what they were. But the moment for that had passed. I was committed.

I stopped him as he turned to hurry out. "Dixmeister," I said, "I've had some complaints from the networks about degraded signals on our transmissions."

"Transmission fade? Gosh, Mr. Tarb, I haven't seen any memos—"

"They're coming along later. I got this head-to-head with the net people. So I want to check this out. Get me a wiring diagram of this building; I want to see where every signal goes from point of origin to the phone company mains outside."

"Right, Mr. Tarb! You mean just the commercial transmissions, of course?"

"I of course don't. I want everything. And I want it now."

"That'll take hours, Mr. Tarb," he wailed. He had a family, and he was thinking of what his wife would say when he didn't get home for First Gift Night.

"You've got hours," I told him. He did. And I didn't want him spending those hours looking for incoming memos that didn't exist or chattering with somebody else's staff about what Mr. Tarb was doing now. When he had the entire electronics circuitry displayed for me I froze a hard copy, jammed it in my pocket and made him join me on a physical inspection of the place where all the lines came together, the comm room in the basement.

"I've never *been* in the basement, Mr. Tarb," he whimpered. "Can't we leave that for the phone company?"

"Not if we ever want to get promoted again, Dixmeister," I told him kindly, and so the two of us took the lift down as far as it would go and then a freight elevator two more stories below that. The basement was damp, dirty, dim-lit, dingy—it was a lot of things beginning with *d* including deserted. There were hundreds of square yards of space here, but too nasty to rent out even to night-dwellers. It was just what I wanted.

The comm room was at the end of a long corridor, choked with dust. Next to it were three rooms of stored microfiles, mostly urgent FCC and Department of Commerce directives that, of course, had never been opened. I looked into every storeroom carefully, then stood at the door of the comm room and gave it one quick glance around. Every phone call, data-link message, facsimile and video transmission the Agency originated went through that room. Of course it was wholly automatic and electronic at that: nothing moved or flashed or clicked. There were manual override terminals for rerouting messages around a bad circuit—or cutting them off entirely—but there was no reason to man them. "Looks all right to me," I said.

Dixmeister gave me a glum look. "I suppose you're going to want to test all the circuits?"

"Nah, what for? The trouble's got to be outside." He opened his mouth to protest, but I closed it with, "And, listen, get all that junk out of those storerooms. I'm going to take them over for a brainroom."

"But, Mr. *Tarb!*"

"Dixmeister," I said gently, "when you're star class you'll understand the need for privacy at times like these. Right now, don't try. Just do it."

I left him to it and went back to Mitzi's condo, wanting very much to find her there. I had a problem or two still to solve. Mitzi was not the person to solve them for me, but she could give me, at least, the touch of beloved skin and the solace of body warmth . . . if this happened to be a night when she would be at home.

She wasn't. All there was of her was a flash-paper note on the pillow to say that she had to be in Rome for a few days.

It wasn't what I wanted but, as I sat staring out over the dirty, sleeping city with an ounce and a half of grain neutral spirits in my hand, I began to perceive that it might be what I needed.

III

My scripts were ready. The candidates to appear in them had been selected and stashed away in hideouts all around the city. It had not been hard to pick them, because I knew just what I wanted; getting them to the city and ready to go had been a lot harder. But they were there. From the condo I phoned in orders for two-man Wackerhut teams to round them up and deliver them to the recording studios, and by the time I reached the office they were there, too.

The actual recording was easy—well, comparatively easy. Compared to, say, six hours of brain surgery. It took all the skill I had and all my concentration, while I rehearsed my actors, and hung over the makeup people while they prepped them for the cameras, and ramrodded the production teams along, and directed every move and word. The easy part was that every one of the actors spoke the lines easily and convincingly, because I'd written them out of knowledge of just what they could do best. The hard part was that I could use only skeleton crews, since the fewer people who knew what was going on the better. When the last one was in the can I shipped the entire crew, production, makeup and all, to an imaginary "remote" in San Antonio, Texas, with orders to loaf around there until I arrived, which would be never.

But at least in San Antonio they wouldn't be talking to anybody else. Then I sent my actors down to the newly completed suite in the basement and got ready for the hard part. I took a deep breath, wished I dared swallow a pill to calm my nerves, exercised vigorously for five minutes so that I'd be out of breath and dashed into the office that once had been Mitzi's. Val Dambois jerked upright, startled, from the figures on his desk screen as I panted, "Val! Urgent call from Mitzi! You've got to get to the Moon! The agent's had a heart attack, the communication link's gone!"

"What the hell are you talking about?" he snarled, the chubby face quivering. In normal times Dambois might not have let me get away with it, but he, too, had been pushed past his strain limit in the last few weeks.

I gabbled, "Message from Mitzi! She said it was crucial. There's a cab waiting—you've got just time to get to the shuttleport—"

"But Mitzi's in—" He stopped, eyeing me uncertainly.

195

"In Rome, right," I nodded. "That's where she called from. She said there's a long priority order due in, and somebody's got to be on the Moon to receive it. So come on, Val!" I begged, grabbing his briefcase, his hat, his passport; hustling him out the door, onto the lift, into the cab. An hour later I called the shuttleport to ask if he'd boarded the flight.

They told me he had.

"Dixmeister!" I called. Dixmeister appeared instantly in the doorway, face flushed, half a soy sandwich in one hand, the other hand still holding his phone. "Dixmeister, those new spots I just taped. I want them aired tonight."

He swallowed down a mouthful of soy. "Why, yes, Mr. Tarb, I suppose we can do that, but we've got a group of other spots scheduled—"

"Switch the spots," I ordered. "New instructions from the top floor. I want those first spots on the air in an hour, full display by prime time. Kill all the others; use the new ones. Do it, Dixmeister." And he loped off, chewing, to get it done.

It was time to go to the mattresses.

As soon as Dixmeister was out of sight I got up and left, closing the door behind me. I would not open it again, at least not in the same world. Very likely I would never open it again at all.

My new office was a lot less luxurious than my old, especially because of where it was: down in subbasement six. Still, considering how little time I'd given them, Housekeeping had done their best. They'd put into it everything I'd asked for, including a wall of a dozen screens for direct display of any feed I chose. There were a dozen desks, all occupied by members of my new little task force. Best of all, Engineering had closed up a couple of old doorways and cut through some new ones, as ordered. There was no longer direct access from the corridor to the comm room. The only way to the Agency's nerve center lay through my new suite of former stockrooms. The little cubicle where the standby engineers had been accustomed to drowse through their duties was empty, and its door had a lock on it now. The engineers themselves were long gone, because I had given all of them a week off on the grounds that the system was automatic and foolproof and I wanted to try the experiment of having it completely unmanned for a while. They looked doubtful until I convinced them that nobody's job was threatened, then they left gladly enough.

The place was, in short, just what I had ordered, with everything I had been able to think of that was necessary to the success of my project. Whether it was also sufficient was another question entirely, but it was too late to worry about that. I put on my best and most confident grin as I approached Jimmy Paleologue at his "reception" desk in the corridor. "Got everything you need?" I asked genially.

He slid his desk drawer back just enough to show me the stun-gun nestling inside it before he grinned back. If there was a hint of strain in the grin you couldn't blame him; after he'd gotten through with the detox center he'd been promised his old job back as a Campbellian technician; then I found him and persuaded him to this unpromising exercise. "Gert and I rigged a tangle-net at the door and another one just inside your room," he reported. "Everybody's armed except Nels Rockwell—he couldn't manage to lift his arm enough to fire. He says he'd like a limbic grenade strapped to his body for, you know, last-ditch stuff—what do you think?"

"I think he'd be more dangerous to us than anybody else," I smiled, though actually it struck me that the idea had merit. Not limbic, though. Explosive. Maybe even a mini-nuke. If things got bad enough we might all welcome a nice clean vaporization instead of the alternative—I left that thought behind me and strode into the suite.

Gert Martels jumped up and grabbed me for a hug. She'd been the most difficult of my people to recruit—they didn't want to let her out of the stockade, even after I threw the Agency rank around; it had finally taken a job offer to the prison commandant —and she was also the most grateful for the chance. "Aw,

Tenny," she chuckled—sobbed—it was actually some of both—
"we're really doing it!"

"It's half done," I told her. "The first spots ought to be on
any minute."

"They've started already!" called fat Marie from her couch by
the wall. "We just saw Gwenny—she was great!" Gwendolyn
Baltic was the youngest of my recruits, fifteen years old and with
a harrowing story. I'd found her through Nelson Rockwell; she
was the product of a broken home when her mother was brainburned for multiple credit frauds and her father committed suicide rather than face detoxification for his Nico-Hype addiction.
She'd been my choice to run the March of Dollars campaign,
soliciting funds for more and better detox centers. I'd picked that
to run first because it was the entering wedge, the least likely to
shock the network continuity-acceptance people into action. "She
was *grand*," beamed Marie, and little Gwenny blushed.

If they had already started we could expect a reaction soon.
It came within ten minutes. "Company coming," called Jimmy
Paleologue from the corridor, and when I saw who it was I ordered
him let in.

It was Dixmeister, hurrying down with urgent messages. "Mr.
Tarb!" he began, but was distracted by the crowded desks. Not
by the desks, exactly; by who was at the desks. "Mr. Tarb?" he
asked querulously. "You've got *talent* here? *Actors?*"

"In case we need them for some last-minute retakes," I said
smoothly, gesturing to Gert to take her hand away from the
stun-gun in her drawer. "You wanted me for something?"

"Oh, hell, yes—I mean, yes, Mr. Tarb. I've been getting calls
from the nets. They've screened your new promo themes, for the
candidates, you know—"

"I know," I said, with my most menacing scowl. "What the
hell is this, Dixmeister? Are you letting them get away with trying
to censor *advertising?*"

He looked shocked. "Oh, gee, Mr. Tarb, no! Nothing like
that. It's just that a couple of the Content Acceptance Division

people thought there was a, well, a kind of a hint of, uh, Co—
Uh, Con—"

"Conservationism, you mean, Dixmeister?" I asked kindly.
"Look at me, Dixmeister. Do I look like a Conservationist to
you?"

"Oh, gosh, no, Mr. Tarb!"

"Or do you think this Agency would put on Consie political
commercials?"

"Not in a million years! It's not just the commercials for the
candidates, though. It's this new charity drive, you know? The
March of Dollars?" I knew; it was my own invention, a fund drive
for expanding detox centers like the one I had been in.

"They're questioning that, too?" I asked, smiling my so-
they're-up-to-those-old-tricks-again smile.

"Well, as a matter of fact, yes, but that's not the part that I
wanted to ask you about. The thing is, I went through the files
and I can't find a topfloor order for that whole campaign."

"Well, of course not," I said, opening my eyes wide in surprise. "I don't suppose Val had time to finish it, did he? I mean,
before he took off for the Moon like that. Flag it, Dixmeister,"
I ordered. "As soon as he gets back, I'll get on him. Good work
noticing it, Dixmeister!"

"Thank you, Mr. Tarb," he cried—grinning, very nearly
shuffling his feet. "I'll take another look for the order, though."

"Sure thing." Of course he would. And of course he wouldn't
find it, there being none. "And don't take any gas from those
network people. Remind them we're not playing for marbles here.
We don't want to have to bring a charge of Contract Breach."

He winced and left, though he couldn't help one last, wondering glance at Marie and Gert Martels, clustered around Marie's
desktop screen. "It's hotting up, isn't it?" asked Gert.

"Hotting up," I agreed. "Is that one of ours you're looking at?
Display it for me, will you?"

Marie moved a stud on her control board, and the first of the
wall screens lighted up with a network feed. It was the Nelson

199

Rockwell commercial, eyes gleaming out of the bandage-swathed head as he delivered his pitch: "—severed patella, that's the kneecap, two broken ribs, internal bleeding and a concussion. That's what they did to me when I couldn't pay for the things I hadn't wanted in the first place—"

Gert giggled, "Doesn't he look cute?"

"Real lady-killer," I said genially. "Have you all got your stun-guns where you can get at them in a hurry?" Gert nodded, the smile suddenly frozen on her face. It wasn't a smile any more. It was scary. I judged that the trouble it had taken to get her out of the stockade was well worth it.

Rockwell took his eyes off his own image on the screen and fastened them on me. "Do you think there's going to be trouble, Tenny?" he asked. His voice didn't shake but I noticed that his left hand, the one that wasn't in his whole-body cast, hovered close to the desk drawer. What could be in it? Not a gun; I hoped not a grenade—I hadn't quite made that decision yet.

"Well, you never know, do you?" I asked, strolling casually to his desk. "It's just best to be ready for it if it comes, right?" They all nodded, and I craned my neck to see what was in the drawer. It took me a moment to realize that it wasn't a grenade; it was one of his damned Miniature Simulated-Copper Authentic Death Masks of Leading Male Undergarment Models. I almost choked with a rush of sympathy. Poor guy! "Nels," I said softly, "if we get out of this I *promise* you next week you'll be in Detox."

As far as you could tell under the bandages, his expression was scared but determined, and I think he nodded. Out loud I said to them all, "It's going to be a long night. We'd all better get some sleep—take it in shifts."

They all chorused agreement, and as I turned to my own office they went back to watching the end of the Rockwell spot: "—that's my story, and if you'd like to help me get elected please send your contributions to—"

I closed the door behind me and went right to my own desk.

I punched up the latest *Advertising Age* and stared down at the screen. They hadn't waited for the hourly edition. They had a red-flashing special. The headlines were:

Shocking New Net Spots from H & K
FCC Orders Investigation

Things were hotting up, all right.

I hadn't been entirely honest with them. One did sometimes know when there was going to be trouble. I knew. And I knew it wasn't very far away.

I followed my own instructions, but not very successfully. Sleep didn't come easily. When it came it ended in a hurry—a worrisome noise from the outer room, a bad dream, most frequently of all an increasingly fretful call from Dixmeister up in the world. He had given up hope of getting home that night, and every hour he called with some new and more urgent Fair Commercial Practices complaint or network blast. I had no trouble with them. "Handle them," I ordered, every time, and handle them he did. He got Haseldyne & Ku's lawyers out of bed three times that night, to hire a tame judge to deliver a Freedom-of-Advertising injunction. They wouldn't stay enjoined. The hearings would all come due in a week or less, but within a lot less than a week, one way or another, it wouldn't matter.

When I peered out now and then I could see that my stalwart crew slept no better than I. They woke, startled, at odd noises— woke up fast and got back to sleep only slowly and uneasily, because they were having their bad dreams too. Not all of my dreams were nightmares. But none of them was really good. The last one I remembered was of Christmas, some improbable future Christmas spent with Mitzi. It was just like memories of childhood, with the sooty snow staining the windows and the Christmas tree chirping its messages of no-down-payment gifts . . . only Mitzi wouldn't stop ripping the commercials off the tree and pouring the kiddy-drug sweets down the toilet, and I could hear a banging on the door that I knew was Santa Claus's Helpers with guns drawn, ready to make a bust—

Part of it was true. Someone was indeed at the outer door.

If I had been of a wagering turn of mind, I would have bet that the first one banging on my door would have been the Old Man, because he would only have to come across town. I was wrong. The Old Man must have been in Rome with Mitzi and Des—more likely, already halfway back on the night rocket to put out this unexpected fire—because the first one was Val Dambois. Sneaky son of a gun! You couldn't even trust him to stay tricked when you tricked him, because he'd obviously tricked me right back. "You didn't get on the Moon ship after all," I said stupidly. He gave me an evil look.

The look wasn't half as evil as what he had in his hand. It wasn't a stun-gun, or even a lethal. It was worse than either. It was a Campbellian sidearm, definitely illegal for civilians to own at all, even more illegal to be used anywhere outside a posted area. And the worst part of it was that Marie had been left alone in the office and she'd drowsed off on her cot. He was past the tangle-net at the door before anyone could stop him.

I was shaking. That's surprising in itself, when you think about it, because I wouldn't have believed it was possible for anything to frighten a person who had as much to fear already as I did. Wrong opinion. Looking at the flaring muzzle of the limbic projector turned my spine to jelly and my heart to ice. And he was pointing it in my direction. "Huck bastard!" he snarled. "I *knew* you were up to something, hustling me away like that. Good thing there's always a Moke-head around the terminal you can bribe to take a free trip, so I could come back and wait to catch you in the act!"

He always talked too much, did Val Dambois. It gave me a chance to get my nerve back. I said, with all the courage I could find, forcing a grin, keeping the tone cool and assured—or so I hoped, though it didn't sound that way to me—"You waited too long, Val. It's all over. The commercials are on the air already."

202

"You'll never live to enjoy it!" he screamed, lifting the barrel of the Campbell.

I held the grin. "Val," I said patiently, "you're a fool. Don't you know what's going on?"

Faint waver of the gun; suspiciously, "What?"

"I had to get you out of the way," I explained, "because you talk too much. Mitzi's orders. She didn't trust you."

"Trust *me?*"

"Because you're a wimp, don't you see? Don't take my word for it—see for yourself. The next commercial will be Mitzi herself—" And I glanced at the wall screen—

And so did Val Dambois. He'd made mistakes before, but that one was terminal. He took his eyes off Marie. You can't altogether blame him for that, considering the shape that Marie was obviously in, but he had cause to regret it. *Zunggg* went her stun-gun, and the limbic projector dropped out of Val's hand, and Val dropped right after it.

A little late, the door to the storeroom flew open and the rest of my crew boiled in, wakened from their uneasy naps. Marie was propped on one elbow, grinning—her cot contained her mechanical heart and she couldn't move away from it, but she had a hand free for the stun-gun when it was needed. "I got him for you, Tenny," she said proudly.

"You surely did," I agreed, and then to Gert Martels, "Help me lug him into the storeroom."

So we tucked him into the room where once the engineers had dozed away their standby shifts, and left him to do the same. The limbic projector I turned over to Jimmy Paleologue. I couldn't stand to touch the thing, but I thought he might consider it a valuable addition to our limited arsenal. Another wrong guess. He darted out into the hall with it, I heard the sound of running water from the communijohn, and he came back with it dripping. "That one will never work again," he gritted, tossing it in a wastebasket. "What do you say, Tarb? Back to sleeping shifts?"

I shook my head. The sleeping room had now become a jail, and besides we were all good and wakeful. "Might as well enjoy

203

the fun," I said, and left them brewing Kaf to jolt the drowsies away. I wanted a look at *Advertising Age,* and I wanted it in the privacy of my own office.

It wasn't reassuring. They were transmitting nothing but bulletins now, with headlines like:

FCC Head Vows Full Prosecution
and
Brainburn Seen Likely in H & K Case

I rubbed the back of my neck uneasily, wondering what it felt like to be a vegetable.

I didn't have long to spend on that unenjoyable task, because I guess Mitzi had caught the night rocket after all. There was a rattle and a squeal and a bunch of relieved guffaws, and when I got my door open there she was. Stuck in Gert Martel's tangle-net. "What'll we do with this one?" asked Nels Rockwell through his bandages. "There's still plenty of room in the storeroom."

I shook my head. "Not her. She can come in my office."

When Marie turned off the juice in the net, Mitzi stumbled and half fell. She caught herself, glaring up at me. "You fool, Tenn!" she spat. "What the hell do you think you're doing?"

I helped her up. "You shouldn't have given me the cure, Mitzi. It cured me."

Her jaw dropped. She let me take her arm and lead her into my office. She sat down heavily, staring at me. "Tenny," she said, "do you know what you've *done?* I couldn't believe it when they told me what you were putting on the air for political commercials —it's unheard of!"

"People telling the truth, yes," I nodded. "Never been done, as far as I know."

"Oh, Tenny! 'Truth.' Grow up!" she flared. "How can we win with *truth?*"

I said gently, "When I was being detoxed I had to do a lot

204

of soul-searching—it was better than cutting my throat, you see. So I asked questions. Let me ask you one of them: In what way is what we're doing right?"

"Tenny!" She was shocked. "Are you defending the hucks? They've despoiled their own planet, now they want to do the same thing to Venus!"

"No," I said, shaking my head, "you're not answering the question. I didn't ask you why they were wrong, because I know why they were wrong. I wanted to know if we were right."

"Compared to the hucks—"

"No, that won't do, either. Not 'compared to.' You see, it isn't enough to be less bad. Less bad is still bad."

"I never heard such pious claptrap—" she began, and then paused, listening. Sudden sounds of a squabble from the anteroom: a man's furious bellow—Haseldyne's?; clipped orders in a higher voice—Gert Martels?; the sound of a door closing. She stared at me, wonderingly. "You'll never get away with it," she whispered.

"That's possible. Still," I explained, "I picked this place because it's next to the comm room. All Agency communications go through here, so the building's shut off, and the Wackerhuts have orders to let staff in, not out."

"No, Tenny," she sobbed, "I don't mean right now, I mean later. Do you know what they'll *do* to you?"

The flesh at the back of my neck crawled, because I did. "Brainburning, maybe. Or just kill me," I acknowledged. "But that's only if I fail, Mits. There are twenty-two separate commercials going out. Would you like to see some?" I turned to the monitor, but she stopped me.

"I've seen! That fat cripple you've got out there, whining about how she was made to eat junk food—the aboriginal that says his people's life-styles were destroyed—"

"Marie, yes. And the Sudanese." Finding him had been a bit of luck—Gert Martels had done it, once I bailed her out of the stockade and told her what I wanted. "That's only two of them, love. There's a real good one with Jimmy Paleologue about how

Campbellian techniques work—on people like me as well as the natives. Nels Rockwell's good, too—"

"I've seen them, I tell you! Oh, Tenny, I thought you were on our side."

"Neither for you nor against you, Mits."

She sneered, "A real prescription for inaction." But I didn't have to say anything to that; inaction wasn't what I was guilty of, and she knew it as soon as she said the words. "You'll fail, Tenny. You can't defeat evil with namby-pamby piety!"

"Maybe not. Maybe you can't defeat evil at all. Maybe the world's social ills are too far along and evil's going to win. But you don't have to be an *accomplice* to it, Mitzi. And you don't have to give up, like your hero Mitch Courtenay."

"Tenny!" She wasn't angry now, just shocked at blasphemy.

"But that's what he did, Mitzi. He didn't solve the problem. He ran away from it."

"We're not running away!"

I nodded, "Right, you're fighting. And using the same weapons. And coming out with the same end results! The hucks turned the planet into ten billion mindless mouths—what you want to do is starve the mouths, just so you can be left alone! So I'm not on the huck side, I'm not on the Veenie side. I'm opting out! I'm trying something different."

"The *truth.*"

"The truth, Mitzi," I declared, "is the only weapon there is that doesn't cut both sides!"

And then I stopped. I was working myself up to a grand speech, and heaven knows what heights of oratory I might have reached for my one-woman audience. But the best parts of it I had already said, and I had them on tape. I fumbled on my keyboard to call up my own commercial and paused with my finger on the Execute button. "Look, Mits," I said, "there are twenty-two commercials altogether, three each for the seven people I'm using—"

"What seven?" she demanded suspicously. "I only saw four out there."

"Two of them were kids, and I sent the Sudanese off with them to keep them out of trouble. Pay attention, Mits! Those first twenty-one are just to prepare the audience for the twenty-second. That's mine. At least, that's me delivering it—but it's really for you."

I hit the button. The screen jumped alive. There I was, looking serious and trouble-worn, with a stock shot of Port Kathy matted into the background. "My name," my recorded voice told us, and the professional part of my mind thought, *not bad, not too pompous, talking a little too fast, though*, "my name is Tennison Tarb. I'm a star-class copysmith, and what you see behind me is one of the cities on Venus. See the people? They look just like us, don't they? But they're different from us in one way. They don't like having their minds bent by advertising. Unfortunately that's made things bad all around, because now they have their minds bent in a different way. They've come to hate us. They call us 'hucks.' They think we're out to conquer them and force our advertising down their throats. This has made them as mean as any agency man, and the terrible part is that their suspicions are right. We sneak spies into their government. We send in teams of terrorists to sabotage their economy. And right now we're planning to invade them with Campbellian limbic weaponry, the exact same way I saw us do just a little while ago in the Gobi Desert. . . ."

"Oh, Tenny," whispered Mitzi. "They'll brainburn you."

I nodded. "Yes, that's what they'll do, all right, if we fail."

"But you're bound to fail!"

Old habits die hard; much though I wanted to get straight with Mitzi, I couldn't help casting a regretful glance at the screen —I was just getting into the best parts! But I said, "We'll find that out pretty soon, Mits. Let's see what they're saying." And, leaving the screen to run through the rest of my spot unnoticed, I punched up the headlines on my desk screen. The first half dozen were nothing but dire threats and sinister portents, just as before—but then there was one that made my heart leap:

207

And just below it:

Brinks Head Says Demonstration "Out of Control"

I didn't bother with the text. I threw open the door to the outer office, where my trusty four were gathered around their desks. "What is it?" I called. "Are we getting a play? Check the news channels, will you?"

"A play! What do you think we're looking at?" called Gert Martels, grinning. As the new wall panels flashed into life I saw what she was grinning about. The local stations had knocked themselves out with remotes to get reaction shots—and the reaction was huge.

"Jeez, Tenny," Rockwell shouted, "it's gridlock!" It just about was. The cameras of the news stations were roving from intersection to intersection—Times Square, Wall Street, Central Park Mall, Riverspace—and every one looked the same. It was morning run time, but traffic had come almost to a standstill while the city's teeming millions listened on portables or watched the building-wall displays, and every one of them was listening to one of our commercials.

I could hardly breathe with excitement. "The nets!" I called. "What's going on in the rest of the country?"

"The same thing, Tenny," said Gert Martels, and added, "Do you see what's happening there, in the corner?"

We were looking at Union Square, and, yes, in the far right corner, there was a group that wasn't just standing still with its jaws hanging. They were very busy indeed. They were methodically, brutally, ripping down a display screen.

"They're tearing down our commercials," I gasped.

"No, no, Tenny! That was a Kelpy-Crisp! And look over there —the limbic area? They've wrecked the projector!"

I felt Mitzi's hand creep into mine as I stood there, and when I turned she was smiling mistily. "At least you're getting an

208

audience," she said; and from the door a new voice said solemnly,

"The biggest audience ever, Mr. Tarb."

It was Dixmeister. Gert Martels had already drawn a stun-gun and it was leveled right at his head. He didn't even look at her. His hands were empty. He said, "You'd better come upstairs, Mr. Tarb."

My first thought was my worst thought. "A Fair Practices squadron?" I guessed. "They're canceling the spots? They've got a counterinjunction—?"

He frowned. "Nothing like that, Mr. Tarb. Gosh! I've never *seen* such hourlies! Every one of the campaign spots is drawing optimum-plus-fifty responses, the March of Dollars is swamped with pledges—no, no, it's not a *bust.*"

"Then what, Dixmeister?" I cried.

He said uncertainly, "It's all those people. You'd better come up and see."

And so I did, and from the second floor of the Agency building I could look out over the street, the square, the windows opposite. And every inch was packed with people.

The funny thing is that even so I couldn't believe it at first. I thought they were a lynch mob—until I heard them cheering.

And the rest of the world? RussCorp, Indiastries, S.A.[2]—all of them? You begin to hear cheering there, too; and where it will end I know not. Old habits die hard for nations as well as individuals. Monoliths are hard to demolish.

But they've started unloading the shuttles in Arizona again, and the monolith has begun to crack.

209